CW01510589

1

Don't Forget to Pack the Humour, Honey

Philippa W. Joyner

First Edition

Précis ~ the letter for my Best Seller

Dear Sir @ Publishing Camels ~ I think you may be the one? Are you the one? Well, I'll send it anyway and hope for the best. (And, I have a student loan to pay back and my Mother appears to be rather beside herself with worry, so I would be very grateful if we could get this publishing lark going on the press as soon as gratefully possible.)

Much obliged and all that.

Love Honey x

(is this editorially correct to sign off 'Love Honey x ? ')

Here goes: Has the world gone mad, or is *Honey Hollings* (me) experiencing her adult life capturing its more cynical side? Chapters of *Don't Forget to Pack the Humour, Honey* judge the ludicrous, the absurd, even, she might add (me), the incongruous side of life as she simply travels to and forth, post maternity leave, upon the Great British Trains, from her chocolate box village of Greater Bungchip to the smog of London Victoria. And beyond.

Honey Hollings is a flighty, intelligent, mildly pragmatic, eloquent, yet totally whacky lady in her late thirties. Okay, early forties (and I did use the largest synonym finder to describe myself.) But, how can she have possibly let *scenario after scenario* pass her by, probably all of her adult years, without at least noting it? Probably, she might add (me), because she simply did not have the time. But now, she has. Then, purely as a pick-me-up at the beginning to amuse oneself on maternity leave, when the children were mature (mature enough to hold their own spoon giving Honey both hands to type) did she start to annotate jocular tales. And she soon realised even *she* laughed at her own literary prowess. Maybe she was *the* only one laughing, but she thought she would give herself the chance to become a novelist. Why not? At least a novice novelist for starters.

Classics in this title include reminiscing over Honey's whirlwind, skimpish, coquettish tour of Europe with Amber; witnessing a murder from an innocent train window; encountering the Posh Porsche Boy; Honey's interview as a PA on the catwalk;

accidentally becoming part of 'the' dog walking club, or shall I save that for Volume Two?; Waga-ha-Joo (the Satellite City of Palmerston, Darwin) that time; La Polizia; and generally meeting every complex personality a plain, Mother-of-two with perfectly domesticated House-Husbandry commuter could even aspire to encounter. Notwithstanding Perdita the Nurse, Wuthering Heights with a certain localised drama intertwined; Chardonnay; the passing of Great Uncle Daffyd and her Father's Cataracts; and the perfect, flamboyant, utterly incorrigible, yet completely flirtatious, Aunty Amber - my sister.

Love Honey xxx

To **Perdita**, who inspired me with her ambitions of *'Living the Dream?'*

And to all of my characters. You fear, but I promise I didn't befriend you purely for your good, free, publishable chats. I *promise*. Cross my wellington boots. It would have been a great disservice to humankind to keep your tales to myself. The coffee beans on the 07:21 at Greater Bungchip for instance? Who would they have been shared with? No employer would welcome a fully hyper-caffeinated employee onto work premises if the coffee beans had been consumed by just that one fellow commuter alone now, would they? It's good to share. *More* than my fair share? I don't think that's a fair synopsis of what happens. Think of the time I replaced them in June of 2018. They were a good batch, a marvellous batch of coffee beans. Superior, I believe. Us working Mums need it more than engineers who dress in a variety of chequered shirts seemingly on their way to lumber-jacking in London? These types of commuters seem to think it's good and correct to carry parts of demobilised cars in pink carrier bags onto trains. That's right, I did see your limb-shaped exhaust pipe stuffed into the overhead luggage rack. Enough to bring the entire transport infrastructure to a grinding halt, if I say so myself. Huh? Sorry? Me plugging my hair straighteners direct into the carriage wall socket is far more dangerous? Why's it there then, the socket? They only smoke a little, my hair straighteners, and that's from the wet hair. Smells like a wet dog on a hot day, but never mind. No chance of short-circuiting the 07:21 from Greater

Bungchip with those. No chance *whatsoever*. ☺ And, if you feel it necessary to tell anyone that I secretly colour in my few stray silver hairs with a Sharpie pen, then, well, I'll steal another coffee bean. Unless, that is, I become parochial, narrow-minded, passionless and cold and decide to slide next to that very colourful character who alights at Upper Krapchip cooking porridge each morning. He has extra for sure. And, on the return journey, he lights his Calor Gas stove and cooks up a vegetarian curry, hanging off the armrest, on a Thursday night. Insensitive? Tactless? Smug? Fickle? I call it wise.

And to *my Mum*, the best mum in the world, who is the only one plausible person to have inspired such delirious literary prowess. She, herself, is renowned for hiccup-free excursions, isn't she, Amber?

"Hi Amber, hi Honey,

Dad had a rehearsal of packing his suitcase this morning. We haven't been on a plane for nearly twenty six years, although it seems like only yesterday your Father had his head in a brown paper bag all the way to Agios Gordios, Corfu. That was the holiday he booked us in as 'Mr and Mrs Smith' before we were married. Then wondered why the hotel manager questioned our surnames and scratched his head as he threw our passports into the slammer. Your Father told me that everyone calls themselves 'Smith' when they're pretending to be married, and was up in arms it wasn't working for him. Why did your sister have to move to France, Honey? Oh yes, the sun. Oh, and that French man. At least we're married now so we can be Mr and Mrs Jostick with no questions asked.

Your Father bought a new suitcase. Yes, you can pick up your jaws from the floor now, girls. He bought a new suitcase only because the one that your Grandad used during the air-raid of 1939 had finally gone to its grave. He put everything in his new suitcase, your Father, that he would be taking to France and found there was a lot of extra space so he has just taken it back to swap for the next size down. "£9.95 refund," he smirked. He wasn't quite so smirky when I muttered under my breath that we'd waste at least that in petrol getting lost en-route to the airport. His hearing isn't quite so bad now, apparently. I said it would have been a useful overflow for me, this superfluous space in the suitcase £9.95 more expensive, but his hearing had miraculously deteriorated again. If I'm struggling with what clothes to omit now I haven't got quite so much luggage area as I'd hoped with utilising your Father's extra bit, he has now said that as mine extends there will be masses of room. I *do* hope so. I haven't been able to take the top half of my beaded bikini anywhere since we exchanged holidaying in Corfu for Wells-Next-The-Sea, but, I must admit (don't tell your Father) that Corfu was a) rather hot, b) full of Greek people with stinking tans, c) rather complacent at the airport when the customs officer thought I was drug smuggling. Don't **ever** take your hot water bottle to Corfu. The residents are beyond stupid. How can they not know what a hot water bottle is? And the police cell was full of lizards. I was nearly totally arrested, but when they couldn't get through to your Father and his obsession with wanting another map of the island as his one was cheap on eBay for 97p and was a child's sketch, they must have been tearing out their greased-back hair. I think your Father thought we were in the tourist office, dears, and was most upset when he had to pay to get me back.

Your Father also said that the advantage of getting a large case alongside a small case is that we can store the smaller one inside the larger one when not in use. But that idea seems to have died a death alongside the suitcase from 1939.

I haven't had a rehearsal of my packing. Once is quite enough! And, Honey dear, what do you *mean* you can't make an Espresso Martini, or even a simple Strawberry Daiquiri on the train journey to work, dear? Don't be so defeatist.

Love Mum x"

Time to Get Up?

It was time to get up.

First day back.

Maternity leave; did it actually happen? Oh. Yes. It did. I glared down at the kitchen floor, my feet stuck in a milky residue of milkiness. *My* milk. I should really clean it up. But, the train. Unless systems had changed, it wasn't going to wait for my arrival just because I now had a balding baby. And no, I'm not referring to House-Husbandry.

Lego. It was everywhere, and it was only because I was mildly stuck to the floor that I didn't take half my foot off. I cast my mind back to the days when Jack relied only on his animal instincts. His food store. Breast-feeding. It suddenly seemed quite an alien concept popping out my mini-watermelons on the…SHIT…the TRAIN! I would see the same people. Would I? Have the commuters seen me at one with nature, not a care in the world, and chatting to them whilst I looked like a wild pig shopping for nappies? Never mind, I didn't have the time to contemplate it right now. Thank God.

The microwave clock ticked on. 06:59.

My blouse wasn't ironed. It wasn't ever ironed 13 months ago, but it looked sort of different and I couldn't figure out why. I turned to the side and looked in the reflection of the fridge. "MY BOOBS! They've disappeared!" Thirteen months of being sucked dry of calcium and my boobs had given up trying to be perky ever again. My blouse looked huge and baggy all in the wrong places, but the button at the bottom seemed to not meet at all. In fact, there was an inch or more that needed more material. Pulling didn't help. So, I decided, my boobs had gone. And, in their place, my hips had decided to have an argument and move apart like repelling magnets. Never mind. I had the excitement of adult conversation again that didn't involve how well their children were walking and talking at just 18 weeks old. Did I tell you that my Jack said "hello" at four months? That's just *16* weeks (and a bit, but we don't need that much attention to detail so let's round it down.)

"My train was stuck behind the Orient Express; There were six lazy sheep on the track, not going very far, just grazing, you know, no urgency; My carriage was hit by a discarded shopping trolley", but the best excuse, ever ~ *"I thought we'd all been sucked up by the Solar Eclipse, but we had just entered the tunnel at Bromley South."*

I mulled over my excuses from previous events before maternity leave. My late to work excuses were plausible, undeniable, true (to an extent), but at least they were all pretty decent. Points for ingenuity, at least, come on. And my Jack, he *did* say "hello" at 4 months, that's 16 weeks you know. Bright, isn't he? But, in later years, when Jack returned home with his school report reading *"Jack Hollings is a lovely young boy with a cheeky twinkle in his eye,"* I knew that his days were numbered. However, delving further into the teacher's wildly frazzled brain,

I realised that Henrietta-Divine's rising intellectuality wasn't the be-all. Boys with cheeky twinkles in more places than one could even imagine were a catch with the ladies and jovial to be around. Who cared about adverbial clauses when centrifugal forces made Mummy a swimming pool? And, it is a life skill to learn from a young age how to zone out and think pivotal thoughts. Take marriage for instance.

So, how can I possibly have let *Scenario after Scenario* pass me by, probably all of my adult years, without at least noting it? Probably, I might add, because I simply did not have the time. But now, I have, so I keep saying. Motherhood, to begin with, was when I taunted myself if my eldest son, Jack, *"absolutely needed"* his teddy three miles into a journey, or my youngest daughter, Henrietta-Divine, *"tragically requested"* seventeen furry creatures for a sleepover. It is funny, only now, that Henrietta-Divine *"could not go on"* if her sunflower collage was not absolutely perpendicular to the edge of the roughly cut paper at aged 3. It is only funny *now*. Like when I went to the office with a sticker of a dinosaur (a Brachiosaurus to be precise) on my scalp because I would rather not say *no* to Jack than face the consequences of a crumpled face turning to a deafening outburst as my last memory that morning. And like the time House-Husbandry simply had to wear nothing but a bicycle helmet and boxer shorts to feed a child, in his high-chair (child, not House-Husbandry), at the stable door, open in the sunshine; just because. Just because they ask us to.

"Just because" has definitely become a title all-encompassing. I think, *just because*, children are smarter than we are; us adults. *Just because* they can push our buttons and we just compute. That was then; this is *now*. Then, adults would prefer a tantrum-free life. Normality. But when children are thrown into that loop, normality rushes out the stable door and embarrassment ensues if it means that the child is even just mildly amused. We did not care as long as *they* were content. *Just because*. We all looked outrageously stupid, most days, but who's counting?

I have since wised-up.

I was proud to be going back to work on the train, I thought. A female bread-winner, House-Husbandry running the home; The Domestic God he was. Oh, how we were acting so incredibly modern. Proud and excited, I was, until I heard this; the first adult conversation of my first day back;

"Oh my God! I don't care, I don't care, I've already slept with someone else anyway, and I don't care!" (Acne-encrusted, enthused, and slightly self-important, thirty-something man, obviously full of prowess, was voicing his mutant lesser than best Kentish articulation.)

I turned and moved seats, and purely by chance encounter, I stumbled upon two seats, the only two seats that endorsed extra leg room.

I sat down.

The conversation in my ears swiftly turned to the conductor. "Maam? Maam? That door is the ONLY one on the train which doesn't open. MAAM, did you hear me?" (I'm not sure why Greater Bungchip had suddenly turned American.) The lady surely did not hear. She continued to press the *Door Open* button from the platform until the train slowly moved away. Her iPhone stuck in her ears. Her hair fizzing.

I sat down. Sloped down. Further and deeper into the same blue seat that I remembered from thirteen months ago. The leg room had gotten longer, I'll give it that. Just. Or was I wearing flatter trainers? I looked down. I was in flip-flops. It was raining. Oops.

The tannoy jumped into action and my ears opened up to hear this. "Apologies for the four coach train this jolly morning. My name's Terry, your relaxed conductor all the way up to London today stopping at the delights of all the normal miniscule villages where not a soul alights or disembarks. We are rather packed; the other four coaches have broken down and sadly the two working toilets were in those carriages which are no longer with us. For health and safety reasons, the rooftop seating is cancelled so that's it."

It was 7.30am. The lady commuter next to me was blatantly drinking a Pina Colada. The man opposite had cracked open a beer. Was I on the wrong train? I wasn't. I didn't really care anyway. I'd just run over a pigeon. Killed it outright in two seconds. It didn't fly away like they always seem to do when I'm a passenger in anyone else's car. It just stood right between the summer headlights which just seemed to pop on. Perhaps that was why it didn't move. I'd confused the pigeon. Headlights? In summer? *I'd* be getting out my own way if I saw me driving towards me. So it just continued. The staring between the pigeon and I. I stared back. *Glared* back. But it just did not move and I didn't fancy the tractor behind careering into the back of the car. Ordinarily I'd have walked to the train station, but the microwave clock was six minutes slow. I'd have missed the 07:21.

I sniffed as hard as I could. And that Pina Colada? It went right up my nostrils and I swiftly passed out to the lull of the grinding wheels on the buckling track of the tipping train screeching through Brixton. I guess the graffiti there is as decent as graffiti comes.

Train Windows

It's quite amazing what you see from train windows.

I always used to think *what would I do if I witnessed a crime? A murder even?* I know, it does sound a bit morbid, a bit farfetched, but it could happen? I mean, it *does* happen, so there's no reason why I wouldn't witness it over someone else having the pleasure. Sorry, I don't mean to say that it would indeed be pleasurable to witness a murder, a robbery, a mugging, even a fight in the school playground. What I mean to say, it would be more fortunate, and far less wasteful, for me, an amateur writer, to witness some such crime, because I could do the tale so much more literary justice over the next.

So, seeing the lesser-morbid, but equally as critique-able, Olympic-style runner on his outside treadmill come rain or come shine was quite an addiction of mine. The first time I spied him (for want of a less stalker-type description) I became rather jealous. I'd love to exercise, to be able to throw open one's French doors, to step out under a clear blue sky and to burn calories without the need of attending a basement gym depleting my bank account of £697.50 per year along with 43 others sweaty urchins. (Not that, I must add, I did.) I mean, I did join my Mayfair establishment 15 years ago. Everyone seemed to be married to this affliction. So me, being a lemming, I followed suit. But it wasn't my entirely my cup of tea and I would dearly have preferred to have taken a jog in Berkeley Square for free than have paid to show my inability to do … anything, it appeared, remotely energetic even remotely flawlessly. Lifting the smallest of dumbbells was a task. My inadequacy to stay centrally on the treadmill wasn't a breeze. Oh and the exercise bike, oh and the cross-trainer, oh and the mountain-climber. It was all rather embarrassing. So, the bright outdoors, free of other like-minded exercise freaks frantically jogging their lives away during the 45 minute break from their computer screen, was *heaven in a tea-cup.* I like that phrase.

So, I spied him. I made it my aim of a morning to seek him out and to make sure he wasn't slacking. *Gotcha.* There he was. A fraction of a mile past Swanley train station, there he was. Running away in his dark grey hoody, on his secluded fake grassy roof-top garden, burning off his Weetabix swimming in skimmed milk. There he was. The exercise freak. I felt jealous. I felt overwhelmingly jealous of his lifestyle. Jealous of his fake roof-top garden lined with minute cherry tomato plants. Outlandishly jealous of his mini sky-light garden heralding the miniaturist of potted Coriander herbs. Zanely jealous of his attack on obesity whilst surrounded by the natural beauty of the lesser-spotted lavender bush, the cutest of which sat, awkwardly, at the edge of his mini-miniature raffia fence which surrounded everything, even Mr Exercise (as I decided to call him from the wide range of synonyms that flooded my brain at 07:44am.)

I felt pathetically, insanely jealous of his kinship with the countryside of which he had heroically built up all around him, along 3 metres square of it, compacted into his little fake roof-top garden whilst he ran and he ran and he ran and he ran within the smallest collection of nature I had ever seen.

Then *zoom*. The train, the fast train which tooted its horn timely each morning as we passed Mr Exercise on his idyllic treadmill in his perfect garden dwelling, shook this man's entire existence as he held on to the machine's bars and grimaced. Yes, at 07:44am each sunny, frosty, wet or blustery morning, Mr Exercise gripped his expensively kitted-out minute outdoor exercise parlour, and he gripped tightly to the metal bars as he continued to run without a third and a fourth hand to cover his ears from the train's impending timely horn Monday through Friday. (For the irony and the purpose of this little chapter and verse I'll write that the 07:44am passing via Swanley train station was always extremely on time.)

And there it was. I, suddenly, after weeks, maybe months, I realised. Suddenly, reality smacked me in the face. Out of the blue, my jealousy didn't gradually fade, it just disappeared *tout d'un coup* as the French say. All of a sudden, my jealousy vanished into thin air and I really couldn't understand how I could have been completely obsessed with this stranger's life. I mean, this stranger, Mr Exercise, he lived exactly where I would *never* even dream of living. In London, well, as close to the capital as Swanley train station was despite it actually still being in Kent, although it was technically near to Bromley South, and although Bromley South was technically still classed as Kent, only one train ride minute down the track was absolutely the periphery of London.

Anyway, geography aside, I had suddenly assessed my situation. *I* was the blessed one. *I* had the North Downs on my doorstep, literally on my doorstep. I could box-kick open my back door, wander up my garden path, wine glass in hand, duck under the enormous damson tree whose low hanging branches, offering the most juicy array of damsons bi-annually, would poke out my eye (but I knew when to duck), I could turn slightly left and continue up my grassy passage following the giant daisy trail which House-Husbandry had created with his mower, giant scented daisies flourishing everywhere with a cute little trail roughly cut down to create a fairy path for Henrietta-Divine. Then, I could continue to meander up the meadow (okay, I'm milking this now) towards the cherry blossom via the apple tree before reaching the in-situ park designed by House-Husbandry, scrummage through the vegetable allotment of oddly shaped wild garlic, celeriac and mandrakes, take a refreshing bounce on the 14 foot trampoline, before opening the secretly hidden wooden Cherry-Oaked gate in order to reveal the wildest built leafy camp where us, the family, pitched up and played in fair-weather.

There. There the North Downs lay. Untouched. Grassy, hilly, infested with beautiful wildlife, naturally. That was me, *ME!* I did not need a purpose-built roof-top copy of what already existed, one thousand times larger. I did not desire an artificial, cut out piece of picturesque landscape as long as you kept your eyes on the speedometer of a treadmill. I already had real, insanely real, countryside at my beck and call every minute of my home-life. And, and I could swear, I could absolutely swear that Mr Exercise used to spy me too, in my pink and grey tea-cosy hat, and my muddied black wellington boots tucked under the train table. I could, without a shadow of a doubt, lip read his words. He wasn't singing *"Rise and Shine"* when he clocked my looking at him. He was grimacing *"God, how she's divine."* That's what I tell myself anyway when the 07:44am rattles Mr Exercise from living his dream.

So, Mr Exercise, you artificial stranger. You only own an artificial fraction in your artificial rural existence of what I own. Me, *ME!* I have the greatest rural retreat existence known to man. I have a rural personal pleasure juxta-positioned with urban working life. *I* was the envied one. *I* was the lucky one. *I* had *both* lives, and I wouldn't swap my never-ending fairy glen North Downs for a thousand miniature penthouse exterior treadmills (unless I had a wee cherry tomato plant pot on the side, and perhaps the occasional toilet closer than when caught off-guard during a lengthy urban jaunt (for the kids of course)), and perhaps, and only *perhaps* would I swap my rural impeccably adorable lifestyle for Mr Exercise, just maybe, if it meant I could then, just once, see me, *ME*, rush by on that 07:44am writing away in this book. Then *I'd* see my smile, my grin, my absolute mad concentration a novice writer tries to hide.

But.

I still hadn't witnessed a murder.

How many times had I trundled, accelerated, crawled or throttled past urban high-rises? How many times had I emerged from the deepest, longest, blackest of tunnels? How many times had my train run so close in proximity to the windows of low-slung apartments that I actually believed my carriage was in their front room? How many? My fingers and toes could continue to spawn and I still would not be able to count. Far too many, that's all I can say. And, I still had not witnessed a murder, domestic violence, not even a toddler having a tantrum (not from my train window anyway.) So, I decided. I must look harder. Surely I was missing a trick? No?

Christ! He fell. That man, he fell. She, that insane blond frizzy-haired power-crazed woman had pushed him, pushed him with her huge, rough, bare hands, and then struck him with a serrated carving knife wielding a burnt orange handle and a blade of which Jamie Oliver would be proud. And, that man, he had fallen, dripping with blood, thin red claret pouring out all over the lower basement wooden floor, his facial skin turning from pink to white to pale elephant grey in a matter of seconds as I, *me*, *ME* witnessed the life rush from his flagging soul, and within seconds, he was dead.

There.

Dead.

For Pete's sake, what was I to do? I had all these great intentions of capturing the best murder ever to be seen by one human, me, but now, now it had really happened, now that my innocent eyes had witnessed such brutality, how on earth could I just write it all down? How could I be so callous to actually be excited that I had finally, *finally*, got a real murder to describe? How could I, genuinely, want to make money and good fortune from another man's dreadful demise? How could I just sit back, as my train trundled on, and pretend nothing had occurred lest me having the next chapter to my Best Seller? How *COULD* I? What a mean, devoutly utterly horrific person I would be if I kept this cold-blooded murder to myself?

Sod it.

I'm going down the callous route to make money out of this.

I could try and solve the murder? I could become the next Mrs Sherlock Holmes? I could report my story to the police, or even better, the *Press?* How could I *not* report this gratuitous violence and get this terrible murderer put behind solid iron bars for the remainder of her lousy existence? Easy. Keep quiet. It was *my* story after all and no one else was going to steal it.

I stared straight ahead.

Slid down into my seat.

And simply stuck my eyes to the bald head swaying in front of me three feet further towards London.

I tried to look gormless. I really did try, but it was no good. My brow started to sweat. Perspiration poured down my forehead, quickly gathering in my poorly plucked eyebrows, before spilling over the long strands and rushing down my nose. Most of the beads of water crept back up inside my nostrils (I could never fathom out the scientific gravitational pull on that one.) And I sat there. I sat there, as quiet as a mouse, and pursed my lips so tightly that I thought my teeth would bite clean through. Bloody hell, I'd just witnessed a murder. And it appeared that I was the only one.

I looked around. Just with my eyes. My eyes darted about in their sockets to see if I could catch a glimpse of anything suspicious, to see if anyone else looked as perturbed as me. Hang on, what was I thinking? Why would any of these passengers look suspicious? The crime scene had been outside. As the innocent train, steeped with innocent passengers, trundled through *Lower Plummerage* and then hastened its speed skirting around the pretty village of *Even Lower Plummerage*, we approached more urban surrounds leaving death behind.

I could not for the life of me work out what in heaven's name I should do? But if that was my first reaction, I was obviously more heartless than I thought. I used to pride myself in putting everyone else's needs miles before my own (even arriving to the office, in Mayfair, with a mass of tangle woven hair an eagle would have been proud to call its nest, never giving my own appearance a second glance of a morning over ensuring Jack and

Henrietta-Divine were porridge-fuelled, reading-booked-out and House-Husbandry as demented as possible.)

But today, even *I* considered myself a heartless cow, a wretched changed human being with a mind full of the selfish desire to keep this bloody murder to myself, as clandestine as possible in order to characterise the motive before reality stepped in. I loved it. I smiled.

I wanted to be the authoress to this crime. Do the murder supreme literary justice ahead of even Jonathan Creek. And then solve its motive and reasoning before even the police. Blimey, did that mean I was harbouring a criminal? Fantastic.

I stared even straighter ahead, so intensely that I swore the worn, threadbare faded blue material covering the headrest of the passenger in front smoked with a burning hole. It was mad. But I liked it. I felt a rush of excitement flood through my body. I was the sole owner of the worst crime that mankind could possibly commit, a *murder*, and it was all, *all* mine. Only *I* (until the victim failed to turn up in daily life) knew of the crime, and only *I* could, would, re-create its story. I would keep it close to my heart and totally undisclosed.

"Shocking! It's shocking! Horrific," I informed Anita at Reception when I fell into the office. *Oh dear.* I was shaking, with fear, with excitement, with bloodcurdling sickness that I thought I might vomit there and then on Anita's well-polished desk.

"Morning!" Anita replied as she rushed back out the door in through which I had just stumbled. She had not heard.

"Oh, yes, morning," I replied to the wind from her passing that blew my messy nest messier. Perhaps that was better? After all, I *did* want that story to be mine, so why was I so verbose in telling the first person I saw? I looked to the floor and went to the toilet. The cleaning lady was changing all the toilet rolls. I forced myself to smile at her like it was just another normal day, pleased that I did not readily know this lady ever so well otherwise I may have been tipped over the edge and spilled all the gory details.

Instead, I locked myself inside the first toilet I came across. The cleaner knocked at the door. "Bugger," I whispered. *"Yes?"* I cried as I sat down on the closed toilet seat to gather my inner strength and muster up what I was going to say as to why I was perspiring so much. Nothing sprung immediately to mind. I pulled open the toilet door a smidgen just to take the huge pile of separately sheeted paper from the Latvian sanitary technician's clammy hands. "Thank you!" I replied, chirpily.

"Liels paldies!" the cleaner cried as I heard her tiny feet patter away.

"Me too!" I tittered weirdly as I heard the Latvian lady walk away not a clue as to what she was muttering but it sounded very enthusiastic.

"Es nevaru ticēt, ka angļu valodā tiek izmantots tik daudz purvu rullītis!"

"My thoughts exactly!"

The main toilet door slammed shut. I was alone. Alone in my locked cubicle. "S**t!" I said to myself as I pictured the murder scene for the third, fourth and 18th time. "S*****tttttt!"

My day was long.

Each time my telephone rang, I jumped.

"Too much coffee, Honey?" Anita cackled. I was known to add two heaped tablespoons to my mug and not much hot water. Barely any at all. I crunched my way through my third mug.

The train ride home was abysmal. I thought that everyone knew I was a murderer. Eyes from the weirdest of people I used to see falling into the train of an evening, just staring either into their mobiles, into other people's mobiles, or just out of the window, were now, seriously, boring a hole into my brain as if to pick-out crucial information vis-à-vis my witnessed murder.

It was awful. I felt imprisoned. But I was surely just a victim of circumstance? Yes, that was it. *A Victim of Circumstance.* If only, if only I had not opened my bleary eyelids at that point on the train this morning (I was having a nice dream about a large fluffy white rabbit which had escaped from its hutch in the village of Greater Bungchip juxta-positioned with the stealing of a wheelie-bin from number 16 Cadbury Row, and I was just about to embark on the Pilgrimage of the Harry Krishna's), then bam. The murder was thrown into my life. I didn't sign up for that. Although I had been hoping for it all my life.

So, I did what I always did in an awkward situation. Nothing. Nothing at all. I found my seat, sat in it, pulled out my smart phone (which I only used for writing Best Selling Book Chapters on a whole heap of computerised memos before piecing them all together at midnight with matchsticks to keep my eyelids from snapping shut) and just typed. I just typed with my right thumb and did not smile. At anyone. Not even did I look at the train conductor with whom I always exchanged pleasantries. I just flipped him my Gold Card and kept my eyes fixated on my next memo entitled *"Murder on the Dance Floor."*

Hang on a moment. That was the song I could hear, pretty clearly, from seven rows up. Enormous headphones have got a long way to go engineering-wise I glared as I shook my head in disapproval. *Sound-proofing not that particular brand's forté?* I spoke with my eyes to the buffoon seven rows up. So, the chapter *"Murder on the Dance Floor"* was obviously scrapped and I replaced *"Dance"* with *"Parlour"*, then replaced *"Parlour"* with *"Kitchen"*, then was about to scrub even that (as on retrospect my mind could not readily recall in which room the crime had actually taken place) when I felt a sudden tap on my right shoulder.

I tensed up.

Christ, was I about to be arrested, escorted off the train in full view of all the commuters I meandered with day in day out? Well?

I turned. My entire body, not purely my low-hung, guilty-impaled head, but I turned my entire body and I twisted to face my onslaught. "Yes?" Gosh, I shocked myself. I was so abrupt. "Well?" Blimey, I was on a roll, a roll of authoritarian status and I could not snap out of it. I knew I had to act a little more demure, a little more like the old me, for my own sake (and for Jack and for Henrietta-Divine and for House-Husbandry. They didn't want an imprisoned Mother whom they felt obliged to visit every third Sunday and at Christmas did they? I had never asked them, but I rather hoped not.) "Can I help you?" I managed a slight curvature of the lip. Just one side.

"Your book. You dropped your book," an innocent, balding, baggy-suited man passed me my book. "It fell from under your arm, what with all those bags it's no wonder you can't carry everything! What have you *got* in there?" He tapped my huge red rucksack. "A dead corpse?" He actually then laughed out loud, laughed out so incredibly loud the entire carriage turned to look at us.

"Don't be absurd!" I retorted, turning red, and shaky, and far too defensive to sound normal. "It's three cartons of apple juice, two pints of skimmed milk, six bananas and a coconut. Look for yourself if you don't believe me," and I thrust my heavy bulging rucksack his way.

"I, I was only joking," and the bald-headed man skulked off. Completely off the train and into another carriage at least five coaches further down the platform. The rest of the commuters frowned and returned to pretending to digest the Evening Stardust, rustling the newspaper pages ridiculously, or to stare, insanely, into their mobiles.

Oops.

I slept on it. My guilty conscience. I slept, badly, with a less than masterful conscience and I (in my elusive nightmare) came to the awful conclusion that I had absolutely no conscience at all.

When I awoke, sleep-deprived, the following morning, nearly a whole twenty four hours after having witnessed the *event,* I contemplated my dilemma. And I was, no doubt about it, quite deep in the aftermath of a cow's dinner. It was awful.

I got up. I washed my hair. And I exfoliated my face beyond belief, as always. My skin burned, but that was no different to most mornings. Over exfoliation. And then I left. Locked the stable door behind me. And left. With my self-made cold coffee on the inside. *Bugger.* If I didn't have enough to worry about harbouring murder information and I'd left my coffee, the only thick black sludge in the world that could sufficiently wake me up (and make me think harder and over analyse my situation) out of reach. *Oh,* I found yesterday's flask in my rucksack. Even better. Very-cold-thick-black-matured-Italian-envied sludge. And there's a Green teabag in there for good measure. Antioxidants will kick-in soon. I swigged the entire lot. God! What if the police are sweeping my text messages? Did I send any, to incriminate myself, tell Anita or the Latvian loo cleaner? Did I? Did I also look a complete guilt-infested freak to the baggy-suited bald man on the train last night? S**t, did I?

Yep. The creosote Ristretto coffee had immediately kicked in. Self-over-analysis. Bugger. And, to top it all, I was only ever used to knowing, determining, moulding my life. Now, I had no idea if this dilemma was, for me, to have a merciful ending. I was out of my comfort zone. I felt wronged, bewitched, I felt pathetically jealous of myself as of yesterday morning, when all I had to worry about was my pencil. Was it sharp or blunt, hence if I had left my smart phone with the children downloading *Spider-Man* would I have to resort to the old-fashioned way of documenting words? Writing with graphite on lined paper. And, even if my pencil was sharpened, did I actually have any lined paper in my bag? Crisis. That was yesterday. That was yesterday's crisis. Today's was worthy of a brain transplant to incorporate both loss of memory and hospitalisation. That was my preferred action of the day, a brain transplantation, but even me and my wacky ideas, I did not really anticipate that to occur.

I walked, a caffeine-jittery style walk, more of a chicken-run, to my train. I got to Greater Bungchip train station early.

I never used to arrive early to Greater Bungchip. I was certain I never had. But that morning it was different. I was authentically early. Four minutes early. So, the opposition of tardiness, I had finally achieved it. But, in all honesty, I wish I hadn't. Under my circumstances anyway. Ordinarily, it would have been awesome to have arrived early; more time to write; 240 seconds more time to write. But I would rather have had a nicer, simpler, far more pleasant reason to being early for the 07:21. Not running from a murder case reason. Anything but that reason for actually waiting for a train and not leaping onto a closing train door, coat hanging off as buttons unbuttoned. I would have given anything for that rushed arrival to Greater Bungchip that morning. I hated being early now. It was like a war-zone in my head, not ditzy tall tales. Oh, anything for a ditzy tall tale now to take away the misery. *ANYTHING!*

"Morning Honey!" Perdita called from her open car window.

"Oh God!" I cried.

Perdita heard. She frowned and wound up her window. It got stuck. She grimaced. *Please, please...* I thought. *Please let the train come. Please let Perdita miss it, dear God, please?* I could not believe my own ears. What *WAS* I thinking? Perdita, she was my closest, funniest, most viable train friend. We were so close, so very close, and we both laughed at society when it freaked most people out. So why did I absolutely want her to be late for work? She was late anyway as ordinarily she would be long gone from Greater Bungchip by 07:21 but that was irrelevant today.

I couldn't, I really could not bring myself to make eye contact with Perdita as I swear she would guess my terrible plight immediately. The 07:21 hooted from a slow distance. Perdita strolled over. I looked into the trees, at the rabbits, even at my long thin knobbly fingers to avoid her. "Oh, Perdita, morning!" I falsely spoke, engulfed with transparent guilt. "You're late."

"No, no," Perdita laughed. "Working in Afflicktone today. Job share. Have a nice day, Honey!!!" She *ALWAYS* gimmicked my name. She crossed to the opposite train line, waved, and ascended into her carriage. *I* was early. *I* was early, and wading in guilt, awaiting a late train, and Perdita, Perdita breezes by and into her day as happy as a box of unopened chocolates that happens to be lurking at the back of the cupboard. What was *wrong* with me? I was a hopeless romantic not a bloody murderer.

The day seemed long, remarkably long. Each time a distant police siren rang in my ears from the depths of behind The Ritz, or along the quagmire of little, intrinsic lanes that led off and back on to Jermyn Street, I flinched. It was painstaking. Strenuous. Assiduous even. Bad. But, before I actually confessed to murder, yes, I actually did feel like I had committed the crime, the clock struck 4.45pm and I was out that door. *Gees, that was close. I had nearly confessed and I was not even at the crime scene. What was I to do?* I knew, I absolutely realised, that I could not continue on like this, to live another day looking over my shoulder for the Old Bill to clap handcuffs onto my bony wrists. What would the neighbours think? It was one thing hobbling up the pavement in Mayfair with a broken sandal, or a hole in my pump which had been there and noticed three weeks on the trot, but an arrest? That was a bit over the top, and probably fairly noticeable amongst the pin-striped suits and the tiny fluffy-pink-collared pooch.

So, I dipped my head low. I pulled my tea-cosy hat over my eyebrows, and just walked, quick-stepped, to the train station. For another, I assumed, dreadful journey home.

But, it wasn't that bad. In fact, it was quite profound. In fact, it was the most weight that could have been lifted from my bony rucksack hung shoulders in more time than I could begin to imagine.

You see, I swore I saw *the man. The dead-corpsed man.* Walking, plainly, along the street between Green Park and the Serpentine. I swear it was him! *Alive.*

I ran. I ran after the dead corpse; he obviously wasn't dead, he was absolutely alive, but for the purpose of my tale he had to be referred to the same as he always had been; to avoid confusion, you know. So, I up-paced and gained on the dead corpse. "Excuse me," I cried from upon his heels. "Ur, excuse me, Sir?" I had no idea what to call him, but he turned around to face me, the breathless wreck whom I had become.

"Yes?" the dead corpse slowly enquired. "Yes, can I help you?"

"Yes, yes...," I puffed, ridiculously. "Yes, you can, please," I added.

"Well, what is it? Are you *quite* alright, missy?" the dead corpse frowned, and then peered over the thin-rimmed spectacles which I had absolutely seen crash to the floor that awful morning; not even 36 hours ago. "Well? What have you got to say for yourself?"

"It's okay, it's okay really," I began. "I can help you, I'm a witness you see, and I'm more than happy to oblige, tell my side of things, I saw it all, you see, so there's absolutely no need for you to worry. You don't need to worry about a thing." *There, I'd confessed.* I was ever so relieved, and I felt the most blissfully deserved grin creep from the tip of my left corner lip over as far as it could go to the right.

"What *do* you mean? Witness to what, may I enquire?" the dead corpse was super friendly for a dead amoeba.

"Your killer, of course!" I was shocked that he even had to ask.

"I'm sorry, dear," the dead corpse edged backwards, still holding my gaze, but clenching his jacket pockets and covering the zips on his briefcase as if trying to protect himself from a pick pocket. *God, is that what he thought I was? A pick pocket? A common thief?* I was about to imprison his culprit and all he could do was to squander my help and believe I was a criminal.

I gave him the benefit of the doubt. Of course he was scared, vulnerable in society, so I smiled sweetly and said I'd contact the police myself and everything would seem better in the morning. The dead corpse gave me a pitiful, sceptical look, and walked off, and only was it because I hung around to make sure he was okay did I notice a possy of girls rush up to him shaking their autograph books and crying *"We love you Corny Brooks, we love you!"*

Corny Brooks? Corny Brooks the actor, the crime actor infamous for all those bloodthirsty, axe-wielding, bone-crunching murder films? Surely not? And, he was now dead? Poor man. Oh, no, he wasn't *actually* dead, but still, you know what I mean.

I pulled out my mobile as if to call the police. Get that murderous cow convicted. But then I stopped, and then I laughed at myself, my ridiculous crime-saturated self, and then I threw my red rucksack, filled to the brim today with five pints of semi-skimmed milk, three jars of blueberry conserve, two ripened sharon fruits and a thin bag of bulging lychees, high into the air; my muscles far too weak from my recent worries to be able to catch it on the way down. Its contents completely smashed to the floor, but I was *free!* And that smashing seemed to symbolise it.

Of course. It was an act! It was all a crazed murder scene being captured for a film, Corny Brooks' new film. The dead corpse was making a film. For all the mangoes in the world, I was let off. I was no longer going to prison. I was no longer harbouring serious inside information. I no longer had to endure breaking into a profound sweat when anybody of authority wearing a bright florescent uniform passed me by. *I was at liberty!* Free as a bird!

I caught a reflection of myself in an ironic police car back window which kerb-crawled past. My hair! What a state. I'd not attended to it for longer than I fancied contemplating. It was, thoroughly, a mess. Never mind, at least I could now face looking at myself in a mirror to de-tangle the masses without seeing a criminal perverting the course of justice stare right back.

Messy hair, it didn't bother me nowadays anyway. My freedom did. I had wised-up. Or, even if I never learned the ability to be wise, calm, hyper-sensitive-free, at the very least I should just plain shut my eyes to prevent any more Cinema-Graphic snapshots from clouding my better judgement; although, I didn't really have the brain capacity to entertain anything other than a crazed adaptation of events. That's for sure. A simple, watered-down, truthful series of events (reality) wasn't my strong point. I would not make a good, fair, placid, strategic cop. Not ever.

Destiny? Was I destined to be guilt-laden? Or, was this all just inspired? Inspired and stretched by the imagination for my gripping Best Seller? Oh, well, seeing as I'd made a big effort, seeing as I'd embellished, for real this time, my murder case, I might as well have sucked you all in.

A film. It was only a film; a bloodthirsty, horrific, snapshot of a murderous film which became such a reality reflected, depicted in the making to me, inside of the train window, that even *I* nearly convinced myself of its authenticity. I say *nearly*, but not quite. But I had you going, didn't I?

That Summer of 1991

London

"Fancy coming? There's no one else I can ask," Amber questioned me over breakfast. That's my sister. That one.

It was July, July 1991, and my sister had broken up for the summer holiday. University was out for the summer and she had a pair of Inter-Railing tickets she had won for 'railing-it' around Europe for that summer, that summer of 1991. A massive tour. I was 17 years old. Was my Father really going to allow us? Well, he was more likely to allow me to go, in order to keep *her* in check, to keep Amber on the straight and narrow. I was 17, she would have been 20? Yep, 20 years old, and we were allowed to go on that road trip, well, rail trip to be more precise, but it did sound ever-more exciting when I called it an Amber-style *Road Trip*. Fabulous. We took Dad's camera and we were off. (Off our rocker, more like.)

Dad dropped us, a rolling stop on his way to Tesco, at the train station. With our ruck sacks. We were clean, packed, all excited and full of beans. When we came home three weeks later, we were dirty, dishevelled, tired and never wanted to see another train platform or a dormitory bed *EVER AGAIN* (until the next time. It is equivalent to child birth, I guess. Searing pain until it's all forgotten and one blindly does it all again.)

Oh, and Mother sent Amber an email whilst we were travelling. Most odd. She must have pressed something. It is very out of context. And, how very uncommon for 1991, unless this has gotten confused with all her other emails between 1984 and 2018? Anyway, it makes for a good read so in all eventualities it does not matter where it appears in this Best Seller. And it kept us in touch with normality (if one could be so bold as to call it that. Please do not judge the formatting and the odd shading which does not easily go away.)

From: Clementine Jostick (Mother)
To: Arbuthnot Jostick (Father) ; Amber Jostick (Sister)
Sent: Tuesday, July 30, 1991 5:15 PM
Subject: Re: wenn up the`orspital

Hi Amber,

With B&C coming Friday as well as P, N & W, *(who **are** all these people?)* we forgot to give Honey a box of blueberry mini muffins we'd got for her and also the cheque for the deposit for the Christmas meal. So Dad posted them - he put the muffins in a Persil tablet box and the cheque in an envelope stuck to the outside.

Honey rang yesterday and said thanks for the muffins. I said *did you get the cheque as well* and she said *no.* I said *it was stuck to the outside of the box* and she said she must have torn it off thinking it was part of the wrapping paper, adding *I hope I haven't torn the cheque.* She went to look in the dustbin.

It gets worse!

Mum?

Yes?

The dustmen have been!!!!!!!!!!!!! She laughed, and I thought there's nothing wrong with a bit of levity now and then. Nothing wrong at all with the treatment of a serious matter with humour or lack of due respect. *Your Father will have to write another cheque,* I said. *And he will have to find another pen as all the ones in his pen pot are "old and blobby",* he had said for the fourteenth time.

Love Mum x

From: Honey Jostick (Me)

To: Arbuthnot Jostick ; Amber Jostick

Sent: Wednesday, July 31, 1991 5:19 PM

Subject: Re: wenn up the`orspital

Hi Honey (and copied you in Amber – Mum had flu for a week which I don't think I told you - or it may not have been flu, not sure. She'll explain.) We went to the Lester Hospital most of yesterday. I'll leave her to say about it - we went at 5.15pm and came back at 1.15am. Must do it again sometime. Anyhow, she has some antibiotics so they should be the answer.

Love   Dad x

Hi girls. It's Mum now. With all the details. What happened was that gland at the top of my right leg was really hurting still on Monday and I was still waking up drenched with perspiration, so I managed to get an appointment with Dr Make-Cuppa in the afternoon (Monday. Funny name for a Dr, isn't it?) I presumed it was a lymph node which was trying to stop infection from getting past.

So Dr Make-Cuppa looked at my right leg and poked it and prodded it and said she wanted me to go straight to hospital (A & E) and give them a letter she was writing. She said it was not absolutely typical of a lymph node and was concerned it may be a thrombosis (DVT.) She rang them up while I was there and explained that she was sending me. (The doctors' special hotline was blocked up it was so busy, so she had to ring the normal number and wait for all the options to be rattled off.) She said they were very busy there that day and to take a good book.

We arrived at 5.15pm and I had to check in at Reception. We were behind a man holding his head. Reception rang through to the doctor's team when I explained that Dr Make-Cuppa had rung. They asked if I was walking. When she told them *yes, I was walking,* they told her to tell me to sit in Reception and wait. (Should have got Dad to carry me in thinking about it, but it's no good now suddenly having good ideas.) At first we only paid for two hours in the car park. Reception also mentioned that I would go to an assessment ward at some point (but not necessarily have to stay overnight which I was very pleased about seeing as all my best nighties were still screwed up in the washing bin.)

Reception was PACKED. There was a girl who had taken an overdose of Paracetamol, a girl who had just smashed up her bedroom and a piece of the mirror had gashed her arm, a boy with something in his eye, three young people - the boy kept saying to one of the girls *you do realise this is all your fault, don't you?,* several people with hand injuries, all the relations of a man who had had a stroke who kept taking it in turns to go in and sit with him, a woman with dreadful stomach pains, a man with horrific chest pains, various limping men, a youth who was lost and thought he was in the Bookies, and some tall people in tall wheelchairs.

After about three quarters of an hour, I was called to a little desk in Reception where they take even more details and also your pulse, blood pressure and temperature. Then we had a wait of several hours before I was called into another room to give some blood samples. Dad bought another car park ticket for more hours. They left a needle sticking out of the inside of my elbow in case anyone needed to administer anything intravenously.

Dad was forced to listen to all the soaps on the TV which was permanently on just below the ceiling.

Another time limit was reached for the car park but apparently someone said no one checks in the night so we left it at that.

Countless people kept being called (but not me.) Dad checked a couple of times - once there was a spare bed but no doctor, and then there was a doctor but no bed. It depended what people were in for and whether doctors were called away etc.

Then a tetchy man with a red knitted hat and black tracksuit bottoms came up and asked me if he could lie down. I couldn't think of a reason not to, so I said *yes.* He then lay across all the seats opposite and started saying *Give me some painkillers. I want some painkillers, please. It is my entire fault.* He started thrashing up and down on the seats in agony. Apparently he'd been in the day before as well and had been given pain relief for the pain caused by drinking. Someone eventually carted him off somewhere and the next we saw of him he was talking to the 7ft security guard while waiting for his wife to collect him. (The patient not the security guard, but I think the security guard wished otherwise.)

It must have been round about 11.00pm that I was eventually called to see the medics. I started off being seen by a nice young female English doctor with red streaks. She then explained it all to a small French doctor. They didn't seem to think it was a DVT thankfully but said they wanted me to have a chest x-ray because of the perspiration at night. I said I take a boiling hot water bottle to bed with me and have seven blankets to feel secure, and for some reason they all looked at each other, rolled their eyes and couldn't seem to get through the procedure quick enough. They wanted to know if I'd been in contact with anyone with TB or had I been to foreign places. I told them about the 17 mosquito bites from 26 years ago. They said when I came back from the x-ray they wanted me to see a surgeon, and if he thought I could go home, then I could go home.

I was ages waiting in x-ray - Dad was writing with the latest *Etch-a-Sketch* from the children's toy box. Takes me back to when, oh, hang on a minute, he was doing it then as well when you and your sister were trying your very best to get your toy back from your Father.

I digress. Then the x-ray man said *you've still got your bra on!* I was thinking *how does he know that?* - But the under-wires had shown up on my x-ray - no one said to take it off. He said *your x-ray is in the computer,* and then he went home for the night. When I got called back they all knew I'd still had my bra on. I knew from the sniggers.

Then the surgeon arrived. He was extremely pale and very quiet and ever so polite. I hadn't realised he did not speak a word of English, and my Saudi Arabian is not as good as it used to be, so we all got by with smiles and nods of the head, which, to me, does not seem the best method of communication when trying to explain a possible threatening illness.

So many people had poked it, my sort of lump, on Monday that it was beginning to object in a big way! He didn't think it was a DVT or a hernia (another suggestion from earlier - I had to cough several times) but that it was in fact *a reactive lymph node.* The area below it was red and a bit lumpy and was feeling a bit hard by now. I did then mention the cat scratch (don't actually remember it happening but can't think what else it could have been) and how infection travels up your leg and gets caught in your lymph nodes. I don't know why it has gone *reactive* though. Best not to ask. Well, I guess I couldn't unless there was a translator present, but seeing as I wasn't on the Eurovision Song Contest that seemed a long-shot.

Anyway, the mute nodding surgeon prescribed *Phenoxymethylpenicillin 250mg* (2 tablets four times a day) and *Flucloxacillin Capsules 250mg* (1 capsule four times a day.) The foulest tasting things I've ever had - (supposed to swallow whole but had dissolved before gone down.) He said if the inflamed area below it gets bigger or the gland itself gets bigger or it is all still the same after the course of pills I have to go back and they will have to do an ultrasound imaging I think to see what's going on. So fingers crossed it all works. Don't want to spend another evening in that place. The cats must have been really hungry - I had visions of them eating each other. We had our tea at 1.45am.

I'm sure Dad could have told you all that, but I see he said I would explain.

Oh, before I forget, I've won a Mohair Throw from a competition in *Period Living* (I belong to *Loquax Competitions Portal* which is free to join.)

Well Twiglet and I had better have our pills now. *That's the cat, one of them.*

Thanks for asking.

Love Mum x

To: Honey Jostick

Sent: Wednesday, August 01, 1991 1:52 PM

Subject: wenn up the`orspital

Did you reply to Pru & Maurice or Florence about the long details of the fire that they sent? *They didn't send a fire; I assume my Father is referring to the email that they sent referring to the Australian bush fires. That reminds me of the time my Father's email account was rather deranged. He received an email saying:*

> *"The cat is dead*
>
> *Happy to be here."*

Rather short and to the point and lacking in any compassion was my first reaction. We then realised the email was badly arranged, and the grammar should have been.

> *"The cat is dead happy to be here."*

We digress, again.

Funny weather here - spring sun and then it pours with rain. Daffs and Croci all coming out though. Sorry to hear about Andrew's job, but wasn't entirely unexpected I guess - though it's still a shock when it actually happens. Good that you can go back, although a bit of a culture change for the both of you - not that that matters nowadays. Can Andrew become self-employed whilst looking for another job, as re-employment (as I found in the early 1980s and 1990s) is tough in recessions?

Still, you have Will to keep you busy.

Love Dad x

I have *no* idea what my Father was talking about to this day. Or who *any* of the people in the email are. I think that last paragraph about jobs and the recession was meant for another recipient who, I hope, isn't still awaiting a compassionate reply from my Father 25 years on.

La France

I just could not put them down. Mother Clementine's tales. Amber was flicking through the *Lonely Planet* to Paris. A Parisian thumbed copy from her university chum who had recently visited this City of Romance (and gotten her passport stolen. Idiot, that was *so* not going to happen to me. I was far too street-wise. I tutted again, like the first time Amber had told me about Rhianna and her passport theft. What a naïve girl. That's just pure candid gullibility. Puh!)

The Great British train rumbled out of Finsbury Park. It was only 23 minutes since Father had pushed us out of the car on the way to buy milk and loo rolls at Tesco. We both hoped that he thought before acting this time. Father went home with one hundred bread rolls one Saturday with absolutely no idea what we would be using them for. Mother's shopping list had clearly meant 'loo', toilet rolls. Not 100 bread rolls.

The train lurched itself towards Kings Cross. We came to a stop. The carriage, packed with part-time workers taking the cheaper after 10:00am service, bumped, and the people tripped as they stood up too early when the locomotive plummeted into its final descent, and this puzzled me somewhat as I was certain these commuters would surely know by now the train's wild antics.

Anyway, Kings Cross. We had arrived. I folded up the collection of old printed-out emails and letters I had brought along for this Road Trip (which I had read and read again on the short train stint from Draycod to Kings Cross) in case I got homesick for a smackering of Motherly weirdness, and slid them inside my rucksack. Secretly, I couldn't wait for a new story to come in. A fresh dilemma onto my phone. The papers squashed my banana and sliced the skin right through, but that, little did I know, was to be the least of my issues for the next three long weeks.

Amber and I threw our rucksacks, stealthily, onto our backs. Our shoulders were broad and strong; then. *We* were strong, ambitious and raring to go. "I need the loo," my sister announced to the entire trainload of commuters, and she heaved herself into the train's one and only rancid toilet which boasted only a terrible stretch, no toilet paper and outrageously boiling water beyond belief in which to wash your hands. Amber got stuck. I don't mean *one too many pork pies stuck*, I mean the ridiculousness of shoving herself wearing her jam-packed rucksack through the thinnest, non-being-able-to-move-nor-turn-around train toilet door stuck. That type of stuck. I rolled my eyes. It was to be a long, garishly long, three weeks abroad. (That was if we ever managed to prise my sister free of the train toilet door which was nearing its departure back from whence it had come.)

At last we managed to remove the female (my sister), with rucksack embedded, from the on-board lavatory cubicle. We were now ready to go. *Really* go.

And, off we went.

Oh God, if only hindsight was a pre-written book readily available for purchase. If only. I'd be a millionaire, and this train, pah, I would not be riding aboard its cosy offerings.

So, we, two unassuming sisters, one older, one younger, one at university, one still just studying A Levels, one blond and one crow-haired, but neither street-wise and both far too discerning and far too naive (one, myself, excessively so I will admit now) headed down into the London Underground for... *"Sorry, sis, where are we going again?"*

"Europe," Amber flicked her curled fringe which always curled up and of which she absolutely detested. In wet weather, one part of her fringe would curl up so much she had once threatened to cut it off. But she didn't. Jack did at school in later years. He cut the hugest of chunks from his fringe during a forfeit playing cards.

"Well, I know *that*, but where *exactly* in Europe?" I looked, haphazardly, at the collection of intermingled, overlapping coloured lines which was the London Underground. The coloured lines printed onto an enormous board were vast, and I had to stand back to be able to take it all in. The board represented a mass of travel options. I looked and smiled and ran the tip of my left index finger across varying lines pretending to look smart and knowledgeable to the random herd of commuters bumbling, pushing and swanning by. I didn't know why I felt the need to appear an intellect to the London Underground system as it was fairly unlikely I would ever see this particular sea of faces ever again, but something I had read in *The Rough Guide to Paris* had instilled a certain level of credit within me and I had the urge to *appear* shrewd, artful even.

"We need *this* one," I harked with my eyes closed and in a state of amusement only a five-year old playing Pin the Tail on the Donkey would endure. And, like a five-year old, I cried for several hours after my choice became non-negotiable when it appeared I could not change my mind.

So, we took the pale blue line, called the Victoria Line, and managed to take in an unexplained detour of Buckingham Palace before heading to Big Ben, Trafalgar Square, and Notting Hill and, finally, Kew Gardens having interchanged across a rainbow of colours on my mini-map version.

We needed Dover.

We got there at dusk.

We called Dad from a payphone and I still wonder to this day why he chuckled, disguised by a coughing fit, when we said we were about to board our ferry to Calais. In retrospect, I suppose we could have flown to Boston, Massachusetts in the 7 hours and 53 minutes we had perused the London tourist trap, but as we so rightly corrected our Father, it was absolutely intentional to use our time wisely and visit London's greatest before taking to the French seas; *La Manche.*

We sat down.

Finally, after a day heaving around those blessed rucksacks filled to the brim with rolled-up vest tops, flowery elasticated shorts, Evian water (to elude ourselves as being Parisians), stolen napkins (and a whole bunch of other accessories from the latest coffee shops and toilets such as flowery loo roll and toothpicks just because they were easy to bag even though we had no intention of even using toothpicks unless we needed to prick a pick-pocket, and even then we would have to find them at the bottom of our bursting bags before the pick-pocket headed off with our passports and money), a velvet hair scrunchie in every plausible shade known to man and three empty packets of Smarties, we sat down and the ferry set sail.

I closed my eyes.

I felt sick.

The sweaty lorry driver slouched next to me smelt of sick, or was it perspiration? And that did not help my cause. We were still within the parameters of Dover Port, and I felt sick. Travel sick. Dreadfully travel sick more than I remembered ever feeling even on those bumpy-tracked roads we used to take as a family to Wells-Next-The-Sea. As sick as that, but worse. In a car, Dad used to stop. Let me get a smackering of fresh air. Here, on the ferry, it was non-stop sailing until we hit the French coast. Literally. I clenched my hands, sweated to death and sucked it up. I was green. I was *verte* say the French. We had arrived to beret-adorned, Espresso-aroma-ed, baguette and smelly cheese land. But all I wanted to do was curl up and die. Okay, sleep, but die sounded far punchier for a Best Seller. Then, as I peered over the side of the ferry, which I pride myself that I was still actually lucky to be sailing within having forced myself to not hurl my entire sick body over the side into the choppy, arid waters below, I changed my mind. I *did* want to die.

The smell of that Camembert was horrific.

A ferry porter smiled, sweetly, his toothless grin perpetuating the situation, and herded us all off like mutton. He stank. Worse than the cheese. His breathe was so unappealing that I actually wanted to re-board the ferry on which we had arrived and notwithstanding the choppier seas as the burlesque wind blew up head straight back to Dover.

We caught the next train to Paris. *Christ!* It was *fast!* The *RER* was like a bullet; making the Great British trains seem heroically touristy and quite frankly like a teenager taking her first driving lesson. That slow, but not cautious like a teenager taking her first driving lesson, just slow. And smooth. Those French trains destined for Paris were so incredibly smooth that I thought I was just lying on the beach listening to the gulls above in the sky float about on the softest thermal there could be. And I liked it. The voyage swayed me to sleep, and when Amber and I were rattled from our dreams of soft-feathered pillows and downy-filled duvets, Paris was right there. Paris was here, the bright lights of the Eiffel Tower sparkled into my bleary eyes, and the gentle floating Parisian dialect flooded in and out of my soft-listening ears. The accordion played its sweet musique, and the smell of wine (authentically unique and personally foot-crushed) drifted our way.

And so did the smell of urine. It was *foul.* Foul, in fact was an understatement; it was such a reeking stench that I had to shove my fleece up both nostrils and get off that train. The platform was mildly better, smell-wise, unless Amber and I had just gotten used to it. Our nostrils had become incenses and we had, luckily for us, become acclimatised to the odours which were about to pop up everywhere as a perpetual daily routine. We better had become used to it as we were now in Europe, and in Europe in 1991, cleanliness was not a top priority. I sipped my water.

"Bonjour!" Angelina called. Phew, my sister's friend from school had arrived at *Paris Gare du Nord.*

We were going to stay at her apartment for a long weekend. Oh how luxurious. I had told all my school friends. *She has an apartment overlooking the Eiffel Tower,* I had boasted. *My sister gave me one of her European travel tickets, and we are going to stay true Paris-style in an authentic apartment in central Paris with Angelina.* I tried to pretend it was just a normal occurrence for me, but I oozed opulence.

The apartment didn't. We arrived at Angelina's apartment and, at first, I thought there had been an oversight. Angelina's apartment did not ooze opulence at all. In fact, the smell of urine on the train a few hours before had been better than the smell right next to where I was supposed to be sleeping.

"Shall we go out?" Amber questioned her friend who was obviously far more used to the stench; it did not seem to bother her at all. Also, Angelina had greasy hair and an unkempt look about her. She had, most definitely, turned Parisian. We had also better get used to it.

"Oh sure, if you like," Angelina replied, and we were both thankful she did not pick-up on our disgust at the petit, smelly, shared-toileted apartment in which we had to sleep for the next four nights. FOUR NIGHTS! If we made it that far without passing out completely.

We headed out.

Angelina looked quite the chic lady of whom I barely recognised. Amber kept glancing her friend up and down. Angelina was wearing tan open-toed leather sandals (with taupe glossy tights, or hold-ups, I couldn't quite see until she bent over and then it was quite obvious she was sporting suspenders.) She had her entire head of hair greased back into a ballet-bun, and her top was silver-sequined. Actually, it turned out it was a dress, and I'm so glad I had refrained from letting her know she had forgotten to put on her skirt.

I was wearing elasticated shorts, plimsolls, a vest top and a ponytail in my hair. Amber was much the same although she had bright white trainers with banana coloured stripes along each side veering towards the fact that she was about to go running. It was amazing how twenty years later, Amber looked just like Angelina, having herself emigrated to Nice and, despite mocking her friend of her glittery, low-slung, extremely eye-catching appearance by most Paris males during our four day *holiday* in 1991, Amber found it absolutely crucial to look like that too after just a few days being brain-washed Niçoise-style.

It suited them. And me too, when I lurked about in Mayfair during some of our better Indian-summer months twenty years later.

So, *Le Paris*, what can I say? The *Metro* was harsher. The train doors snapped shut unlike in London where health and safety is, for certain, far more paramount. The French drove fast, walked fast, cycled fast and even swigged their wine fast (although with the latter, I could not decide if that was the *Brits Abroad*.) That said, red wine, pink wine, white wine and even purple, I swear, flowed, and the four days in Paris flew by in a vociferous, dysfunctional, French-style haze. It wasn't until Amber and I were air-kissing Angelina and talking with our arms, both of us dressed in newly acquired matching sparkly denim shorts, and not having even used Angelina's shower, that we realised Paris wasn't that smelly after all. It was us Brits over-analysing life.

Still blowing kisses and waving white starched hankies, our train left the romantic lights of Gai Paris in its tracks. Amber and I watched, open-mouthed, as suburbs appeared and the opulence retired. *Versailles* came and went. *Duveuney* came and went. Even *La Fabieujeux* came. And went. Delightful Parisian urban titles of areas named outrageously nicely, but graphited as if this was thing of which to be proud, producing high-rises and conglomerates as far as the eye could imagine, waiting to be double-glazed soon, disappeared.

Then fields. Oh! Cows! Sheep! Goats, I think. Rural farms and red-tiled farmhouses appeared out of nowhere. It was heaven. Green and grassy and, oh, blimey, the worst manure stench I had *ever* had the misfortune to have up my nose. The train halted. It had an unscheduled stop at *Wyvieux.* Three old peasants needed a ride to Pisa, so the city train was alerted and briefly ceased its journey in order to collect these random passengers from their random stop.

Wyvieux was beautiful. Insanely beautiful, and these three old dears had absolutely no idea that their request helped my yearning desire for rural-ness after a frantic time spent in the whirlwind of the Parisian highlife where I felt I had had no sleep at all for in excess of 96 hours. It was fabulous (the rural lush greenery, not the tiredness my eyes were now experiencing.) And then, for no other reason than sheer politeness, the conductor helped the three old dears with their luggage, pulled the enormous train cord which in turn puffed huge clouds of dark grey smoke onto not only the three old dears and their luggage but the entire village of Wyvieux too, gathered speed and caught up the time we had lost to avoid the 09h16 train from Paris to Pisa running late. *Did you hear that Great Britain?* I called into the wilderness. We were not to be late.

Pisa

We arrived bang on.

There was a thunderstorm.

It was massive. We had no umbrella but the hotel was so '60's and appealing with old Victorian open-levered metal lifts run by cogs and ropes that the horizontally sheet rain blew away any cobwebs that would cloud my judgement of Pisa. It was nice. Pisa, it was nice. The lifts with their cogs were so incredulously slow, but juxta-positioned with the liveliness of Paris, the deceleration that Pisa offered was insanely nice. The apathy was, to be honest, divine. The hindrance of the waiters and the delay in which the porters denied you any chat was so welcome, and the gradual deliberation to listlessness was heaven.

But, I was hungry. It was strange. In a country where I thought even snails would overtake the normal tourist mooching along the pavement, in a place where I thought the cars were continually pressed to exhaustive acceleration as if the driver had died and gotten his flip-flop stuck on the gas, in a city where I had only ever thought lethargy was not a word to even whisper unless you fancied a term in jail, it was idle.

Amber and I went out (once we had dejected the metal cog lift as a way to exit the building and took the steep winding staircase that surely had far more steps than was possible to go the same distance as the lift would have covered if it were ever to have arrived.) We, reluctantly, went out. It was still sheeting with rain, but not quite so much unless we were so delirious with hunger that we failed to notice our shoes filling up with water and our hair growing more than three inches weighted down with precipitation. It was like Paris; once there, any etiquette learned from previous existence fell away like a bad dream.

I visited Pisa years later with House-Husbandry and it was nice then too. There was a horrific thunderstorm also, again, but Pisa, it was still *nice*. Pleasant; not romantic like Paris, nor glamorous like Nice, nor ancient and vast like Rome. But simply Pisa; with a river, a tower and a *Nice Modern Pub*. The river Arno and its mythic, Napoleonic bridges are classic, but not over-bearing, and Pisa's niceness was essential for that point in our travels. Calm. Calm before the midnight storm.

We went in that *pub* on both visits (with Amber and with House-Husbandry) to shelter from the rain. We stayed all night too, on both visits, and I now come to the conclusion that on the second visit, with House-Husbandry, was by far the calmest. Even the ale pump ceased to work as the tower had been struck by lightning. It was *that* calm. Then, we walked back along the river to combat pretty much vastly similar hotel encounters with far too many oddities akin to both visits that it's too scary to mention considering the decades apart in which there had been ample time for building works to fix the lackadaisical lifts and the indolent swivelling doors, and even the reluctance in which the chambermaids could, on both visits, ever engage us with their presence to simply make the bed. Decades apart from the other, we walked that river. It was full both times, the river, more than full; the water gushing, mediocre in its ebb, and not particularly dramatically, downstream.

Amber and I had sat out in the warm evening breeze after the cracking tropical storm had departed, and chatted with some local Italian boys in 1991. (Decades later I had probably seen them again, sleazing at other girls then in their mid-forties.) My sister had done most of the talking back then, flirting should I say. I had just propped my stick body up next to her to appear interested but I had never been interested in smarmy, flirtatious strangers leering at me. And those smarmy strangers being greasy Italian in origin did not make the situation any less vomit-inducing.

It made me vomit. I always tried to fit in, and smile, and hitch up my skirt to a lesser degree a level than Amber's but I always thought it was more revealing because I was so tall. Amber was three years my senior, but I was always taller than her by a good few inches. She made up for it in other areas. However, *my* agenda? I always couldn't wait to curl up with a big fat adventure book and a dark hot chocolate.

That night, that *first* night in Pisa, by the fast-ish flowing river, with Amber, I got none of that. We ended up staying out until past 2am. My sister had become quite tipsy on the local brew, and the Italians were quite broody seeing her like that (mind you, I think Italian men are born broody and it would not surprise me in the least if their Mothers still nursed them well into their twenties.) I was more than happy for *La Polizia* to move us all on; arresting one for jumping bail or even murder by the sounds of the loudness and the vocalised dramatic gestures and the abuse that was coming out of all of their mouths in unison. Nothing was intelligible. (Mind you, having seen Italians conducting politics on prime time television, there was not much between it and that night on the bridge.) Either murder or one of the Italian lads was the policeman's son. Verbosity had escalated to the highest piercingly mind-blowing degree and in Italian the simple ordering of a cup of tea could sound, to the English outsider, like World War Three had actually begun. It most probably had but the Italian voices rose higher in decibels, disguising any such onslaught.

Amber and I crept in at nearly a quarter to three. In hope that our Youth Hostel room was still just for a duo, we fell asleep too tired to even look if the other two bunks were occupied.

By 05:55am, our question was answered. Four ghastly loud female Texans were zipping bags, unzipping bags, re-zipping bags, rustling maps and *whispering* about how many rashers of bacon they would consume to soak up last night's beer before their flight to Rome. *Flight?* I had thought. *What's wrong with the train?* I shoved my head further under my pillow to stifle my nausea, and I wasn't even hung-over.

Pisa in the daylight was beautiful. Arty, quintessential, and beautiful. It was beautiful, not just nice, but *beautiful* during the sunshine which flooded onto the *Campo dei Miracoli;*

translated as such as *The Field of Miracles*, and quite rightly so. We sat, in the *Square,* on the neatly cut heat-scorched, but still green, grass and looked up at the Tower. *The Leaning Tower* was, absolutely, leaning, and we did the touristy thing and stood way in front holding our arms out to one side so, in the clever photograph, the victim appeared to be holding it. Then we ate an extortionately priced double-chocolate *Gelato.* It would be rude not to have done. It was delicious, the ice-cream, but the deliciousness of the extortionately priced double-chocolate Gelato was sucked up by those bloody Italians from the previous night rocking up again. They spotted us, and this time I walked off leaving Amber to flirt alone.

I went to look at the *Mother of the Earth* stalls, as I always call them; still nowadays. These stalls sold fake leather bracelets, candles, flags, t-shirts, tie-on cloth sun hats and all sorts of other things that we absolutely did not need (and would absolutely not fit in our already jam-packed rucksacks.) I sauntered around still licking my Espresso strength ice-cream. It was worth it. *I* was worth it!

And, whilst Amber battered her eyelashes at the *Marcos* and the *Valentinos*, I became inherently aware, and became an intrinsic part, of the excavation that took place right in front of me. *Quelle chance!* Archaeological remains from the 5th century BC confirmed the existence of a city at the sea, trading with *Greeks and Gauls.* The presence of an *Etruscan Necropolis,* discovered during excavations in the *Arena Garibaldi* in 1991, confirmed its Etruscan origins. I was there, but although I searched and searched, there was not a Garibaldi biscuit in sight.

Florence

Pisa had been lush. Historical, Gothic, educational, even intellectual (despite the Italians.) But we ambled along to the train station to head for even lusher *coins*.

Florence. Now that was better. It was every bit as nice as *The Rough Guide* depicted. Extremely Florentine in all its culture, art and beauty. And, not a sleazy Italian Romeo in sight, so I had gotten back my sister.

Amber, she was an intellect for sure. She was studying Business French at a university built under the busy architectural design called *Spaghetti Junction;* Maston University. Now, that wasn't nice, but Amber, she was. She was very intelligent, and very modern, and very, very driven. Towards men. She liked men. I did too. I really did. But Amber, she was enticed towards the Brad Pitt type, and me, well, I was more of a Jonathan Creek type of girl.

So, *Palazzo Pitti* was a favourite of mine, or *Pitti Palace* as I liked to call it. I actually got lost inside this museum, but if it hadn't been for my lack of knowledge of the Italian language, hence my inability to completely understand the signs, I would never have found my *own* Marco. This curly-haired Italian equivalent of Jonathan Creek showed me the best way to order an Espresso and definitely endorsed the best way to flirt even by my smallish standards on direct flirting with an unknown entity. I was more of a personality-type driven hopeless romantic rather than a looks-type of lover (hope House-Husbandry never takes time out from his masterfully building of tree-houses, or his Neanderthal plucking of fish from the local Bourne for dinner, to flick open this Best Seller at such a page.) My House-Husbandry is rugged and good looking *and* hopeless, sorry, I mean hopeless*ly* inflicted with romance in his own way. Despite proposing for our marriage wearing *Marigolds* and offering a bunch of garden daffodils doused in bugs (and a sparkly ring), and hoarding 27 bags of *on-offer* luxury cereal to himself having calculated they would indeed last him 18 months at 3 scoops a day if no one else helped themselves, he *is* kind, and he *does* do so much more than a general man-of-the-house would do, I am sure. House-Husbandry takes on rugby, cookery, spellings, art, music and playfulness with the offspring whilst I trudge up and down from Greater Bungchip to London each working day, and, in all honesty, if the cooking and the cleaning and the vacuuming and the reversing of the car at ballet and at rugby was in fact up to me, all the aforementioned would, undoubtedly, never be done on time or indeed at all. In fact, I'll stick to organising high flying bankers and dictating in prose this Best Seller, and House-Husbandry can absolutely stick to unsalted butter in cooking and de-monsterising the orchard from entanglement-anonymous.

Anyway, Florence. There was not a little brown-haired girl followed by a springy robot or an orange whizzy dog in sight. Nope, Florence was not just a wee sweet character from *The Magic Roundabout*, Florence was divine. Florence is the capital city of the Italian region called Tuscany. In later years, House-Husbandry and I went to Tuscany too. We hired a villa (pre-children) and we met the odd nun, and we accidentally gate-crashed a wedding, and we saw the estranged pizza place dug into the hills of which we only fell upon because the key attendant for our villa arrived five hours late (and even at our rolling of the eyes and tapping of the watches she regarded *us* as if *we* were the oddities; 5 hours? What's that between friends?) And we made love in those said hills, being overlooked by that said nun who appeared from bleedin' nowhere.

With Amber, it was inherently different. I did not meet any nuns; in fact we barely set foot outside of the ramparts of the Tuscan walled city save our bus taking us to *Fiesole.* Fiesole was impeccable; an absolute stunner, which is more than I can say for the hordes of people (generally gypsies and the like) which lined its thin, twisting, cobbled streets up to the top. Fiesole lies 8km above Florence, and when finally at the top (the bus drove us up, thankfully, and we fast-paced it down according to the gravitational pull of the architect who apparently laid those streets pissed at an angle.)

Amber and I decided that the intrusion of the dark-skinned gypsies (or were they the burnt-to-a-frazzle auburn tourists? – it was hard to tell them apart once altitude sickness had set in) were too much to see mile after mile, so we opted for a more cultural afternoon before even more dark-skinned Italians lined the already packed streets to entertain themselves of sorts; generally students and young ruffians with nothing better to do than drink wine and wee into the river on a hot summer's evening. Much the same as London really, but the climate in Florence was far more appealing and the wine could readily be stolen from a parentals' cellar without anyone noticing whatsoever. In fact, the mere fact that children aged seven were cruising the streets at 11pm did not bother their parents. They, in fact, wholly commended the entire affair.

So, Florence Cathedral it was. Its terracotta-tiled dome roof, engineered by Brunelleschi, and the Bell Tower, designed by Giotto, were sights for sore eyes. But to get there? That was not. A vague, rugged Fatherly whisper at the back of my mind suffered something like *perspective* and three hours, blistered from head to toe and parched to death's door, later we arrived. It was shut. Only open for the mere miniscule of less than one hour a day for tourists did not quite seem right. How on earth were the Italians to pay off their national debt by use of charitable donations *for the church* (nudge nudge, wink wink) if the largest attraction in the city was closed for 23 of the 24 hours that Florence was alive? Never mind. As long as the siestas were long and the dining out even longer, then who am I to complain?

Rome

Stepping off the train at Rome from Florence with Amber was the equivalent of having bathed in soft pink rose petals to now find oneself walking on chipped broken glass.

Florence had been velvety green and Rome was as dry as my Father's Christmas turkey with no gravy in comparison. He liked that, but it wasn't for everyone. No one, as I found, as the years went on.

The Roman sun was scorching, the gravelled roads were cracked with heat, and my sunglasses were 153 UV Ray protective too low. Perhaps I should have been less thrifty when it came to eye protection and not purely used my £10 Dorothy Perkins voucher, with change given.

Crack! I had happily, and light-footedly, stepped off the hefty maroon-coloured train in Southern Italy, but it appeared that my sister hadn't. In fact, Amber was clutching her head and howling in searing pain. I frowned, not quite realising the seriousness of the situation. I had initially thought Amber was just moved to tears with the heat-wave Rome was exuding. She was quite a sun-worshipper, and in 1987 on her first trip abroad with *the girls*, her black body on her return from the Canary Islands was enough to make our tarmacked drive appear positively snowy in comparison. But no, her head was actually showing a trickle of blood.

"Christ, *Amber?*" I cried, trying to run back to save her, my heavy rucksack determining me to be a turtle mooching along however hard I paced.

"I am zee mostio terriblio sorrio," a dark-skinned, dark-haired, dark-eyed muscle-embossed man-of-a-man stepped down out of the train behind Amber. "My guitario just slippioed out of my handios and it landed on your friendio's headio," he continued.

"You-o are not-o for realio?" *God, did I say that out loudio?* I replied, just as the car park barrier also then quite out of the blue fell on poor Amber's head, on top of her already bruised guitar incident, and her expensive sunglasses smashed to smithereens. *"Thanko heavensio for Doroth-io Perkins-io,"* I had muttered, completely at a loss of what else to say.

Amber huffed, picked up her rucksack and we left the train station for good-io. Her sunglasses, wrecked, stayed on the car-parkio-floorio. A guitar and a car park barrier hitting her on the head made her never, ever want to go to Roma again. To this day, she has kept to that.

That night was hot. Very hot. But our accommodation was quite snazzy. We had been tipped off that instead of Youth Hostelling; we could actually pay the same amount and get ourselves something quite upmarket. It called itself a *Pensionne.* That was like a guest house. So we could get a room just for us, with a balcony just for us, with a wind tunnel just for us on said balcony just for us which could blow all our hand-rinsed underwear and partly-washed towels into the dustcart that felt the need to park stationary directly below; all just for us. Nice. It was though, nice. And at the very least, our rucksacks were lighter of clothes and towels, and we did not have to endure god awful Texans at 05:55am.

Instead, we had to endure the Rome Embassy as I had gotten my passport stolen. Okay, okay, it wasn't my fault. And, I suppose, I should never have mentioned that Rhianna was a stupid naïve fool getting her passport stolen before I had even left the parameters of my safe house in Draycod, but I had to hold on to something on the packed bus back from the Vatican City after my sister had rushed in, totally embarrassingly, completely flaunting the law of Catholicism, past the Vatican officials in her off the shoulder t-shirt and her above the knee shorts. She nearly got us arrested. But no, it was me. I had to hold on to the bar on the rocking bus, the rocking packed bus, whilst the gypsy three foot tall below was scavenging in my bum-bag.

We waited. And waited. And waited in the Rome Embassy. Amber was nearly thrown out of by some frantic Italian official when her solitary bottle of water could have supposedly been acid. *Yes, really?* I thought that too. But she flirted with him and all was seemingly brushed under the carpet. That is how all Italian politics and scandals are straightened out I had come to realise. So we waited for our turn, our turn to call our Father and get him to bail us out. He sent us some money, we bought a new European Train Pass (I failed to mention, and was rather embarrassed to mention earlier, that my entire contents of my £2.99 bum-bag had been taken.) Father Arbuthnot qualified we were who we said we were, in our matching flowery elasticated shorts, I had my mug-shot taken for an emergency passport, and we left Rome well and truly behind us. We had not stayed long; we had not actually intended to stay long even before our minor theatrical robbery. It was smelly, big, and colossally big to be honest, dusty, cramped, and loud (very loud) and despite the images of the Vatican and the Colosseum and even the Trevi Fountain looking promising from the guide books, in reality, Rome, it was rather crud.

When I opened the facsimile my Father had sent to the Rome Embassy, he also included a letter. *"There are thieves in Florence too,"* he had typed. That warning was too late as we had already visited Florence. A better experience than in Rome. But, the funniest, was an article he included about *Top Gear*. It said:

Letter in today's Telegraph says 'The BBC should change to proper programmes about cars and motoring related news. This would make a welcome change from the barmy antics of three elderly buffoons who should know better'. I couldn't agree more.

Arb. Xxx

Lucerne

I stared at my Italian passport. I don't mean I had completely changed nationality and become an estranged *Bambino*, I mean my passport was now just a thick cream coloured A5-sized piece of paper valid for one year stamped by a bronzed official telling me in Italian not to fall foul to gypsies again, I had been warned, and I was a naïve, pale, inadequate 17 year old English girl destined for failure. I understood every last word. He just smiled and I smiled back. What more was to be said? I suppose I had presented myself to be every one of his descriptions, but needless to say, it was pointless arguing back. I would only end up in prison, and I'm sure Arbuthnot Jostick had not the slightest intention of accepting reverse charges from abroad again. He didn't sound too enthused the first time around, but, I suppose, he felt obliged. His youngest daughter had been robbed to an inch of her life. If she ended up on the wrong side of the law, he would probably tell the officials to keep me there until I had earned enough money to bus-it back home.

So, instead of a multitude of greenish pages whereby I had collected numerous pretty cool stamps from various countries over a prolonged exciting period of my life, this new identity card was just that; a card. A flimsy card which probably, seen by authoritative figures, means *loser, she got her proper passport stolen, airhead.* But, the photo, I liked it, so that was about all I cared. My Italian mug-shot. I liked it. My hair was glossy, my eyes were enormous, and my nose not quite as stubby as I had always assumed.

Switzerland seemed a long, long, *long* way away. It was. A long way in mileage and a long way in culture. But, it was worth it. As much as Rome had been hellish, Lucerne, it was angelic. It was divine. It was, absolutely, my favourite destination; a compact city in central Switzerland sitting amid snow-capped mountains on the northern tip of Lake Lucerne. It even sounded heavenly. It was so clean, squeaky clean, and so incredibly crystal-watered that I spent my first 48 hours in Lucerne with my jaw scraping along the silver-rimmed pavement. Cars turned off their engines to preserve petrol and to protect the ridiculously pure, unblemished, Swiss air at traffic lights. Hand-held road-sweepers hung around waiting for cars to pull away from sidings so they could absolutely brush underneath. Machine-led road-sweepers reversed to sweep parts of the concrete the hand-held road-sweepers had missed leaving no tiny bit whatsoever unkempt. But, the main height of complete amazement, which will stick with me for always, was that everyone just drank the water from the copper public street water fountains which popped up everywhere. Phallic symbols that they were. It didn't matter. Everyone in Lucerne seemed to quench their thirst by drinking water from the tip of some famous man's knob. That was cool. Very cool. I was thirsty, but even if I hadn't been I would most definitely have sipped huge mouthfuls believing the spring H2O would cleanse my soul (and made me feel rather sexy inside to say the least.)

The hills were alive. Truly alive. I felt like Julie Andrews; who wouldn't, who couldn't in all honesty? Switzerland was just stunning. And I wanted to stay. So we did. We thought about Italy and we cast our minds back to Paris and we even mulled over our brief jaunt around London a couple of weeks previously (but we skimmed over Spaghetti Junction and Birmingham, 'nough said.) Lucerne, as I always like to paraphrase *Heaven in a teacup* (this time sprinkled with *Tate and Lyle* icing sugar.)

Our Youth Hostel, (by *The Lake of Shining Waters*), was not in the same league as anywhere else Amber and I had ever, ever frequented. Anywhere. It was paradise. The words *YHA* (Youth Hostelling Association) and *Paradise* had never, ever, been coupled together in the same sentence as far as I knew. Never. It was just not possible. At all. But here I had found an exception, the only exception for which I was certain.

The *hostel* was built out of the purest Apple Wood, so the literature described (no other YHA hostel even possessed *literature.*) The building structure in cross-over beams would be worthy of an architectural award for design both in complexity and location. Each glass window was the largest, cleanest most aspirational lit surface area imaginable. And, each lake-facing window was just sublime. It was enviable of a retreat; a spa away-day; a remarkably placed five-star hotel boasting lush forest and natural beauty alike. It was the most amiable place I had ever had the fortune in which to reside. Amber and I loved it.

We split up. Amber marched off to exercise her leg muscles. I walked around the forest looking for inspirational mushrooms (not to eat, okay, maybe just the one…or two, but then I met my *Gilbert Blythe* from *Anne of Green Gables* and dreamt that I was *LM Montgomery's Anne Shirley.* Amber was exercising having jogged the periphery of the entire *Lake of Shining Waters.* I was swooning in the effervescent grasses drinking raspberry cordial.)

"Shit, we left dad's camera on the pavement. You had it, no?" I had said the following day after we emerged from our misty mountain trip.

"I thought you had it?" Amber had replied.

Neither of us had it. It was gone as we rushed for the bus. Exhaustion had set in after climbing *Mount Pilatus.* Here is what I thought of it. Maker of weather, dragon's lair, home to giants and grave of rulers: Lucerne's very own mountain, Pilatus, is one of the most legendary places in Central Switzerland. And one of the most beautiful. On a clear day the mountain offers a panoramic view of 73 Alpine peaks. On a bad day, you lose your camera right after having taken an entire collection of breath-taking shots. I was not about to climb it again. And I didn't have a camera to re-enact the shots anyway. So I wrote it all down instead.

A dragon rock supposedly fell from the sky in the year 1420. The Roman governor Pontius Pilatus might have been buried in Lake Pilatus. Legend has it that a petrified man stands guard in front of a cave. The mountain massif of Pilatus, which towers above the region with its 2,132 meters in height, indubitably captures the imagination. Even today Pilatus is a source of mystical discoveries and is home to places of natural beauty that are steeped in legend and lore. The mountain can be reached from Lucerne by gondola lift and aerial cable car and from Alpnachstad with the world's steepest rack-railroad. Thus a special roundtrip tour is possible, involving journeys by paddle steamer, rack-railroad, aerial cable car and bus. The trip can be combined with various types of sports, hiking tours, or a visit to the summer toboggan run. During summer, the best way to become acquainted with the dragon mountain is with the steepest railway of the world (ascent 48%), or the spectacular aerial tramway and modern soundless panoramic gondolas. For those people who like boat rides and mountains, the Golden Roundtrip is a wonderful journey. To Alpnachstad by boat or train, then to Pilatus Kulm on the world's steepest railway. Descent by the cable car and gondolas to Kriens, Lucerne or the whole tour vice versa. In the region of Pilatus, you will find tracks not only for hikers, but for mountaineers and alpinists as well. Another very particular attraction is the longest summer-toboggan run of Switzerland - a funny and sportive experience one should not miss. At Krienseregg you find a large children's playground, a recreation area with way-marked hiking trails and picnic areas with tables and benches and open barbecue.

Up on top of the mountain, the gravity had been light and the air transparently thin. Here, back *at base,* it was harsh reality and I could hear Father Arbuthnot's words of wisdom ringing in my ears. *Take this camera, it's full of charm and is worthy of great pictures. Make sure you look after it, for it is an heirloom, descending from my Great Grandfather, Lawrence Arbuthnot Charlie. Be wise...* Well, Father Arbuthnot, you should not have chanced your luck and been so quick-spirited entrusting your two daughters for we are even lacking in the art of finding Dover. Blaming Father's kind, but too foolish, offerings made me feel, but only slightly, less guilty.

Was it time to go home yet? I really needed a strange, odd, random collection of news via Mother Clementine to lift the spirits. So I delved into my well-travelled rucksack for some old news which was entirely in need of a second, or even a third, read. I had printed them out in Paris from my phone.

From: Clementine Jostick

To: Arbuthnot Jostick ; Amber Jostick

Sent: Thursday, August 08, 1991 5:15 PM

Subject: Re: Marie-Claire

Hi Amber and Honey,

There was less of a thud than usual when the postman just delivered your April issue of *Marie-Claire*, the reason being that it only measures 8 and three quarters x 6 and a quarter inches. I am wondering if this is an error, or whether *Marie-Claire* has gone over completely to this small travel size? Have you seen any large ones for April? I'll have a look next time I'm somewhere that sells them too. Honey, if you are in a newsagents in London or at the train station can you see if there is a big April one please? If they have discontinued the large size, is it still something you'd like to keep having, Amber? Of course one advantage is it won't take up so much room/weight in luggage when flying. You can perhaps decide after reading this one. Maybe they are cutting down on postage?

We're just trying to think why the amount of gas we've used is much higher for this quarter than the identical quarter last year.

Ruth sent Dad a card with the husband saying *I'm going down the pub - get your coat on.*

The wife says *Ooh, am I coming?*

And he replies *No I'm turning the heating off*!! I remembered that one you sent, Honey, with the monkey covered in ice saying he was going to tell Dad it will soon be time to put the heating on.

Been very cold/hailing here in Draycod.

When Ruth came back from taking her parents to the airport her nine dogs had burst out of their gate and ripped all her cushions to shreds with stuffing everywhere!

She left her cast iron imitation log gas fire on 24/7 for 7 weeks while her parents were here and, aside it making her dogs barmy, it has broken. £900 for new one! (Courtesy of her Dad.) Her parents gave Dad a Swiss watch for his birthday as a thank you for all he does for Ruth (like raking up the leaves and taking her colossal collection of dogs for a walk all at the same time. He is out for ever such a long period each morning but by the time he has re-arranged the entanglement of leads at least a dozen times it's nearly lunchtime so in effect he has only ever gotten as far as Ruth's enormously high gates and then turned back. At least he got a Swiss watch out of it to add to his collection.)

By the way he (your Father) went to the cardiac Nurse re: his *bundle branch block* yesterday and he hasn't got one. It must have only been temporary (in ambulance and at hospital) after his faint at the Carvery that time. So his ECG was fine. But she gave him a home BP (Blood Pressure) monitor to do twice a day for a week as it was on the high side. First time he tried it wouldn't stop inflating and beeping and was going tighter and tighter - he hadn't read the instructions and had it upside down on his arm (cable coming out the top.) Having to keep record of results to take up in a week. He (your Father) had three walks before taking it - not sure if that affects reading. He went once to get the paper followed by mowing the lawn, followed by walking to *Poots* on the Retail Park to spend a voucher. He then went on another one with me later (walk.) I know lots of walking is meant to be good, but wonder if too much causes high BP.

I'm still on *Ramipril* for same thing to try and stop the *spikes* of high BP which happen at certain times.

Poor Peter Potter is also poorly. It is taking him an hour to get dressed and he has had to stop everything workwise for now rather than just cut down. He is very weak and can only just get across the room with three sticks. I did tell him that three sticks would surely hinder his getting about as doesn't he have only two hands like the rest of us, but I don't think he heard me. He's being investigated. He hates being indoors and is not at all happy.

A very large rook landed on the bird feeder yesterday and has bent the pole!

Love Mum x

P.s. Safe travels, did your Father drop you off okay at the train station? And, we just got this response from your Marie-Claire, Amber. Hope it doesn't affect you. It's better the smaller travel size. Maybe I should not have drawn attention. Maybe we can get it back to the smaller handy travel size?

Dear Mrs C Jostick,
I am writing to let you know that an error was made in the distribution of the April of Marie-Claire, which has been despatched as the Compact format size instead of your usual Standard edition. Please accept our apologies, and I hope that

this will not affect your enjoyment of the magazine. I would like to confirm that both editions contain exactly the same articles and information. Again, sincere apologies for any inconvenience caused.

If you have any questions about this or any other issues, please call us on 0330 010707 or e-mail us at magazines@mc.co.uk

Kind regards
Colette Greenwood
Customer Service Deputy and Manager in Excellence

If the European tour wasn't eventful enough as it was, we had brought along some useful amusing reads in case we got home sick for Mother, and it had worked. The heavy weight lifted off my shoulders. Mother Clementine's *Marie-Claire* story, true story but edged with far more excitement and inference than in reality it bore, made me feel human again; carefree to be brutally honest. I didn't mean to have been so terribly slapdash and leave Father Arbuthnot's ancient hereditary camera behind, but if it was to be left behind at any one point during that summer of 1991, then to be left behind in the riches of Lucerne's train station would have been my choice; if I was an inanimate object.

Brussels, Oostende

Nope, it was too much. We did not get off the train neither in *Brussels,* nor in *Bruges*, nor even in *Oowenerds.* Just stayed asleep until our train no longer had rails on which to roll, and even then we felt like keeping our eyes tight shut when we saw the delights *Oostende* offered.

It was quite black really, a slate-grey black, like coal. I hoped we would soon be in *Birmingham* instead, and years later, *Downtown Perth* was much the same. *Fremantle* a dream, but the urban periphery of Perth was like having landed in Birmingham, not even Solihull, but Maston, under an underpass, at 02:00am on a Saturday night, morning, you know the time I mean.

Disbelieving that *La Manche* between England and France could be any different in distance than that between England and Belgium in reverse, was something that my mushed brain was not able to comprehend. It was 5 hours; *FIVE* hours long the ferry journey on the smallest of boats on the longest of crossings and it was 02:00am. We arrived in Dover at 06:00am. Something made me put the hour back to British time. It had been a long, choppy night and I looked like exactly how I felt. Tired, smelly, grey, and ashen and in need of a good slapping to get me home in one piece. In fact, Amber and I *were* one piece, stuck together with some sort of super-glue that had us mooching along in a tiresome unity. I felt gritty; my eyes, metaphorically, my feet, physically, my clothes, absolutely, and my mind, sympathetically. Every bit of me in mind, body and spirit felt gritty. Yuk.

We passed out.

Amber and I passed out across two facing trio-sets of seats on the slow bumbling train back to London. It seemed an age, a real *age,* since we had been taking in the delights of the unforeseen Rhododendrons of Kew Gardens and the marching of the black-hatted soldiers along Pall Mall. I swayed as the train meandered in a dedicated, delicate steady pace along the North Downs way and supposedly towards the *Capital.* There were no bright lights sparkling towards the crescendo of an Eiffel Tower, there were no double-deckered city trains speedily connecting the country, there were no brightly-suited jovial business men zipping off to work like they all seemed to adhere to on the European Continent.

And, thank the Lord, there wasn't a single Italian sleaze-bag in sight. That was why Amber was sleeping. There were no males at which to bat her eyelashes, or with which to be abashed, but in reality, her eyelashes were as dirty as the rest of her.

I jingled my bum-bag. The slightest chink resonated from inside. I unzipped its worn silver teeth, and, once open, three coins shone back. I had three Francs left to remind me of my trip; my journey; my absolute eye-opener of a jaunt around the most beautifully culturally-designed continent on Earth. Three Francs, gritty eyes, holes in my plimsolls and five rolls of camera film (minus the sixth which had had the foresight to remain oozing opulence in Switzerland embedded in Father Arbuthnot's prehistoric misplaced camera. Good on it!)

Amber still slept. Her mild snores were peaceful, and I felt blessed. My sister, my sister had chosen me, *me, Honey Jostick* with whom to travel the Earth. Me, Amber's younger sister had had the privilege to take in the raptures of Europe, to understand the differences between our England and all those other countries littered across the English Channel. Amber had chosen simple, honest, trustworthy, Christian, boring even, me with whom to share her summer of 1991.

Father Arbuthnot had allowed Amber to travel because her younger sister could, perhaps, keep her in check. We could both learn off each other; her extroverted-ness could rub off on little old me, and my goody-two-shoe-d-ness could triturate on her. We were a team; always bickering yet simply there for each other, helping each other through cities which threw all sorts our way. I was truthful and prudent, Amber flighty and sexy; I was meek and honest, Amber brash and an exhibitionist; I was shy and predictable, Amber was rash and secretive; I was timely and tidy; Amber was slapdash and cocky, gregarious to an extent. I always told the truth otherwise I would blush, obviously, Amber would just get by. I became like that too. It's such fun! But then, back in the *summer of 1991,* I could not have tried to tell even a white lie. It was just not me. Truth to the bitter end.

I breezed in to school to re-tell my friends after that *summer of 1991. Europe? Magical,* I had said. *Angelina's apartment, words cannot describe. It was simply enormous, palatial, and lavish. I had my own personal en-suite.* I had raised my eyebrows and rolled my eyes as if to personally re-call the domicile. A sickly feeling of vomit exploded within my stomach and I smiled, sweetly. *Paris? Irresistible. So chic and only ever smelt of expensive perfume; even the lavatories. Men? Oh, the Italians were delicious, adorable; couldn't keep them at bay.* I shuddered at the greasy remains that were left in my mind. Improvements certainly could be made in that domain. *Pisa? Divine. The sun shone so much it was like heaven. Florence? Simply cannot do the place justice with my verbal descriptions. Lucerne? Got some irreplaceable photos up Mount Pilatus, must show you some time but presently my Father is sending those particular photographs in for a competition, and he must place his expensive camera back in the safe. Oostende? Oh, sheer opulence, to die for. You must travel some time.*

Well, a little bit of bollocks goes a long way. Who do you think wrote *The Rough Guide, Sandals, the YHA literature?* Little old introverted professional liars like me, of course.

Commuter V *"Sandwich on the Moon"*

I see them all of the time. I see all of the commuters at commuter time all of the time. Every day. And, and I see them at playtime. *My* playtime. They must recognise my tea cosy hat? But this time, at playtime, I am with four children, at least. Not all mine, but it feels like it.

So, the business aura had most definitely been erased from my persona that day, and the hassled mummy look had most definitely appeared. Oh, but actually, miraculously, *mysteriously,* that notion was just in my head. I did not seem to have taken on board the insipid, notorious, pre-empted inevitability of a Mother taking out four children, all day, on the train (a commuter train.) No. It was fine. Really, it *was* fine.

My day out, all of us together, four adults, four under-sixes, all of those combinations were pathetically absolutely fine. My two (three if you include House-Husbandry) children and Aunty Janey with her two wee ones; Treacle and Poppet. Indeed, they were the names of Aunty Janey's earthy children. They were dandy. It was like an episode of *Swallows and Amazons* spiced up with sporadic explosions of *Annie* and intermittent discussions revolving around *The Clangers* to keep all amused. I was very amused, very amused indeed, and, strangely enough so were the commuters all around our mini-outing.

You see, sticker books, nursery rhyme books, sticky-taped together colouring pencils, my wooden hairbrush for keeping us all in an orderly fashion, four exactly the same *Roses* chocolates (and I mean *exactly* the same; no one was larger, smaller, differently angled, shinier, thicker, thinner, Best-Before-Date any longer or shorter; you know what I'm getting at.) They were all in my bag; all of the afore-mentioned items plus more stuffed in for effect amongst the mini wine bottles. My large red animal-patterned bag was growing. My enormous, over-filled red animal-patterned bag was over-flowing. My gigantic, larger than me, red animal-patterned rucksack with three internal pockets and eight other varying zips was full, very full, rammed full to zip-bursting point. And my two other adults (save Aunty Janey with her Treacle and Poppet) did not know how, what-for and really why it was so incredibly full as if a five week camping trip with an entire pre-school of children was imminent. Nope, it's simply a day out.

"It's *just* a day-trip to London," Aunty Amber implied, flicking her hair.

I smiled, sweetly.

Aunty Amber, yes, she was our fourth adult. She'd had time that morning staying with us (she'd arrived for a week's stay-cation chez the Hollings) to brush her hair, condition her skin, place chic perfume in all varying sorts of places I shan't dare to write down, sip 2.6 cups of tea, ruffle her scarf to *the* perfect position and polish her kitten-heeled black leather boots, then exchange that footwear idea for pink-cushioned trainers for comfort. I shoved my tea cosy upon my unintentionally ruffled hair and hoped for the best. It was a miracle that two-fold mummy only had smiley coffee streaks up her cheeks and nothing else, noticeably, untoward.

"Aunty Amber, she's coming to *staaaaaay!*" Jack and Henrietta-Divine had cried, burst my eardrums, and danced around the garden. Anyone would have thought Aunty Amber was the Princess of Monaco by the reaction, but, I guess, to Jack and Henrietta-Divine, she was. Aunty Amber came to visit three or four times a year; the voyage from Nice to Greater Bungchip was marginally comparable in time to my train journey to London, but the end destination was more than marginally different.

"Aunty Amber, she's coming? HOORAY!!!" Henrietta-Divine created again.

Okay, OKAY, I thought. Aunty Amber is amazing. My sister, *that* Aunty Amber, is so so *so* amazing. I mean, how anyone can not be so so *so* amazing who lives in a place called *Neece* as the children pronounce it. I'll leave it to you to work out. It rhymes with *Police.* And, trains in Nice are nice, I have to admit. Very nice indeed. Double-deckered, I have to add. And, 93% cheaper per mile than that for a seat (if you get one) on a Great British train (but let's take that percentile figure with a pinch of salt.) Well, *Opposites Attract*, and we were; *Polar Opposites* Aunty Amber and I.

Aunty Amber arrived with her many sequined dresses and sparkling beaded jewellery that I thought Henrietta-Divine's eyes had actually popped out. Even House-Husbandry shook his empty head and empty-pocketed trousers and non-existent bag.

"What can you possibly *have* in there?" House-Husbandry had pointed, laughingly my way. "Any room for my wallet, keys and mobile *(which I shan't ever switch on?"* I added under my breath) he enquired.

I smiled, sweetly, and ignored him. What did *he* know, or care even, about women, Mothers and the multitude of *things* required for a few hour jaunt? Not much. He shopped and he cooked and he drove and he washed-up and he dried-up and he built sheds and he filled sheds and he vacuumed and he cleaned and he made the most scrumptious pasta dishes, and the most saintly apple crumbles, and what he didn't know about roasted vegetables wasn't worth knowing, and he did the school run every day and very very *very* occasionally he dusted and he scrubbed and he always chopped our orchard garden to an inch of its life. But, *bags*, carrying *unnecessary* stuff about was not on his (or *ANY* male) radar. Stuffed pockets, fine, but bags, a big fat no *no.*

But, it worked. My over-filled bag to entertain not only the multitude of children for which I was being guardian, but the creative drawing and reading and singing and necessary wee-munching of healthy chopped carrots kept all munchkins within a three-mile radius bloomin' happy for the one hour and 29 minute train journey to the capital. *"See,"* my glare implied to all of those who *still* did not understand.

It was heaven.

I would not have swapped it for the world.

I actually felt proud that I was so simple and two-fold that I could always appear happy on the outside (and I mean I was always happy on the inside too but I want to re-iterate that I was happy on the exterior so everybody could see) when I was being both *Business Woman* and *Mummy*. Those glass ceilings had been greatly reached and I was deemed an adaptable creature of not pure habit, but of human make-up. What an analogy! *I* even impressed myself as I sang *"The Sun Will Come Out Tomorrow."* For me, it already had. I was totally ahead of the game. So mature and responsible.

"HENRIETTA-DIVINE, GET YOUR HEAD OUT THE TRAIN TOILET, AND THE NICE MAN OVER THERE DOES *NOT* WANT A JELLY BABY STUFFED IN HIS TROUSER POCKET…OR HIS LAPTOP CABLE, DARLING!" I found myself whispering.

It's funny (in a strange, angelic, preposterous kind of way) that adults get more cynical and more flustered and more totally set in their ways as they grow older. You'd think we'd learn from experience and become mature and understanding, but life seems to take a curve ball and we adults become rather narrow-minded. Some adults; but not me.

Take our day trip to London, for instance. Earthy Aunty Janey is amazing. She guides her children in the most independent fashion, so she is an exception to my rule. Aunty Janey appears unflappable, homely, graceful, and even with two young head strong girls, she flies through life with her head held high (she does, I must add, possess *the* longest legs in the village so that does help the highness of her head.) She is *the* most amiable yet determined young lady. She even makes my husband three cups of tea when his delicacy has been forgotten. *Three;* lucky fellow that he is. The first cup that particular day when he was helping her find two escapee chickens was black tea with honey (the sugar bowl was empty. He didn't actually require sweetness, but that's fine, the thought was there.) The second brew was purely milky bubbly white with lashings of honey, and the third an *enormous* cup of *just let the teabag see the water* style. As I cast my mind back to his liking of a perfect cup of English Earl Grey, I am not entirely sure that any of those varieties offered fitted the requirement, but hey, it was a free cup of homemade tea. I asked House-Husbandry that evening which of the three he had chosen after the shock of the triplet of obnoxious brews awaiting on his return from the toilet ~ Henrietta-Divine had soaked herself swinging over the bath as it had filled up. Drat those badly plumbed pipes, wired up wrong, something like that, when flushing the toilet. Anyway, I asked which cup of tea had taken his fancy, but what with the long legs and the mad chickens and the dishwasher fascia needing sticking back on for which being the reason House-Husbandry had the initial purpose of going around for tea in the first place, and the extremely long front stable door which needed a crucial plane to reach its purpose and potential in life of opening to let people inside, with all that going on, I believe he said he drank all three, and when earthy Aunty Janey had her back turned to brew the red wine in some sort of scientific experimentation going on in the background he filled up one of his empty tea cups with homemade Italian Soave and played with those mad chickens (or was it the children, his mind was rather foggy.)

Anyway, back to cynicism and tolerance on the train. We (most of us save Aunty Janey and I), we become vastly intolerant, as a nation, as time passes us by. But that day was simply gorgeous and became the reason why children fascinate me. That day, that day in London was a vast collection of sporadic and continual hope. (Before sleep that night.) They should dearly be in charge. Clearly be in charge; these children.

The South Bank. The South Bank along Waterloo had been enthralling. The theme was *Mad Hatters Tea Party*, and the venue was packed. Varying Fathers looking like they had been primed to an inch of their life to take their children along, join in the Irish Maypole dancing for two hours *and* make it look like they are, genuinely, enjoying themselves stood around the outside of the hall whilst us earthy Mothers (having already face-painted our children, kicked off our shoes and slugged a large white crisp wine in secret) took centre stage.

I loved it.

I even removed my tea cosy for the event.

Henrietta-Divine loved dancing too so, thankfully, she became my partner when 100's reduced to 10's ruled. Aunty

Amber jigged on the spot with House-Husbandry in the background, on the periphery, both searching for the nearest exit and the nicest riverside bar.

We found it, the most gorgeous waterside watering hole. Well worth the wait until I had finished my Irish dancing (even Henrietta-Divine had slyly sloped off.) French, it was, this exclusive brasserie. French, and chic, and fine wine laden. "Well deserved, that was quite an exercise routine," I commended myself, with a reply from a voice I did not readily recognise but with which I absolutely agreed, "Please, *please* accept our apologies for the lateness of your wine," the Polish waitress spoke out without any realisation from our party that the latency had actually occurred. "Please, *do,* accept our apologies, and we insist, absolutely, the bottle is on the house," the blond, beautifully au natural, waitress obliged.

"Not a problem," Aunty Amber replied, pouring us all a well-deserved beverage. "Not at all!" Aunty Amber had worked hard that day.

I smiled, sweetly, as I emerged from the toilets, for the third time that afternoon. Perhaps the children had, regrettably, consumed one too many healthy train snack-prunes from my awesomely, super well-organised fun-packed rucksack. Oh well, we still had the train ride home to finish the *Annie* songs, learn our times tables backwards, colour in 99 home-made Easter cards, revel in supremely baked white chocolate and raspberry muffin cakes, read 82 religious psalms and enter it all onto Facebook.

"Sssssh! I can't *sleep!*" Aunty Amber and House-Husbandry sneaked off to slump into a hidden duo train seat together.

"Sleep?" I enquired, still revved up for the sing-song home. *"Sleep?"* That idea was alien to me. *"Sleep? Preposterous."* To which the reply from Henrietta-Divine was as adorable as her ridiculous name suggested.

"Mummy-Pig?" Henrietta-Divine enquired. "Mummy-Pig, if I was a *Clanger* on the moon, the sandwich I would take is a cheese one. Shall we go *there* next time?"

How could I possibly refuse? I mean, Mummy-Pig, she's the one who created all of these crazy ideas. "Of course, Baby-Pig. Daddy-Pig will take you there tomorrow."

Daddy-Pig's overly loud snores seemed to be telling Mummy-Pig otherwise, but that would be telling.

The Nurse. Perdita from the beginnings

"You *are* rather *furry* looking," my new bestie chum announced when we finally exchanged names. Luckily, we are both quite forward in personality and neither of us let weeks drift by without a firm handshake and an *"I'm Honey...I'm Monica,"* type of conversation. Okay, we didn't do the firm handshake, not even a limp gesture if I am to be brutally honest, but we exchanged names quite soon after meeting, first casually, then quite playfully, as we travelled home together slating our contrasting days. Sorry, did I say *"slating"?* Sorry, I meant talking, happily, frivolously, descriptively about our glorious office hours.

"*Furry* looking? Nice!" I replied. I felt like we were soul mates, to be truthful. We did not travel on the train together in the mornings. Monica is a Nurse. She takes the unearthly-houred train of 05:40 (05:36 in autumn when the train companies add an extra 4 minutes to the schedules due to potential "wet leaves" on the track. Anyway, that's another story.) Monica used to chuckle (in jest she said, but I think it was jealousy to tell the truth) and tell me I was *"part-time."* But, she can't be a part-time Nurse. I mean, if she became a part-time Nurse, then there would seriously be some lacking train stories for me to narrate. We would be catching the same trains in both directions to and from London, and my book would be half as short. No, no, no, that is a resounding *"no."* Monica, the Nurse, *had* to stay full-time just so as I could feed off her tall tales. She's good at telling tall tales

(saves me having to embellish them as they are already rather overly-stretched.)

"Not *furry*, stupid, *fairy* looking," Monica cackled back. "A *devious* fairy, I might add."

"Devious?" I chortled, yearning for more information. "Devious, how's that?" I chortled again, telling the entire carriage who probably dreaded seeing Monica and I on the 16:52. They would get no sleep no matter how hard I tried to whisper our conversations. "Devious?" I laughed even louder, and had to divert my eyes away from the tutting I heard from the crowds around us (obviously jealous of our kinship.)

"Yes, I think you're part of the MI5 gathering information. You act all innocent, but I don't believe you at all. You're too coy," Monica rolled her eyes, and I rocked the carriage with my incessant silliness.

"Me? MI5?" But I suppose she was partly right. I mean, I wasn't gathering information for the Secret Service to sell on to some sort of high-ranking intelligence, but I was prying, digging, delving for a few funny stories. "Oh, I couldn't rattle a snake let alone drain you for info," I lied.

"You lied," Monica said when she read this book.

"Yep, I lied," I replied, truthfully.

"Well, we can rectify that," she said. And, we did.

"Femme Fatale, is that okay?" I asked as she read the next draft; the next draft of how I was to procure her life in my book.

"I suppose that will have to do," she said, smirking and looking out of the window; a window in which I could quite clearly see her smirking reflection of positive gestures. *Femme Fatale* it is then. It went like this, and, I deemed from her smirk at the end of one particular train journey when I read her my captive thought on how I perceived her, that she actually quite liked it.

"Femme Fatale," she said, the Nurse.

"Sorry?" I replied. "That was my idea."

"Femme Fatale, *Living the Dream*," the Nurse continued, eagerly. "Look, if you really are the MI5, in disguise, obviously, because it's so easy to see no one could be so explicitly obvious as you in your pink and grey tea-cosy hat," she announced to the entire carriage of annoyed commuters never entirely being able to nod off or to read or to puzzle, intelligently, over Sudoku or the *easy* crossword. "If you really are planning to write a book, *The Best Seller*, you may as well embellish *my* life. I always wanted to be Shirley Valentine. Shall we get off at Ashford International and wait for the Eurostar to Lille?"

I creased up in ruptures at the thought of us. Me; tall, dark, appalling hair tied up in a side bun beneath my striped tea-cosy of a crocheted hat, black heeled wellies and a kid's rucksack. And her; full of life, with a bag full of Giant Cadbury Chocolate Buttons, three cloth bags and curly black hair. Both of us odd-bods alighting four train stops further into deepest darkest Kent because…we are rebellious, because we are adventurous, because, we thought, we'd be *"living the dream"* at the Ashford

Outlet Shopping Centre, with 60% off shoes and a Millie's Cookie Shop with 15 year old waiters. Us, two Shirley Valentines living the dream, outside, at night, in the middle of nowhere, mid-winter, cold, wearing a very *very* loosely crocheted (so obviously letting the Great British frosty air right through) hat (that would be me) alone. And, there was no Tom Selleck. Just a random, unknown coffee shop and a long, long, *long* wait for the next train back. So we didn't. We didn't live the dream. Not that night anyway.

Some Time Later (texts to Perdita)

"So, I ran in my tea cosy to the train station with my boss's out-of-date free range eggs, actually, they were at their *Best Before*, so that was okay, and to prevent any further cracks of not very well padded eggs, I then wrapped the entire box in my tea cosy hat (not still placed on my head, I might add), and I am positive they started, one by one, to hatch out," I texted Monica.

"Oh."

"So, your new name?" I texted frantically excited.

"What about it?"

"Perdita. It suits you."

"Thanks."

"You're welcome."

"Good luck with that one; the eggs. I'm on the 16:52 (your local time.) Carriage 5. Off work today. Am with Gavin (my son) if you want a lift home?"

"I had better start counting the carriages. Fifth from the front or fifth from the back? And which end is the front and which is the back?" But then I realised we were on different trains. "Perdita?"

"What?"

"I'm not on your train."

"Shame."

"Perdita?"

"Yes, Honey?"

"The conductor just crackled this from that dusty old speaker normally above both our heads. *Sorry about the late departure of this 17:12. Unfortunately, I was not made aware that I was to be the driver of this train and I was in the coffee shop, having equally been in the toilet on the opposing side of the train station just minutes before. So, you're lucky that I'm here at all.*"

"The usual then, or is this just your interpretation of the facts?"

"No, that was the real excuse. Promise. "*Miles*" gave me a lift all the way home last night."

"Oh. Any interesting tales?"

"Told him about my book and that he was in it; called *Miles* in a coal-mining hat. He must think I'm quite odd but he can't wait to buy my Best Seller. He said you're super friendly. Your son teaches his son football?"

"He must think we're mad. Could give him the wrong impression about us."

"Oh, no, he was fascinated. I didn't mention his coal-mining hat though. How's Jury Service?"

"Jury Service cancelled. Priscilla came round for a cup of coffee so fun chats instead and the man who colours our hair kept 'popping in'."

"Oh yes, him."

"God, Miles must think we *are* mad, crazy."

"No, he thinks we're fun, seriously."

"OMG, perhaps he wants a threesome? Better polish my nipple rings."

"PERDITA! But, yes, he did request that. They do that type of thing down the coal mines."

"Thank goodness he doesn't know what we're really like."

"Oh, he does. I told him that too, about your cream choux pastry fetish…Hello, *hello,* Perdita. Are you still there?"

Deathly silence.

"Damn, there go any more story embellishment ideas from the Nurse. *Hello?"*

Texts on a Train (Continued…)

"How are you, stranger?" I enquired one remorseful morning. "So, I got bored of writing children's parallel universe books and thought I would really get going on my life around me. Get this, I'm *really* excited about my equivalent to *Bill Bryson.* Aspects of life really cannot go unpublished at times."

"I expect royalties if you use any ruminations on my life. Had half-day leave today. Oh to be part-time all the time." *Sighs.*

"Part-time, yep, know it well. That was to be my next question. You may well get a mention, Perdita. A *big* mention."

"I would have liked to have been described as a *Femme Fatale*, for sure. However, are you listening, Honey? After watching *Mama Mia*, I realise I am more Julie Walters than Meryl Streep."

"And I will be one of those impish Hobbits in "*Lord of the Rings*?"

"Absolutely."

"Thanks!"

"Have a nice evening."

"Hope House-Husbandry has lit wood burner, and having wine?"

"That would be nice."

"I had to rush for the train this evening. Just managed to get seat. Creepy man keeps staring at me. Asked pregnant lady if she wanted to sit down."

"Thoughtful fairy, aren't you?"

"She wasn't pregnant, Perdita."

"Oh, Honey."

"Why *can't* we always travel together? Then at least I could cry into one of your many cloth bags."

"Oh."

"Hmm."

"There are two theatrical girls talking in loud voices here, constantly, worse than us, Honey. I miss our live chats now you get the later, quicker, more efficient train."

"Me too."

"Liar."

"Perdita!"

"Theatrical posh girls now making costume drama. I'm learning all about camera angles…as is the whole carriage. Think they might ask me to be an extra…with my Giant Cadbury Buttons. They are looking for a buxom wench."

"Excellent, all duly noted, Femme Fatale. I've woken up, so a good few Femme Fatale pages written. I will use Pen Name as discussed previously, or course, Perdita."

"Please can you make my character slim?"

"What's it worth? I am also using the sour-faced lady and calling her Chardonnay."

"I was going to enquire if she had a role in your Best Seller."

And we didn't quite live the dream, yet. Not tonight. "I have to take my kids to the Panto. They are in it."

"Oh dear, Honey."

"The Brain Surgeon is on this train and asking me to wander along the carriages to find him, but I have an enormous Christmas cake and I'm not lugging it about."

"Christmas cake? It's February, Honey?"

"It's got lights on it, inbuilt. And it's still within its Best-Before-Date. It's for my Dad's 70th. My sister comes this weekend, for the half term. I better start to use the Fossil purse she bought me for my birthday."

"In your novel, you could have tryst with the Brain Surgeon. I would like to have an affair of the mind with an 'andsome academic."

"What the f**k is *tryst*?"

"Why Christmas cake, and why not candles?"

"M&S on sale. Do you think my Dad will notice it has Christmas trees on top?"

"Yes, Honey. Stick flowers on them and pretend spring has come. Look up *tryst*."

"I thought tryst was a predictive text error."

"You are meant to be the clever one."

"It's all a guise. I feed off your tall tales. Coming to the Panto?"

"Well, being a spy you should know about those things, tryst. No, village pantos make me shudder. Seeing adults in odd clothes from the village is worrying and gives me bad dreams."

"I helped Henrietta-Divine into her costume at stage door, and I saw three random male areas."

"Really?"

"Sorry, *Arses*, bloody predictive text."

"Could you identify without looking at faces?"

"No, thank heavens," I texted, but perhaps if I dug for more information, there would be a whole heap of stories to publish.

Chardonnay

I felt guilty. *Ever* so guilty. Terribly guilty. Oh my God, I was getting closer, I was getting closer to her, I was getting closer to Chardonnay and I felt obliged, so obliged, guilty as hell. My knees started to shake, my fingers started to tremble, to get irritable, my eye-lids were flickering, my huge heart was pounding, my intakes of breath were short and erratic, and my footsteps were ridiculously stumbly. For goodness sake, what was wrong with me? I coughed. My throat, it was dry but, but I could not hold back, I tried, I tried my hardest, I really did try my *very* best, better than when I know there is chocolate in the kitchen cupboard and my mind is trying to resist the temptation. I was trying even harder than that (and that is bloody hard, I can tell you.)

I was getting closer. I was fast approaching. She was there, mauve dyed hair, standing still, staring forward, into space, oblivious. No, surely not. Oblivious of me? Oblivious of me, me, *me* in the pink and grey tea-cosy every day? Oblivious of me, approaching her, every day? "Really?" I snapped.

"Morning!" I smiled and nodded, sweating. *Why did I have to say that? Acknowledge her.*

Nothing. Silence. She said nothing. Just like yesterday, just like Tuesday, just like Monday and all of the days last week too. Nothing. Chardonnay's ease of ignoring my happy *"Morning!"* was as easy to her as it was as hard, desperately hard, for me to stay quiet. I knew, I absolutely knew, Chardonnay was not going to say *"Morning!"* back to me in return. That was one thing of which I was certain. But, I simply could not resist. You see, I can't. I simply cannot resist saying *hello,* making a simple morning task a happy one, making someone's early morning a happy one, a smiling one, a blissful start to the day. But that's just me.

Okay, *okay,* OKAY! You've already sussed me out. I wanted her story. I wanted to drain her system of all she knew. And more. I wanted to pound her, politely of course, for information, for free information. But Chardonnay was oak-aged. Chardonnay was ancient-spirited. Chardonnay was corked.

So, well, I would simply have to make it all up whether she liked it or not (the name too, of course, I always liked that name, Chardonnay, and Perdita agreed with me. Chardonnay was perfectly suited to her.)

We had both tried, you see, Perdita and me. We'd both tried to say *'Morning!"* We had both tried to make a simple morning gesture to Chardonnay, but three months in, and me saying *"Morning!"* each day, I felt like I was kicked in the teeth and mortally wounded each time I heard no resounding reply. So, we agreed, Perdita and me. We agreed to stop. We agreed to cease our one word of acquaintance and just make it up. So, although my knees still knocked, and my legs still twitched, and my mouth always ran Muscadet-dry as I approached Chardonnay along the long winding train platform of Greater Bungchip, I zipped my lips and I said nothing.

"Morning!" Chardonnay spoke out loud. And I tripped over my high-heeled muddied wellies from my weekend, child-binding walk. My mouth ceased to work and my vocal chords ceased up and with my meekest squeak of a voice, blocked of any such sound at all, similar to what I could only think was stage fright, I tried to say *"Morning!"* to her, but I'm sure all I could manage to achieve was a mumble. And that was it.

Chardonnay, *Chardonnay* for weeks on end had ignored my little morning one-worders every time, plugged in to her smart phone, staring into the winter trees, standing alone in the open air at the top end of the platform (even when it was drizzling, plopping with icy rain, snowing even) Chardonnay had blanked tea-cosy lady. Now, the one time I ceased my *"Morning!"*, the one time I sweated and I twitched and I tried to plainly stare ahead, the first time I had commuted to Perdita's pact, she, *she,* Chardonnay had replied. Well, she didn't reply because I had not actually said anything. She had instigated the conversation and I had ignored her. I felt awful. I felt guilty. I felt like I wanted the next train to blow me off my feet. (Okay. That would be an excessive outcome but still.) I felt bewitched. Actually, actually, I thought, as I pieced it all together. Actually, that was about right. Oak-aged, corked Chardonnay had called my bluff.

I smiled. She rolled her eyes. We both went our separate ways. Life's funny, isn't it? And it was then I rummaged around for some pieces of paper I remembered shoving in my bag before I popped out the baby. It was another random letter come email from Mother Clementine back in 1994. I am so pleased I am a hoarder, but even if I wasn't these letters and emails I will take to the grave.

37 Pomegranate Road

Draycod

Herts

DR3 9SF

England

26th October 1994

Dear Honey,

In case I forget to put it later on, Cath rang the night before last asking for your telephone number.   Unfortunately I don't have it. What is it?   Anyway, she said she would write to you as you had said you were going to visit her - I think she wanted to talk to you about that.

I'll just go through the little pile of things which has accumulated for you on the doormat. It is rather annoying as the heavy items keep knocking out the cats. Actually, you may not need some of them until you come home for Christmas, so I'll tell you what they are and you can let me know if you want them (thinking of the postage as all together they will be quite heavy!)

They are:

- An envelope marked *'Ritzy, in Wunstable.'* Isn't that a nightclub which is frequented by people who haven't had a good night out until they have gotten into a fight? I do hope not.
- Brochure and leaflets from Frittania Music (we have sent back the thing about not having the Editor's choice.)
- Photocopied Giro Payment Advice for £1.15 signed by Dad.
- A fat envelope from 'Choice' which says 'This envelope contains your statement'.
- A fat envelope from 'Gays' that says 'Hurry!'
- A fat envelope from 'Umpire' regarding a prize draw. I do hope you win, but seeing as it's sitting here, unopened, I better enter. I promise to let you know if we are suddenly holidaying in The Bahamas as we would need someone reliable to look after the cats; and the neighbours are sure to be away at the same time.
- Another fat envelope from 'Gays'. Pray tell what this is, please, dear?
- Another fat envelope from 'Umpire' that says *'Open immediately'*.
- An envelope marked 'Gus'.
- A letter from the Practice Nurse at Bangor (the one you asked me to open) regarding your next smear

which is due! (They do them at our surgery - Dr Make-Cuppas is nice - she was in the local paper for winning an award for going beyond the call of duty in her treatment of an old tramp, visiting him in the street and treating him with compassion and dignity until he died - let me know if you would like me to make you an appointment - specimen required!)

- And; two packets of photographs - one containing two pictures of Johanna and that Spanish girl and one of Johanna with a carnival bear plus negatives, and the other packet containing that lovely picture of three men sitting in a speedboat in Ibiza. I want to put it on the mantelpiece with your old school pictures, but I'm unsure who these men are.

- PG Tips are now doing 'endangered animals' and the first one I got was a Dolphin! I'll send it next time I am sending something lumpy.

Oh yes, before I forget, when I put your old jeans in the wash (I always check the pockets first) I found 50p and a compliments slip from Draycod Police Station (Property Office.) I'll keep it for you. Pray do tell why you have a compliments slip for the Police Station? Is this something your Father and I should know?

I noticed the enclosed write-up about a French Assistant which I thought you might be interested in reading.

I am also enclosing the article about Welsh men getting taller which is making their voices get deeper as their larynxes get longer. And I have also enclosed the article about that woman who died while snorkelling in Zakynthos. - Well, these *are* varied enclosures!

You asked me to send you *'Moonlight Sonata'*. I've looked right through the piano stool and it isn't there, but Dad says he remembers you sorting out some pieces of music and thinks you took some with you - might that have been among them? I do hope so.

We ordered another tape by the Heartfelt Cafe, called Flamingo Orchestra but it was so dreadful that we have had to ask if we can exchange it. It consisted mainly of someone shaking his maracas, plucking a rubber band, droning on a ukulele and banging bongos. We have ordered the same one as yours as we know we like that.

I forget to tell you when you rang that poor Alfie T. had to have Jess put down. She had gone blind and kept bumping into things. That's not his wife. It's the dog. He rang me really upset and said *'You wouldn't think anything else could have happened to me would you?'* I don't know what exactly has happened to him recently so I can't really compare. Every time he comes or rings he always asks if we've heard from you or Amber. If you have got time to drop him a line at all telling him what you've been doing, I know he'd love to get a letter as he keeps telling me how lonely he is. His address is as follows, but make sure you don't send him anything edible as the budgie tends to escape and rifle through his belongings. I don't want his dead bird on my conscience as I still can't decide what tiles I'd like your Father to put up in the bathroom.

> Alfie T.
> 14a Birdie Close
> Draycod
> Herts
> DR2 3SF
> England

Did I tell you I now work for Bertie Petersen from Applebridge Common who is the Manager of The Applebridge Common Sports Centre Trust Ltd (connected to the Swallow Stadium)?   Anyway, he's really nice and brings Dictaphone tapes every week containing reports and letters.

Then there is Jake Williams, also from Applebridge Common, who is the Editor of 'Militaria Anonymous', a new magazine containing, among other things, contributions from people who have sent him war experiences, and I type these experiences for him. He gives me all the photographs to go with the stories as well - old brown ones of young soldiers (some of them are only 19 or 20 and look far more intelligent than those men in the speed boat, but I'd still prefer the Ibiza muscles on the mantelpiece if I had to choose. Isn't life complicated?)

And there is also an author (Marjorie Maximartum) for whom I am doing a great long Logistics report, John Blake, Ralph de Comte, Brian Wonderland, Janet le Grande, George Georgie George (odd name, not sure about him), Hakki Aggar - a farmer from Trippile (his wife came this morning), not forgetting Arbuthnot (Dad) - a workaholic with two broken shoulder blades. I've done a lot for Andrea recently as well. They have just come back from Crete. Her husband nearly drowned. The red flags were out which means you can swim but keep to the edge, and he went too far out and there was a dangerous undercurrent which made it almost impossible for him to get back. Andrea said she stood up and saw he had raised his arm which was a prearranged signal, but she couldn't remember whether it meant he was all right or if he was in trouble! She realised he wasn't getting any nearer the shore and rushed up to the shop and just as help was coming he got to a shallower part where his feet touched the ground. He was completely white and it was half an hour before he could talk. He got really told off for going so far out!

She also told me that her best friend got into similar difficulties when somewhere in Spain. All the men on the beach formed a human chain and were throwing her towards the beach across the waves which were dragging her further out to sea. Her husband had gone out to rescue her before the other men arrived but he drowned before they could get him. The lady was unconscious when she was thrown over the last wave, but recovered in hospital only to be told her husband had drowned.

Shall I bake blueberry or lemon muffins when you come home next?

So please be careful when swimming out there even if it looks calm. Andrea said the sea was totally calm when these two things happened - it is the currents underneath which caused them. Tell Amber.

Andrea also told me that her daughter, Nadine, is so ashamed of their house that she won't bring boyfriends home. One day she painted the bathroom when everyone was out, and when Andrea got home she refused to thank her as she had painted over filthy walls and had even painted over the cobwebs which were now stuck to the walls! She is still going out with a woodcutter who she met while working as a barmaid. I told you *her* budgie died, didn't I? Anyway, it did. And Hermione isn't having a baby in April.

And now for something completely different! It is 5.15 pm and Pearce Smith has just rung from France. He has bought a car to come and visit you in the holidays! He said if you ring us, to give you his telephone number which is 010 33 86 46 95 51, and you have to ask for *Salle des Assistants* who you contact through the caretaker. He said you can get him until 6.0 tomorrow (Thursday) and until 6.0 (Friday) but after that it is the holidays. Well you won't get this letter by then as I haven't posted it yet so I will have to wait till you ring to tell you. He seemed very keen to visit you anyway. Apparently it has been his 21st birthday.

Muesli had a birthday card from Sheba (cat food) the week before last. Ages ago I filled in a form with all our cats' birthdays and how often they ate Sheba. The first prize was your cat painted by a famous artist. Perhaps a birthday card was better as I don't think they'd sit still long enough to be painted! Twig would disappear for good!

Dad was given some exercises to do at the last Clinic appointment. He has to bend down, let his arms hang to the ground, let them swing backwards and forwards and slowly raise them upwards, and also rotate them from the same position. This is less painful than doing anything from the upright position. He has actually been out in the car three times now. Once he only drove the Escort from outside the house to Melissa and Mark's drive (next door) as Mark rang to say they have sold the house but they aren't moving in yet so can we park the car there to make it look occupied, once to the town and once to the station (that was today - he can't drive long distances yet so had to get the train from Marylebone to High Wycombe and back).

Dad is still sleeping in Amber's bed as it is easier to get out of. I wish he'd never over-stretched up that ladder and fallen off. It was such a shock, and it is a terrible inconvenience that he has broken both his shoulder blades as I cannot reach the smoothie blender on the top shelf.

That hotel where you saw Keith Chegwin rang the other day to see if you could work so we said when you'd be back!

Dad was washing his hands at the kitchen sink yesterday when suddenly he was standing in a big puddle. The waste pipe (where the water goes after it goes down the plughole) had burst, and, in trying to get it off with his broken shoulder blades to take it to the shop to get a replacement, he cut his finger (I didn't know about any of this until he came up and asked me to stick a piece of sticky tape over a kitchen towel bandage as he couldn't find the plasters) and when I went down to look there was water and blood everywhere and all the cats were standing in it!

He couldn't buy just the bit which had burst - he had to get a great long thing with a plughole on the end of it - so we have now got a nice new plughole.   (I bet you can't wait to come home at Christmas to see it!)

BMW have gone from the garage at the bottom of the road now. It is now a Rover garage, crammed full of cars.   It'll be handy for Dad anyway. We have a green Rover, but I'm sure you knew that?

I sat up by myself two nights ago and watched 'Rosemary's Baby' with Mia Farrow.   I was sure I'd seen it before but I only remembered two bits.   Dad has wiped 'Gremlins 2' as I had recorded it on 'his' tape and there were no spare tapes when he wanted to record something.   I hadn't seen it yet. Is it pretty much like 'Gremlins 1'? Should I bother hiring the DVD?

We walked to the Retail Park on Sunday and sat in about 100 settees.   There was this really comfortable soft leather one which was really supportive underneath whilst the outer layers cushioned every part of your body and the top nestled into the back of your neck.   The cats would have wrecked it in five minutes though.

The builders have been here most of today as the garage roof is leaking a lot - huge puddles have been appearing on Dad's workbench every time it rains. They traced it to one tile on the balcony which hadn't been sealed after being put in to replace a broken one.

Peter Potter has just been to borrow the tape machine and the Platters are sizzling in the oven (we're having a 'no washing up' meal today as Dad won't be home till late and 'Between the Lines' is on.)

I still haven't found a replacement for the raspberry shampoo. I've tried Todyshop Grapefruit, Poots Body Boost & Shine Apricot & Almond Protein, Poots Two in One Lime flower & Pineapple, Poots Mineral Spring, Gainsbury's Nature's Compliments Sea Kelp & Cornflower, and in the cupboard I've still got Make-Cuppa Field Organic Therapy Shampoo. Dad is using up the one's I like the least.

I can't remember if you've seen the new vacuum cleaner? It has got several height settings which you have to change between carpets. You have to do the stairs with the attachment and put it on boost. If it gets to a particularly dusty bit on the normal carpet, it automatically goes on to boost. Fascinating.

Continued Thursday

It is now 4.30pm on Thursday and I have been doing Peter Potter's work all day since 9.00am with a brief pause for parsnip soup and a jacket potato. Peter keeps ringing wanting to dictate something else. It is all rather confusing. I don't know why I didn't become that opera singer like my music teacher suggested back in 1954. Next time that happens I am going to press 'Two Way

Record' and he can dictate onto the Ansa phone! Have just discovered that facility! Have reached end of page. Thanks again for both postcards and letter. The enclosed bank statement came today. Hello to Amber if she is there when this arrives.

Love Mum x

The Flats

The Flats. Gosh, *The Flats* between *Lower Putteridge* and *Even Lower Plummerage* are vast. And, I mean vast. If I had wanted to invent my murder scene here, then the leverage for that would have been supreme. But, the murder, it had already happened through that dratted train window, so it would be insane for me to have witnessed yet another. Improbable, for sure.

So, *The Flats.* They were surely imported from Wuthering Heights? If so, my Greater Bungchip train to London Victoria was worthy of the £4440.00 annual return fare as it most definitively took in the Yorkshire Moors. Most definitely. My train absolutely past through the murky landscape that only traipsing through and re-enacting the scenes Wuthering Heights could define. The flat, on-going, mist-covered gorse-filled hills were second to none to the outskirts of Greater Bungchip. No quibbles there.

Two girl's voices sounded from not too far away, probably just the next carriage. I could hear a talentless commotion brewing. Females, they were, and conversing with not my type of conversation, rather colloquial for my liking and, hoping the people attached to the vocals wouldn't come my way, I stared out of the window.

The train was slowing. The countryside outside was becoming less blurry as we decelerated. My carriage started to judder, and those less than polite female voices became louder, heading my way. I stared, really intently this time, at the dark green prickly gorse and the rabbit-warrened deep-set paths. They led somewhere. The mist lowered and the bright silver moon depicted shadows, figures, on those Moors.

My eyes widened to the great outdoors. Two figures were playing, so close to the window I could place my palm on the glass and nearly touch their souls. The two figures were happy. *Oh Heathcliff...,* I sighed as the male figure held hands with his female counterpart, Catherine. *BANG!* The train rocked. The two figures outside ran away.

The female voices of atrocity were now very close. Nearing. Soon to be invading my personal space. *Christ.*

So, *The Flats* stood still. Oh. We had stopped. *Hell.* We had, yep, we had stopped. I only realised my train had come to a less than manoeuvrable action due to my black tea not slurping over the paper sides of its cup. Yes, we were going nowhere fast. And if that wasn't bad enough for a Friday night, it was a Friday night in February, and the train had stopped *in No Man's Land; The Flats.* In the dark. With not many souls left in my carriage to sweetly smile and say *"I'm sure we'll be on the move soon."* Having said that, those particular choice words of a quote would have been the least likely line of conversation even if my carriage had been packed to bursting point. Far too polite. Not enough use of well-placed swearing.

Ordinarily, I would not have been fussed. But today, the train had even turned off its engine. *The Flats* were eerily placed and heroically misty, so says Emily Bronte in her first publication of the book of those Moors in 1847. I could have sworn, through the double-thickened glass train window, I spied a shadowy outline of *Wuthering Heights*, the farmhouse where Bronte's story unfolds. It could equally have been the collier dog, its reflection from the elderly furry creature across the aisle, bedraggled and wretched from its twilight stroll in the 21st Century, but that was not how I felt at that time.

What I saw through the toughened, scratched, frosted window was absolutely the jealous and vengeful Mr Lockwood haul himself from the stench of the Moors, arms outstretched to a ghostly apparition in which I most adamantly saw his lips call "*Catherine.*"

"**Catherine, *CATHERINE…COME 'ERE!!!*"** a loud vociferous voice disturbed me from my own literary mind, and the worst foul-mouthed teenager ventured past my seat in search of her friend, Catherine. It was them, the *uncouths*. Did she absolutely need to cry so verbally and piercingly that my ears juddered? The train was a mere four carriages. There was little room for two friends getting lost? But my mind-set was completely lost, and I was wuthering in disbelief that her screeched ***"I'm gonna get yer, I am, girl,"*** made me so angry.

I had completely lost the moment whereby my Bronte characters faded back to their social stigma, dingy era in time. I was no longer in the wilderness with Wuthering Heights a lonely house on a blackening hill. My brain had now de-functioned back to an awful reality. I was no longer widely regarding the classic English literature, with Lower Putteridge a little distance behind, with deeply polarized souls; in a controversial depiction of mental and physical cruelty, unusually stark, challenging strict Victorian ideals of the day, including religious hypocrisy, morality, social classes and gender inequality. Instead, my fiendish mind in this fiend of a tale (an incredible monster out on the Moors, and actions such as relationships breaking down in full view of society laid in hell and seemingly immortal for a fraction) blew apart. ***"Oy, wait up, you bloody cow!!!"*** the vulture of a girl screamed this time.

I just put my fingers into my ears and sighed, *"Delinquents,"* under my breath, I thought.

The girl stopped, in her tracks, right next to me. She turned her head. "Watch'yer say?" she grimaced, scratching her oily scalp.

I did not move. Perhaps if I pretended to be asleep, this cretin might go away?

"I said, *watch'yer say?"* She poked me. She certainly had not gone away.

I still just stared, blankly, at my black wellies. It was becoming increasingly interesting, my footwear, the boots which I wore day in day out as they were the easiest and simplest items to put on. Just left by the back door, I could readily slip in foot left followed by foot right and head out. Anyway, she was still there.

One of the female, uncouth voices from further down the corridor, was now a reality. And this reality was throwing her accusations at me.

I muttered, aloud. "In 1801, Mr Lockwood, a wealthy man from the south of England, rents Thrushcross Grange in the north for peace and recuperation. He visits his landlord, Mr Heathcliff, who lives in a remote moorland farmhouse, *Wuthering Heights*, where he finds an odd assemblage. Heathcliff seems to be a gentleman, but his manners are uncouth; the reserved mistress of the house is in her mid-teens; and a young man seems to be a family member yet dresses and speaks like a servant," I replied like that thinking if this girl thought I was mad, a crazed-individual spouting extreme oddities, she might stop bothering me. I was convinced she would not have heralded the slightest clue as to what I was referring. But, I was literally like Lockwood; snowed in, digging myself deeper and *deeper* whilst the train did not budge and I had to face the challenge this bludger was about to throw my way.

"Wuthering Heights, nice," the oily-scalped girl said back to me in return; peering at my grey coat from way, way taller than little old me sitting down in a partially graphited seat; my eyes the level of her ripped-jeaned-knees. And, she sat down next to me and unzipped her plastic leopard skin bag.

I was speechless. What was this person, this supposed new train friend of mine, about to wield? A gun, a knife, a packet of Maryland cookies to share? My mind was awash with wonder.

No, this greasy teenager, who had a better bag than me I surmised as she sat right close, her leg rubbing on mine as she jiggled in obvious need of the lavatory, this person pulled a crumpled up *First Edition of Wuthering Heights* from her bottomless pit of a large purse, and echoed my little teaser back.

"Oh," I replied. "Fancy that, Mr Lockwood and Heathcliff would be so proud of how they have influenced all manners of today's society."

"Yeah, reckon they would, dirty old fools. Wha' I can't get me 'ead around is why there was so much social stigma back in those days. I mean, if you luv someone then go for it; that's what I say. All this drunken wretchedness from society's social graces caused sh*t and depressions. All 'eathcliff wanted was 'is Catherine. So *what* if 'eathcliff was from a broken debauched background, the poor dark-skinned gypsy of a boy. So bloody *what*. And that Catherine, well she should have just stuck up her fingers at the lot of 'em. Education, respect, only marrying within your own social classes and not beneath irrespective of true luv? Bollocks to that."

"Right," I agreed, quite enthralled and totally enjoying my chat with my new soul-mate. "Indeed, oh yes, totally."

"Watcha doin', Catherine?" the teenager screeched. "You finished in the bog yet," she hollered at her friend. And Tamsin (I spied an inscription on her blinding gold necklace) slapped my thigh and said in parting. "You should read it all, this *Wuthering Heights* thing. It'll be the makin' of yer, it will," and as she blew a pink bubble with her gum and kicked her mate Catherine up the posterior for running off, she winked my way, and then disappeared out of view.

The train engine turned over and the lights flashed, and I could have sworn I saw Catherine, Catherine and Tamsin, race off back over the misty moors. They were, indeed, nowhere to be seen in my carriage, and the toilet door swung, alone, on its hinge. I blinked. I paused, and I contemplated the quiet of the Moors, *The Flats, My* Flats. I suppose I did want a Classic to become a reality but I certainly wasn't expecting that.

Sri Lanka's Ups and its Downs

It wasn't long after we said *"'til death us do part"* that we crashed into Sri Jayawardenepura Kotte, Colombo. My eyes were weary. My legs were weary. Even my elbows felt more than mildly bruised, and it wasn't from the bumpy landing commandeered by Flight Lieutenant Jim Maria. It was from falling down the stairs on my wedding day (coupled with my Bucks Fizz glass landing in my eyes.) Anyway, we had landed. I peered at the itinerary. It was upside-down and torn at the corner. Not much different to my state at that particular moment in time. I swigged the remnants of my post-wedding complimentary Champagne which had been topped-up five times since take off at London Heathrow and stared at my husband's watch. "JESUS!"

"SHUT UP!" Husband glared back.

"Sorry, but it's just dawned on me that you're my HUSBAND! JESUS!" I cried it louder this time.

"You can now remove your... "

"... incoherent wives from the plane?" my husband interrupted the air hostess as she explained over the tannoy that we were now allowed to remove our seat belts.

"Meany," I recall, smirking.

"Don't mention it," I remember him replying as he disembarked ten people ahead of me whilst I battled with my wedged-sandals which had gotten stuck under the seat in front. "Any chance of a top-up?" I held my Champagne glass high, but as I looked around

I realised only the cleaners could hear me, and the strict flight schedules probably meant that if I didn't disembark soon, I would be in a luggage rack straight back home.

The crazed-chauffeur drive to hotel number one was memorable to say the least. Well, I remembered falling asleep. Husband recapped at dinner (or was it in fact breakfast, lunch, tea or snack-time? Who knew? Who in fact cared?) that he would have preferred to have had his toenails slowly extracted without pain relief whilst listening to me asking if he'd extended the wardrobe's inside capacity as yet as opposed to *that drive.* I clearly realised it was far better to have been asleep, dreaming of the coconut-lined roads, than actually seeing the onslaught of masochistic lorries drive at our heads whilst removing us from the road twenty one times. Husband just scratched his eyeballs trying to delete it from his brain muttering, "I paid £2,789 per person when I could have gotten it for free in a car with my WIFE?"

"I know. Damn waste of money, if you ask me. I said let's take a mini break to The Lake District but I think your ears were under the bath water at the time."

After that first dinner of curried cheese sandwiches (that isn't the norm in Sri Lanka. Do still go there. The Tamil Tigers have long made friends with the others and only because I'm an extremely extraordinary eater was I presented everyday with curried cheese sandwiches) we were met once again by Roman; our Chauffeur for the next three luxurious weeks we were to endure. We got back in the low-slung gold car. Roman drove us through the rainforest. Husband had pleaded he would walk, still traumatised from the three-hour airport transfer, but he had a momentary glimpse into his finances and thought he'd paid for Roman, so by golly he was going to use him. We got out two minutes twenty six seconds later (inclusive of three stops to drop herbs at Roman's Mother's, his sister's and his uncle's houses.) And we ventured slowly inside.

It was bloody boiling. Steam rose everywhere. Rose smells lingered in our nostrils. Little women seemed to be running around chucking hot towels at each other and pouring scalding water into wooden coffins.

"$100," Roman announced, hand held out.

"Sorry?" Husband replied, coughing and spluttering whilst he was dragged onto a meat cleaver-type table.

"You're right, sincere apologies," Roman replied. "Miscalculation on my part."

"Phew."

"$200. For the both of you. We only take cash."

"I beg your pardon? As far as I recall, I haven't ticked any optional extras yet. Can't we just enjoy our...."

".... curried cheese sandwiches?" I intervened.

"But this is the best massage parlour in Kandy," Roman replied in a way that meant we should already have been dying to get here. "It would be a travesty if I didn't let you experience Mme. Goude and her twin's exceptional hands," and with that,

Roman plucked the crumpled dollar notes from Husband's palms and slunk back to our car for a sleep.

"Daylight ROBBERY!" Husband cried before Mme. Goude's palms sent him into wild sleep from which he was to wake three hours later, sweating profusely and scratching his pulsating crotch. "And, WHERE are my PANTS!!!?"

I so needed coffee, Ristretto coffee, intravenously pumped into my veins. That would have been so nice. Glorious. But, we were given rose petal water in a rusty tin cup. "Oh well. When in Rome," I smiled.

"But. WE'RE NOT!"

"We can pretend, Husband! Look how shiny your buttocks are!" I shrieked, quite beside myself with lies. They were coming thick and fast now I was a wife.

"Shiny, my arse," Husband grunted.

"Exactly."

And then we were once more whisked off by Roman to our next relaxing adventure; a sleep deprived, excruciatingly boiling trip to the largest Elephant Orphanage this side of the world; *Pinnawela.* I'd never seen such strong mouths swallow thirteen litres of milk in ten seconds. (That was before experiencing Jack's arrival. He sucked me like the world had already been doomed to explode.)

The beautiful city of Kandy, we realised after a good night's sleep, is without a shadow of a doubt much more ably appreciated after a good night's sleep. "Husband!" I cried as I flew back the thinnest of thin pink curtains that first morning on our first whole day.

"SHUT UP!"

"Righto! Espresso?"

"Hmmmm," Husband grunted. I took that as a resounding "yes, please, sexy cheeks!" and heaped six large Espresso-spooned granules into each of the two tiny cups which sat in two equally opposing large saucers. I poured on the water, which was constantly boiling, and stirred. Husband slurped his. "VILE SLUDGE!"

"Thank you! But it's working! Your eyes are so hugely awake it's fearful!"

"Hmmmm," Husband grunted for the second consecutive time and then rolled back over. I held the Espresso beneath his nostrils. "CHRIST!"

"Thought it might buck you up. Ready to climb Sigiriya?" I crackled the brochure over-loudly just in case the six heaps of Espresso weren't having their fastest effect.

"Sigiwata?"

"Sigiriya," I repeated, tutting and rolling my eyes as if to call anyone who hadn't heard of such a place a complete amoeba.

"Oh, you mean Sigiri*yaaa*?" Husband pronounced it differently. "The most exquisite example of ancient Sri Lankan art, architecture and landscaping. Built over 1,600 years ago? *That* Sigiri*yaaa?*

"Might be.

"The sinister-looking 600 feet high black rock once appearing like a huge dazzling white cloud floating above its surrounding forests. Its sides painted with beautiful frescoes of semi-naked nymphs with a massive gatehouse in the form of a lion guarding the entrance to the innermost sanctum of the city – a *Sky Palace* on top of the rock bursting briefly into pre-eminence and then abandoned and now lying hidden in forests for nearly 1,500 years. *That* Sigiri*yaaa*?

"Rings a bell."

"It is definitely a must visit site. What are you waiting for? GET DRESSED!"

"I am," I muttered, and chucked the rest of the five and a half spoonfuls of Espresso down my throat (but mostly down my shorts.)

"When in Rome!" Husband shot up.

"SHUT... UP!"

And all I can say is that the rock climb was pressing far too much on Husband's nether regions. I am *so* pleased that Mademoiselle Massage Goudie-Woudie, or whatever she calls herself today, pummelled extra *extra* deep. (I did slip her another fifty dollars.)

Roman was a nice man. He was. *Really* he was. Perhaps us Brits are just too quick off the mark to appreciate when someone is genuinely being nice and kind and helpful? It is just purely a slower, more cultural life-style which Roman follows. His intentions are gracious, and his manner is polite, and his knowledge of Sri Lanka is really next to none. It really is. He carefully drives us anywhere we want. Oh, did I say *carefully?* See, we are at home already. The danger has disappeared. Roman is as nurturing and as bona fide and as genuinely attentive as one could care to hope for on a romantic honeymoon jaunt. A treasure. *"Sorry?"*

"I would love to come and live with you, please?" Roman asked with his head turned to face us as he narrowly missed a sacred cow. "I have a cousin in Essex, and if I could just come over and spend some time in your house before I track him down it would really help my plight," Roman smiled as he drove us into a hedge.

"I guess he did say, *please.*"

"Anyway, let me know," he slowly nodded his head and turned to look at the road. "Have you decided yet?" he lurched back.

"I think we're here!" Husband wound down the window and let in a mellow stench of elephant dung. "Yep, that looks like hotel number two. Habarana. LET ME IN!" and Husband leapt out into the wilderness.

Roman smiled and let a random tree halt his manoeuvre. It was time for Roman's seventh sleep of the day. I grabbed the nearest pamphlet on the marble hotel Reception table as we glided into the most beautiful array of cottages imaginable accessed through the largest dessert café I'd ever laid my eyes upon. And read. It was *my* turn to memorise the attraction of the town.

Habarana is a small city in the Anuradhapura District of Sri Lanka. The location has some mid-range and up hotels aimed at package tourists, and is a departure point for other nearby locations of greater interest. Habarana is a popular tourist destination for safari lovers as it is the starting point for safaris in the nearby Habarana jungle and the Minneriya sanctuary which is heavily populated by elephants. Elephant-back riding is also an attraction in this small city. Habarana is situated nearby to the ancient rock fortress and castle/palace ruin of Sigiriya (OH GOD!) and is situated on the main road
from Colombo to Trincomalee, Polonnaruwa and Batticaloa. The population of the city is expected to be in the area of 5000-10,000. (Plus us and Roman.) The area has some of the best hotels in the country and the greenery and wildlife has added value making the location attractive for tourists.

I looked around. We were pretty much alone. In fact, *I* was totally alone. Where was Husband? Our suitcases had disappeared, so I could only assume they had been placed in our room, which I was yet to see, or the monkeys had stolen them on arrival and had started to sell our belongings. Seeing as I could not, and had not at all, seen any other humans, I opted for the latter. I didn't like my choice of knickers anyway. I had packed in a rush. The monkeys were welcome.

I glared about some more. Habarana was the complete opposite of Kandy. There were no rainforest-covered massage parlours. Equally, there were no lorries locked on to our gold car

135

like missiles to MIGs. There were no rose petal tins of drink being shoved our way. And, there were no mosquitos ~ at all! Habarana was perfect. I spied a *Rough Guide to Sri Lanka* sitting discarded on the same table from which I had plucked the hotel pamphlet. It fell open just at this spot. Mind-blowing. I cackled and read aloud. *"Sitting on a major road junction almost equidistant between Polonnaruwa, Anuradhapura and Dambulla (and close to Sigiriya and Ritigala), the large village of HABARANA is of little interest in itself but has a decent spread of relatively upmarket accommodation, making it a convenient base from which to visit any of the Cultural Triangle's major sights. It's also the handiest point of departure for trips to Minneriya and Kaudulla national parks, which offer some of the island's best elephant-spotting. The main attraction in Habarana is the fine Habarana Lake, encircled by a small footpath around which it's possible to walk in 90mins or so. Alternatively, a number of hotels and tour operators offer elephant rides by the lake and elsewhere (around $25 for 1hr), although the sight of these mighty animals trudging lugubriously through town beneath a surfeit of chains may leave you feeling almost as uncomfortable as the elephants themselves."*

I didn't believe a word of it. I only had six bruises, and nausea was a thing of the past after two hours in a Jeep. And, the less said about the monkey which stole my slippers and locked itself in my cottage garden bedroom with me inside with it the better. I had called for rescue, but Husband was too busy snapping pictures of the largest goldfish in the world.

When we left Habarana behind us after three long, sandy days, the next part of the holiday was tasting chocolate straight from the plant, rubbing it on our bodies and heading straight to the beach at Bentota. I'll let your imagination run wild with that one. I haven't much more paper.

For Morris Dancers, when Health and Safety had their say and took their sticks and bells away, they had not seen the Bentota Train. The Bentota Train was infamous, the Bentota Train was crazy, the Bentota Train was not, I warn you if you did not take it fully on board the first time, the Bentota Train was *absolutely* not for the faint hearted, and, yes, it's not staged if you ever see it on the TV. The Bentota Train is just as you see it. A fun-packed rusty old ride that gets one from A to B, if you're lucky. I re-named it *The Sri Lankan Roller Coaster.* We just viewed it from afar. That is three feet away when we used the tracks to cross into No-Man's Land for 97% Aloe Vera. We had been fleeced again. £19 for the tiniest pot of freezing pure Aloe Vera could only be bought in Bentota Town. "MY ARSE!" Husband cried again. We found larger pots in the hotel for a fraction of the price, but hey, if we hadn't been fleeced, again, we wouldn't have experienced the wind of the Bentota Train rush past our burnt ear lobes as we crossed the tracks, perils to come.

I rubbed on the Aloe Vera to Husband's burnt palm-tree shapes on his chest, and Husband's voice rang out again. "CHRIST!"

It was a fun honeymoon. We had thought of making hundreds of babies, but the thought of them popping out nine months later with an innate sense of fleecing tourists and wanting to lick cocoa from our privates sort of changed our minds. And, to tell you the truth, the reminder of Husband's burnt chest and pulsating nether regions being flopped about by the hands of brash little masseurs didn't quite make the grade. And the thought picturing Husband's face ever again at Customs. I mean, why would a newly-wed be wearing knickers going through Customs? Ridiculous one might say. I mean, I'm not a Clairvoyant. I didn't know that departing tourists are frisked to an inch of their lives. And knickers, I mean, how would they protect you when your skirt is already round your ankles?

Thinking back, years later, the strange thing was no one, none of the Bentota Train's passengers looked in the least bit perturbed. House-Husbandry and I had walked along the railway bridge, a railway bridge that appeared to us newly-weds, on our honeymoon, like a dilapidated ancient bridge that was surely outdated, its railway tracks even broken in a variety of places, and the thin little pedestrian section for pedestrians who were certainly not expecting, let alone anticipating, a cracked-up, seriously over-crowded, incapacitated, derelict wreck of a train to just appear, ram shackled, on the railway bridge just feet in front of their noses. OUR noses. That's right, our idyllic walk, House-Husbandry's and I's romantic, sunlit, tropical walk, I recall, was flung, dramatically to the side. House-Husbandry and I had been thrown, in our turtle-patched sarongs, into the wire fence, if one dared to call it that; it was more of a torture implement ready to pierce and castrate any unsuspecting walker ridiculously stupid enough to simply not give way to that rumbling Bentota Train. We had, of course, checked the train timetable, for a giggle; it was never going to run on time, I mean, even the plane only landed, just about, give or take, the correct side of noon.

I needed not only a Ristretto, but a dose of something far stronger after Sri Lanka. A dose of Clementine Jostick's tales. And, I recall this. On sifting through my drawers, I had once re-found some fantastical instructions from my Mother Clementine on how to look after the house for the first time when they left me at home. I will never be able to dis-engrain it from my mind.

Honey's Instructions & Info when we go on holiday!

"If the smoke alarm goes off it means something is burning. Get out of bed straight away and rescue the cats. If it isn't serious (just burnt toast or something) you can disperse the smoke by flapping a newspaper under it and the noise should stop. I don't know how you stop it apart from that and in any case you need both hands to put your fingers in your ears or the noise might burst your eardrums. Please don't tell anyone like Jehovah's Witnesses, Tea towel men etc. that your parents are on holiday. If you entertain anyone on the balcony, please remember to warn them that there is a dangerous gap. Please remember we can't use the proper shower yet as there isn't a door. Please recharge cordless phone every night and put its aerial down after use (unless we have unplugged it in which case forget this). If anyone says I told them we weren't going till Sunday, please explain that we booked it with the son and he made a mistake. Please remember to turn the iron off, and even after you have turned it off, please don't leave it touching the curtain. Please do not use Tippex to paint on the letters which have worn away on my keyboard - it will damage the plastic - I will order some replacements. White self-adhesive envelopes are downstairs in brown 'lots of drawers' cupboard. PLEASE KEEP A RECORD OF ANYTHING YOU TYPE (HOW MANY ORIGINAL PAGES AND HOW MANY PRINT-OUTS OF EACH THING), HOW MANY PAGES YOU FAXED (WHETHER IT WAS THIS COUNTRY OR ABROAD), WHO IT WAS FOR, AND HOW MANY ENVELOPES THEY HAD. I will give you the money as soon as I get back and add it to the clients' bills. Please feed the cats (including PB!) every day. Please give them milk every day. Please inspect their litter daily and remove things in it - put them in a carrier bag, tie a knot in it and put in dustbin. Please comb them if you have time - please put loose fur and any bits in a piece of foil (scrunched up) or a bag (with a knot in) and put in dustbin. Please try and get all cats in kitchen at night. Muesli and Twig can get in the shower room little window and Truff can manage cat flap but Corrie and Nutmeg have to be waited up for. Vet's number is 354599. Hope you won't need it but basket is in cupboard under stairs. If they are all ill at the same time, they won't all fit in it but you can borrow a wire cage from the vet for about £20 deposit returnable when you return it. Please explain to Mrs Wilson (or whichever vet you see) that we are away and will settle up next week. As the doorbell doesn't work, please listen for people banging on the window. If you use your bike, please re-lock garage door again.

DON'T FORGET YOUR FRONT DOOR KEY!"

After all of this, Mum and Dad still phoned and I was having a BBQ for ten school friends. I distinctly remember that a boy went to use the loo and Twiglet the cat jumped out of the bathroom window two flights up. I didn't ring the vet. He was fine.

Great Uncle Daffyd <u>vs</u> Arbuthnot's Cataracts

I was on holiday in Mozambique when the news came in. Poor Great Uncle Daffyd had passed away. He was 94, a true Welsh character. He played his tin whistle to Amber and I in his youth, he had a pond on his smaller farm when he was middle-aged living on a vastly reduced-sized homestead acreage than during his later life when he had up-sized. Now, he was gone.

It was sad. But oh, how he had *lived.* Lived quite a varied life with sheep twice my age even. Great Aunty Kaitlin had married an exquisite man. He had been a Banker, in London, when she had been a *wacky hippy CND-marching fanatical in-her-twenties type of gal.* And now, they lived, they had lived, on the largest, most super-sized farm in Monmouthshire which I had ever seen an 88 year old woman and a 94 year old man running, and running very well. 91 sheep and growing.

Great Aunty Kaitlin, Dad's eldest sister (who apparently ran away to Marseille when she was 17, dated *hip* men and dressed like Audrey Hepburn with the longest cigarette holder I had ever seen a lady adorn) ran the show. 88 though, that's quite a feat. Amazing, in fact.

When I was pregnant, with baby No. 2 (Henrietta-Divine) I had bought my husband a voucher for a three-day, two-night stay at any of the *Classic English Inns* in Great Britain. Yes, *I* had bought it for *him*. I had bought the voucher for *him* but for some inexplicable reason (must have been the hormones) I suddenly used it, and before we all knew, I had redeemed the voucher for *Peroni-on-Wye*.

This beautiful riverside town close-by to Great Aunty Kaitlin and Great Uncle Daffyd (close-by so the hotel literature said but that was exclusive of the 59 minute commute through the extortionately heavy-trafficated delightful city of Jumbeanie of which I can only describe as a drive through the outskirts of a shanty town but Jumbeanie was far more roguish than even I can give credit) was quaint. Peroni-on-Wye is a small market town built at such an angle even the River Peroni-Wye loses its battle with gravity. With a population of a mere 10,089 (not counting the four of us and the seven Bulgarian tourists who were lost thinking they had alighted at Wylam which I had to try and explain was in another county altogether far, far, *far* further north than where they actually were and to this day I swore at least five of them scarpered into a nearby Pret-à-Manger to escape being deported) - falling to 9,454 at the 2011 Census. Peroni-on-Wye is found on the northern edge of the Forest of Dean which I swear at any point in the year just oozes mist and low lying cloud just to cover up the enormity of the hills a tourist must climb to reach any given destination.

Our hotel boasted that. Height. Our hotel was a re-designed castle that even Kevin McCloud would be abashed in which to reside. It oozed grandeur and history and even the deep burgundy colour of the carpets running through the hallways insisted that royalty surely had lived there once too? The scenery from our hotel room left us lost for words it was that breath-taking and, apparently, Peroni-on-Wye, somewhere, boasts the first purpose built tourist hotel in England, standing proud on the sandstone cliff overlooking the River Peroni-Wye Goat-Shoe Bend. Hailed as the birthplace of modern tourism, Peroni-on-Wye was central to the 18th Century Reverend Bilpint spotting a great opportunity and then establishing *The Picturesque Peroni-Wye Tour*. I assumed that this hotel aforementioned was the one in which we were residing, but the cloud was so lowly slung not even a Brontosaurus would be able to tell.

"Noice trip, mayte?" the waiter at the bar introduced himself and from that point on we knew we had landed on the outskirts of Wales, or was it Devon, or was it Brisbane? I was not at liberty to guess.

The following day, after a hearty burnt vegetarian sausage-ed breakfast (why I felt obliged to dictate I was of that persuasion; I dreaded dinner that night), we drove the longest ever jaunt (after exiting Jumbeanie; that was the easy bit) down a pot-holed driveway; Great Uncle Daffyd's pot-holed driveway which was more like a Z-road to another town which had not yet quite made it to the *Ordinance Survey*. I knew we were absolutely headed in the right direction when the car was flicking mud up its panels and it appeared we were completely lost. I always knew when we were a stone's throw away from *Frégate Farm* because it appeared we were doubtlessly nowhere. Then we arrived.

Morning sickness was nothing in comparison to that rutted, jarring drive.

Back to the hotel. Phew, it was bliss, the hotel, seriously, I had chosen the most amazing place and, despite putting baby No. 1 to bed, quietly (he was fine, honestly, when we left our hotel room and closed the door. The baby monitor beneath our table in the demure, romantic ambience of this *Classic English Inn* three floors down did not seem to agree.)

It roared. The baby monitor actually *roared* so hard the red flashing lights which depicted the baby's desperation all lit up. At once. And the volume? I had forgotten to turn that down. That was quite annoying as the cry from desperate lonely baby No. 1 upstairs masked the reply I was hoping to hear from the loved-up couple at the next table. The male had just proposed over Pink Champagne. The female looked happy, and they clenched hands tightly across their dimly lit table for two, but whether it was a sorrowful, heart breaking *no* or a tearful, unbelievable *yes we're so in love I must sob my heart out yes* I never heard above the wailing at my feet. My glittery shoes actually vibrated. So, we turned the thing off and drank our demi-carafe.

Anyway, *Frégate Farm* near Peroni-on-Wye. Great Aunty Kaitlin and Great Uncle Daffyd had up-sized their domiciles every decade I had known them. Up-sized the hectares, up-sized the farmhouse leverage, even up-sized the number of barn cats to catch the inevitable up-sizing of the barn mice to match the ever-populating farm sheep and the odd imposing cow who happened to lose its way. They were wool, and meat, not dairy, my Great Aunty and Great Uncle. Anyway, beside the point, a bit of a tangent there.

The farm, *Frégate Farm,* was earthly, heavenly, and marvellous. When House-Husbandry finally put on the hand brake, and our Saab-93 came to a fizzling halt on the enormous clay-mud-partially-bricked driveway, we looked in awe. It was fabulous. My ancient Aunty and her ever-aging husband (who I could barely understand, but what I did understand, did make me hold my sides with raptures) had the most immense farm imaginable. And the sheep, well, they were miles away, grazing in the sheered grasses of *Frégate.*

Great Aunty Kaitlin had the best farm any child come dream up. And, for me, it was also *heaven in a tea-cup with droplets of silver light falling from the skies.* That is what I had remembered from my youth. I was so excited. *MUD!* Earthy, crunchy, deep brown, soily MUD enriched with vitamins and iron which so got my saliva taste buds salivating like there was no tomorrow.

You may now absolutely be thinking, *okay, I could cope with her wishing local cows good morning, and drinking wine at 07:30am, well that's forgivable, but MUD, salivating with the desire to eat MUD, well, that's just wrong. Wrong!* No, you, *you're* wrong, seriously. I had a condition, and no, no, no, don't take this Best Seller back to the library or quietly pass it back to the kind person who leant you this great read saying *thank you, good book... but I'll stick to Bill Bryson in future.* No, keep on reading. You see, my condition, this quite common (fairly, amongst pregnant women) condition, it's real. It's called PICA. Seriously, PICA, it's the unfathomable desire to eat earthy, iron-enriched products due to an insufficiency of iron in the bloodstream (especially when pregnant.) House-Husbandry calls it *Pretty In descript Carrot Anxiety* (as with this condition I inhaled carrots - complete with soiled skin, that was the entire point - day after day, hour after hour until PICA faded out although I do still lick my lips when my train to work crawls slowly through Swanley and the tracks are packed with hundreds of pieces of iron-enriched coal.)

Anyway, we *WILL* get to *Frégate Farm* (and at some point to the reason my Father's cataracts whilst travelling are such a crucial turning point for him.) Yes, we had arrived. *Frégate Farm.* Blissful it was. As blissful as an unwashed iceberg lettuce (another top contender for PICA sufferers.)

We had arrived, black stiletto boots 'n all. God, what on earth possessed me? What *on earth* possessed me to dress up like a model (a pregnant model) when visiting a farm? Okay, I hadn't seen my Great Aunty and my Great Uncle for a few years. The last visit, well, they were twenty two miles closer to civilisation, but in their defence, it was still a farm, and, like all farms, they come with mud (yum!), and dirt, and rusty machinery (indoors), and uneven splintered wooden flooring (indoors and outdoors) and Tom cats and waxy lanolin-coated sheep.

Frégate Farm was no exception. It was enormous. *Frégate Farm*, it was just, well, enormous, and enormously filled with all those farm-like traits outlined above. And, my 8-denier silk tights topped with knee-high thinned-heeled black suede boots, a black mini dress and furry designer (British Home Stores) coat were maybe not the best items of clothing to have worn. Never mind, I had not seen my barmy family for years and I wanted to make a good impression.

Jack fell *splat* on the driveway. My son. House-Husbandry accidentally stepped on the Saab's accelerator causing the wheels to spin wildly out of control and drowning me with mud and Great Aunty Kaitlin roared with laughter, the scraggly barn cats used my nice silky legs as a scratching pole and I just smiled sweetly.

And Jack loved it. That was okay then.

"Hoooooooney, darling! How ARE you?" Great Aunty Kaitlin had announced.

I smiled, again (my ears starting to hurt with the forced pulling of the lips and the cheeks to awkward angles) and picked my son up from the floor. He wiped his muddied palms across my designer coat and kicked his crocodile wellingtons onto my thighs. The clay stuck. It dried instantaneously. I smiled again. *"Great! Never better!"* I lied, but secretly picked some brown patches of driveway from my fake fur, and inhaled to satisfy my PICA craving.

"Come in, come in, Daffyd is inside. Playing with his balls. Oh, and YOU must be House-Husbandry? Nice to meet you at last. Kaitlin shouted back over her padded anorak shoulder as if to warn her husband of our impending arrival "You're very soave, Honey! I'll lend you some wellies."

"Oh, it's okay. I did bring mine," I replied, quite pleased I wasn't going to be taken for a complete fool. I removed my suede boots at the doorstep and walked inside the farmhouse. It was old. It was uneven. It was stone-stepped and I tripped up straight away, over my own suede boots which I had placed at my feet, I thought, but I was obviously mistaken. *Hello Great Uncle Daffyd,"* House-Husbandry and I called out together.

He waved us further into the winding living room, and I followed Jack, afraid what he (and I) might see. Great Aunty Kaitlin had quite clearly stated that *Daffyd was playing with his balls.*

Hello, I said again, and he pulled me down to his level for a kiss. Worried I might catch an eyeful of balls, I restrained myself just a little, but goodness me, me and my filthy mind in the gutter; it was simply his therapy ball. One of those enormous rubbery exercise balls women use in labour (and I sincerely hoped I would not be in need of it that weekend. It looked like three oily sheep, two skinny cats, one Welsh Great Uncle and perhaps a farming neighbour (of whom we had come across bumbling with his wet-woolly dog covered in pond-life (the dog not the neighbour although I couldn't be sure))) had taken a liking to this grey sports ball. *What was I thinking? I was only eight weeks gone, and Great Aunty Kaitlin had said that I was probably thinner than most non-pregnant women when I was eight months pregnant. That was nice of her.*

Wales? How's Wales? Daffyd enquired.

Oh no, that was University, I went to Bangor University in Wales, but Kent, we now live in Kent, I replied.

Dat's whhot I said, Welsh-Irish Daffyd pulled out a cunningly placed map of the United Kingdom and ran his index finger down the west coast. *Kent, dat's a lon whay darn deer. Near ta Luntun,* Daffyd pointed to the Capital, vaguely.

Oh, London, House-Husbandry piped-up at last.

Dat's whhot I said, Daffyd rapped his finger on Camden. He smiled; one of those smiles of recollection of past times. *Mmmm,* he mumbled, and played with his balls.

Oh Daffyd, really, Great Aunty Kaitlin tittered away to herself in the kitchen as she recollected too, and House-Husbandry and I watched the garden peas on the hob boil over, and the potatoes roll into the cat basket, and the fish cakes actually set fire to themselves as House-Husbandry tried to pick them free of the grill's element, spiking his thinning hair as the electrodes zinged through his body. It went bang, the element. House-Husbandry shot back. Jack threw Great Uncle D's gargantuan rubber ball down the cellar steps, I wet myself (terrible pelvic floor nowadays) and Great Aunty Kaitlin announced *"Anyone for a cup of tea with soya milk?"*

You're the Best, Great Aunty K, I welled up inside. *Everyone needs a Great Aunty K. Yummy fish cakes. We all love them,* I laughed whilst we all picked off the carcinogenic substance soiled onto each fish cake crust. Great Aunty K and Great Uncle D were none the wiser how the lunch actually arrived on the plates, and Jack giggled, whilst wrestling with the hay bale on which he was poised. Great Aunty K's best ever made chair. She had tied our son to a spiked hay bale with tractor rope, as if he were Flossy (sheep 49.)

***

Kaitlin's phone rang whilst we were having our Earl Grey in the orchard. Kaitlin had had a text from her friend concerning another neighbour. All very cosy and very well connected these farming people. It's like they all lived on a set of *Neighbours* in Australia. It read:

Just spoke to Claire - she told me she has a persistent low grade infection and is on 3 intravenous antibiotic drips to try and combat it. It will be reviewed in 24 hours.

Chest x-rays clear.

She's enjoying the rest and it is nothing sinister. May be home in 48 hours. As she's the least ill in the ward they are moving her later on to another ward.

She had tachycardia a couple of times but that was just due to the infection.

She only had one and a half hours sleep last night cos of other patients making a noise.

The coffee is ghastly! Tea not much better.

She enjoyed speaking to you, Kaitlin, and has received your text - she says thank you and that she can't always hear the phone ring in her handbag as the hospital is noisy.

Her Dad is talking to her at present. It is all rather convoluted. Lots of people of whom I am unsure. But, I guess that's life.

Jayne, by the way, said your lavender bags and card just arrived - thank you! Yes I'm always tempted to keep them when I buy them but always give them away! Thanks too for the other envelope which I will keep. And your carnations are blooming in the kitchen. Zoe.

We all laughed as we read it as "Your carnations are in the blooming kitchen!"

Love Claire.   Claire writes longs texts, I had said.

Why they did not take the train?

So, Dad did not really have the best of vision when his cataracts were at their full potential. But, he was a man, and that's what men do. They carry on regardless despite the consequences. So that's what he did (just like when he drove into my friend, Laura's, garden wall and knocked it clean down, then drove home as if absolutely nothing had just happened in spite of the deep paint-stripped section of car door missing and a pile of dusty rubble outside Laura's house. (If it had been anyone else but my Father, AJ (Arbuthnot Jostick) they would have been sued.)

So, Dad, Arbuthnot Jostick, Father of us all, carried on his motoring pursuits as if nothing was a problem whatsoever. Nothing a problem at all, apart from pretty much everything to do with safe, legal, healthy driving. He was practically blind. But that was fine. Arbuthnot Jostick used my Mother as a verbal map.

Now, the words *Mother* and *map* (whether it be me, or my Mother, or probably in fact her Mother and her Mother before that) did not greatly go hand-in-hand. It took me three attempts to pass my driving test, my Mother in fact passed first time. So, at the point, driving home 666 miles from Monmouthshire to Hertfordshire post Great Uncle Daffyd's Celebration of Life was one that was on the top of my Mother's list to absolutely forget, and on my list to absolutely debate, describe and embellish 'til Flossy (sheep 49) came home. She never did, Flossy, come home;

apparently she met that lost cow from 13 hectares as the crow flies from *Frégate Farm*, and lived her days out there.

So, Mother became human signage for Father and his impaired vision. Through the blurry tears the Celebration of Life had induced, Mother had to reads sign posts which were greatly in Cymru, and translate in-situ. *Piece of tinkle.* She did not think so. She mildly expressed her opinion of sorts quite well over a glass or two, or three, of chilled white Chilean wine that evening. I did not get a word in edge-wise as she told her tale of events. And the wine still flowed.

"On the way down I was holding an enamel jug full of water and an arrangement of scented stocks. I spent 8 hours trying not to spill it. The jug, sloshing around, made me terribly needy for the loo. We had only got one 20p piece for the public loos, so Dad went first and I held the door open while he went so I got in free - got some funny looks as people walking past could see him going.

While I unpacked, Dad went to get a takeaway. We had to eat it with our fingers as we were in a wooden chalet in the garden of the owners and they only brought cutlery and crockery at breakfast time.

We were a bit early for the church service the following day so Dad suggested going for a walk. I still had hold of my jug of scented stocks in water and we were walking up the hill away from the church when a man stopped his car and said *"Have you come for the Celebration of Life?"* I said yes and he said we were walking the wrong way - the church was down the hill. I tried to explain that we had just come from there but that Dad had St Vitus Dance and couldn't stand still for five minutes. I called up the road to him, but he was out of earshot by then. He got back just in time for the service, not realising I was no longer with him but was following a strange man down the hill trying not to spill my water. He was Daffyd's Grandson over from Ireland.

I was relieved to finally place my jug of water and stocks at the altar. Just like baptisms and christenings, Celebrations of Life are held during the normal morning Mass, so although we were all there, the vicar couldn't start the service until he was sure no more ordinary members of the congregation would be arriving.

The journey to the Crematorium was like a speeded up film. The hearse shot off like a rocket and we all had a job to keep up. But at least we had it to follow. The hearse turned into the area by the entrance, and Dad drove the wrong way for the parking spaces.

On the long and winding journey back for the lunch (with no hearse to follow), the only man who knew the way was right at the back.

At *The Angel,* we sat next to a man who told us that he was thinking of spending thousands of pounds buying an automatic milking machine. His cows know when it is time to be milked, so they would come into the barn, get into individual cubicles, and the machine would milk them without the farmer even having to get out of bed. If there was a problem, the machine would ring the farmer and tell him. I had had two glasses of wine and said it sounded like *Wallace & Gromit*.

Daffyd's brother and his wife had to miss pudding as their ferry was leaving soon.

Kaitlin hopes she won't be knocked over by her sheep again (she broke her hip last time) and has bought a quad bike to round them up. (She hasn't got a sheep dog.)

The B&B owner and her husband came out to wave us off when we departed. She thought we were staying for weeks with the amount of luggage I'd brought to cover all eventualities. The car alarm went off just as we were waving so the departure took longer than just a quick wave. Couldn't stop it for ages. Dad kept saying "What does *that* sign say? And, *that* one?" but I hadn't got my glasses on.

We were in the wrong lane (the inside lane) on a very busy road when Dad suddenly veered right across two lanes of fast moving traffic to get halfway across a space before changing direction. I was saying the Lord's Prayer. Next, we got to a hump back bridge on a blind corner going very fast and only just stopped in time when a lorry suddenly loomed into view right on top of us. And then not long after that, two men were sweeping up after an accident in a country lane and were indicating for Dad to slow down. The accident car was on the verge and glass was strewn everywhere. I think Dad thought they were waving at him socially, so he waved back and sped through all the carefully swept up debris. He didn't hear them shouting as he has gone rather selectively deaf.

We stopped for our packed lunch at Thourton-on-the-Lakeside. I wanted to look at the Christmas cards which had just come into the shops (in August) but Dad wanted to get going. It took us even longer than the journey down to get home. We went wrong about fifteen times. We passed the same hospital three times. Then we got to a roundabout where everyone was going clockwise round it - I thought we were in France - in fact we could have got to France quicker. Dad had been round this before luckily, so apparently he knew the set-up. I closed my eyes.

As we sat down with a cup of tea when we finally pulled up the drive, Dad said. "It's been a funny sort of day. One couldn't make it up."

Seven Untold Truths

So, **Seven Untold Truths** about myself. List them, I thought one day. I needed something to pass the time awaiting delayed trains. So, sat between the gent's urinals at London Victoria and the bursting oodles of customers at the nearest bar where grown men, once dapper in their suits, tightly gripped the Financial Times in one paw and crystal-fluted Champagne and brie and grape for appetizers in the other, I fecklessly joined the marauding commuters to drown our raging sorrows.

The 17:12 train home to Greater Bungchip had long since been deleted from the departures board and its replacement was yet to surface. So, just to start a craze, why not jot down some jocular tales to share? Perhaps share in the bar with the ever-increasing, overly-sized queue ordering overly-sized drinks, I thought? And so, I did. And this is how it all began.

And thank you, House-Husbandry *not* on Face-bottom-book; as he so rightly commends himself for saying. "Why would I want to snapshot my dinner and post it for the world to view? It'll be cold by the time I get round to reading everyone's comments on my cooking, let alone eating it, and why, oh *why,* for God's Sake, would people want to 'like' it? Then same said people complain there are not enough hours in the day….for what? Taking more photos of someone wiping their kids' arse, 'like'! It just goes on and on and on and on, does it not?"

So, yes, as I was saying, thank you, House-Husbandry, thank you ever so much for nominating me, for enticing me to start such a craze. Was it just to keep me quiet so as you had the unenviable chance to watch an entire episode of *Top Gear* uninterrupted? I shan't say it was. But, it was.

So, here they are. Here are the seven things I generally never admit outside of my sober-self, I suppose. I now nominate my sister Amber Jostick, Eva Glockenspiel, Beverley Brown, Arthur Krochet-Pryce, Kathy Snowders, Prudence Hall and Rosy Smiggens. Oh, I feel I cannot stop here. I also nominate Lyn, Mia, Joey, Em, Kiki, Sandy and Prizzy-Lizzy.

1) I once climbed Snowdon in my t-shirt as I did not realise it would be far colder at the top than it was at the bottom. It was sunny at the bottom; ever so sunny, and I did not want to boil, dehydrate and die;

2) I used to be ginger;

3) When my friend got a puncture as we drove back from Bangor, I called my Dad saying we were at Watford (not too far from home) and could he help us? He drove up, bought a new tyre, fixed it on the camper van and let the entire van of friends (plus dog) stay with parents. He later said we were not in Watford, it was in fact Watford Gap about 100 miles further North for him to collect us......bless;

4) I broke a yellow wax crayon at primary school and never owned up to Mrs Veldon despite her scalding us all;

5) I so want to be able to reverse the family car first time (or even second, third or fourth time would be a good start. And not even is it just our family car that poses me a problem, I am sure it would be any car no matter of class, size, peerage and so on an so forth);

6) I went for an interview at *L'Oréal* to be a Language PA, and was taken into the catwalk studio (a mix-up as I was tall.) Mildly more exciting than when I came out, shook hands and walked into a broom cupboard. (I stayed 'til all was quiet and I deemed it safe to come out);

7) My favourite childhood programme was.....*The Waltons.*

There, did it. As I said, I love to write, to embellish, to glamourise my existence even, but these are entirely true, hopelessly and entirely an honest account of the seven items (of which there could be dozens more, but luckily the nomination was purely for just seven), and if you knew me, *actually* **knew** me, you would absolutely swear that there is no other person likely to have done these seven things than me, let alone lie about it.

Replies, comments, whatever is deemed as an appropriate answer to these issues which I received in answer to my seven bullet points;

1) I love number 6!!! x

2) These are gold! Did you *seriously* used to be ginger?! xx

3) The broom cupboard one is hilarious!

4) Oops, that'll be my puncture! Sorry! X

5) I don't remember you being a ginge? Also can't believe you let us take the Veldon wrath over the crayon. x

6) Ginger rules!

7) You were bottom half hair ginger and top half black, but it grew out aged 4, just before Mrs Veldon's when we all met you! Hope Mrs Veldon's not reading this!

7a) She is most likely to be dead. She was at least 74 when she taught us back in the '70's.

8) Yay, Lucie-Lu, you remembered your camper van! I like this game!

9) Brilliant, loving the L'Oréal one. x

10) That's a good list. X

11) I nominate YOU now, Lucie-Lu Bloomers. Was your Dad a magician? I remember that much from primary school.

11a) Oh arse. I knew I should've kept quiet. X

So, here is how Lucie-Lu reacted to her nomination, which, in reality, she enjoyed tasking out just as much as I did.

1) I once drove the Play Bus into a police car;
2) I have been cut in half and had my head sawn off. Yes, my Dad is a magician, so he said;
3) I have slept through various concerts at Applebridge Common, The O2, Wembley etc.;
4) I appeared at the Royal Wedding for William and Kate as the Queen (a paper mask at any event);
5) I didn't break that yellow crayon, Honey, but I did tell on *you;*
6) I broke a green crayon and told Mrs Veldon it was Honey;
7) My head, it was glued back on after number 2).

Maternity Reprieve

I found the *Seven Untold Truths* game enthralling, inspiring, amusing, very amusing. Glad I started the craze. Glad I started to write, glad I was considered amusing enough, and crude enough, and generally cynical enough to write it all down, write it *all* down; other people's entertaining tales and droll situations that enabled me to make a career out of a few chapters of enchanting anecdotes and cathartic sagas, and perhaps get others to write it all down for me, and comment on it all and weave a web of funny truths to make a book. My book; my Best Seller on the shelves. *Imagine?* Who would have thought? - Not anyone that I could name from my childhood as I was, as my Father told the nation at my wedding, an introvert. Not that I knew, but, apparently, I was. Oh.

I didn't think I'd return to work. I really and truly didn't think I would. I suppose I thought along the lines of how former lives ticked along in the '70's, and I followed suit. Arbuthnot worked. Clementine stayed at home. Amber and I got paid to go and do the shopping and we visited separate shops for vegetables, bread, meat and 'tins.' Simple. We got 10p for a pick 'n mix for our help and efforts. I used to buy ten white chocolate mice. I remember it well. Anyway, as I was saying, I suppose I followed suit, in theory, and *I* would raise the children (with my wacky ways and my exciting scholaric teaching twenty four seven until even the neighbours would get bored with me singing times tables but, but, in reality, I was born to be quick-witted; it just took a while for me to realise, and when I did, well, to be frank, there was no stopping me.

But, I wanted everything. I wanted to be a Mother, a full-on Mother teaching phonics and singing *The Wheels on the Bus*; I wanted to be constantly able to breast-feed whilst drinking wine and vacuuming with one hand and vacuuming the same god damn spot on the carpet with the other hand afterwards (and that was only by 09:30am); I wanted all of that, I did.

But, I also wanted to write, and I also wanted to travel write, (as in not about far flung lands, I had done that already, but to local places, to local places with local amusing stories that I could pinch); and I also wanted there to be 15 days in a week and 72 hours in a day, but, of course, that would never come true. Would it?

Anyway, the maternity year ended, and I stopped drinking wine with one hand and vacuuming with the other, and I passed that job entirely onto House-Husbandry - who does it differently to me. House-Husbandry just vacuums without wine as a distraction which, I must admit, did not think was possible (not at 09:30am anyway; not that I am aware; and he doesn't just vacuum the same spot as his mind is on the job and not on Pinot Grigio Blush.)

But come to think of it, I could not, I would not be able to have the capacity and the time and the sense of delightful free tall tales if I was at home getting drunk. I would not be able to sit on the train, a train, *any* train and write whilst I was drinking wine and vacuuming. I do not have three hands for a start.

I didn't think women actually returned to work full-time once they had children; what I mean is, I might add, return to work as the main regular bread-winner. I pulled out of London Victoria Station, 6 weeks before my first son was born. Six weeks? I mean, what was I thinking? Six weeks of sitting at home getting bigger and bigger, and grumpier and grumpier, and hotter and hotter in the blistering summer we had in 2008. *Six weeks.* Then Jack was born. Then I had my year off. I had my year off, and sometimes thought of that last time I had pulled out of London Victoria to Greater Bungchip for the last time, and I smiled at the people, and I smiled at the conductor, and I smiled at the platforms, and I waved at Chelsea Bridge, and I said *aaaaaaah* to myself as I thought of that last time I would see Battersea Dogs Home, as I sat in First Class for free for the last time after each day that I was getting gradually bigger and bigger, and grumpier and grumpier as, ladies, if you did not know, you can sit in First Class for free if there are no seats in Standard Class whilst pregnant. I sighed to myself as I thought of that last train journey out of the smoggy city of London, my entire desk of pencils stuffed into my over-sized bag, and as I chugged further and further into the Kentish countryside for the last time, I thought of apples and tea shops and fudge-making and hay bales.

And I sighed, just as indignantly, as I chugged *back* into London Victoria for the first time again from Greater Bungchip after my year off on maternity leave. We had turned over a new-age Green tea leaf. *S-A-H-D. Stay-At-Home-Dad* was what we did. What *he* did, anyway.

So, I got on that train headed for London Victoria, none the wiser, bur far lighter than when I had chugged out over a year ago carrying on board not only a ticket but a very large baby, and went back to work. Rocking. I went back to work on my first, day, and for probably at least the next five months, or perhaps until I was pregnant again with Henrietta-Divine, I was rocking a virtual baby as I had little control over my limbs. I had been rocking a sleeping baby for a long time now, with the trains truly in the distant past, and now I had no control over the baby now not being in my arms, or hanging from its tied-on carrier to my, now extremely flat, chest. And, I had no ticket. Fatal.

Being read my rights at London Victoria wasn't what I had planned. But I was pleased that the Police Report reported I had *shiny auburn hair and a very thin physique.* I was not particularly phased, not at first anyway. Having given birth to a very large baby boy, I was pleased to be described by an outsider as 'very thin.' Not sure about the auburn-haired bit, but hey, I was very thin. That was vastly due to the largely overly-sized baby boy sucking at me like I was, in fact, one of those cows in the long cut grasses through the meadow at *Frégate.* One of those. A milk-maid for 11 months, but hey, I was officially, officially in a Police Report, thin

Okay, okay, I had been read my rights. It was now starting to sink in. But, Greater Bungchip is one of those miniscule villages and it does not possess a ticket machine and showing my weekly pass to *Greater Bungchip's Baby Led Weaning Group* was, strangely, denied as an option. Some people!

So, my Annual Gold Card was not there. I hadn't bought one. **"I was planning to Officer,"** didn't wash. **"You see, I was stuck to the floor in my own residue of milk, and the baby was about to…"** wasn't acceptable either. So I cried. Nope. Bugger! **"What do you need to do these days, Officer?"** were my last words before a penalty letter, a grand description of myself and the expectation that I would receive my dues in the post within eight weeks? The Inspector at my destination had not listened to my plea. Did he not have any compassion? Did he not have children? In his defence, I had already been told to buy a ticket at the booth but tried to escape out a side gate. But hey, I was *THIN!!!*

Eight weeks later to the day, I was summoned to court, and, for a while, I believed I was going to prison to *"be made an example of"* my husband said, just by the by. It didn't seem to matter to him that we now had a baby; that I was the bread-winner; that me, going to work was, in fact, the way we were to get by financially. No, he just casually let me know that I, supposedly, could go to prison, I could be all over the national newspapers, but he had to get the wording correct. *"I was going to be made an example of…",* and all I could then think of (after I had gotten over the being described as very thin bit) was F***K. I was, of course I was, going to buy my train ticket, my entire £4176.00 GBP train ticket (exclusive of the London Underground), of course I was going to purchase the most expensive over-lander train ticket in Europe, and the entire world I should imagine, train ticket, but Greater Bungchip was an un-manned station. And would he listen? Would the London Victoria Train Station Inspector in his overly-sized navy and silver striped cap listen, would he? No. Instead, he took my name (I didn't falsify it), and my address, and my penalty letter came.

I walked to work on my first day back after an entire year, and, I burst into tears. *"Aaaah, it's her hormones,"* said Anita. *"Welcome back, Honey."* And, I burst into tears again, before being given my Nespresso after four minutes.

And, I burst into tears for the third time when I heard this. *"How much?"* my new colleague asked.

"£4176.00," I replied nonplussed. I was quite used to it. "A disproportionate amount to pay for the level of service which goes down just as much as the fares to travel on it goes up," I continued to explain. But the new colleague had just walked off.

"She's new," Anita commented to me as she looked up, fraughtly, from her thickly bound Reception Bible that every switched on Receptionist could not do without. Was I the only one to see the funniness in all of this?

"You're funnier, funnier than I think you think," Anita commented as I strode, casually, in my lilac knitted hat, black wellies, and strained ripping orange Sainsbury's carrier bag out the office one crispy frosty Friday night. The carrier bag stretched its looped handles so far to the floor not even my raised arms at the jointed elbow and heeled rubber footwear could prevent the plastic rustling along the polished office tiles. "And, it's Pussy Willow, not Catkins," Anita continued to call after me as I tried to escape for the weekend. She had spied me taking (taking, not stealing) the office flowers. Us PA's have a rota, you see. This rota is so well colour-coded and so well executed with algorithms behind the scenes that it would be hard to fail to recognise whose turn it was to steal (sorry, take) the office flowers. But I did. In fact, I failed to even read and decipher the 'flower stealing rota' as I, in fact, forgot it even existed. I only wanted the foliage anyway; not the 3foot high lilies which the last time I took rubbed up against my cheeks pre-Mother's birthday meal. My face was entirely orange one side. When I say entirely orange, I do mean exactly that. Entirely orange, orange like a satsuma, that orange, not a mere tiny smidgen of pollen, no, not that, I mean blatantly coloured in like I had been the unlucky victim of a stag-do where every Alpha Male had wanted some type of revenge. That type of orange. And, it stained. I pretended, of course, to the collection of passengers squished up around me on the Piccadilly Line that it didn't matter, of course I didn't mind, I mean, why would I? Being stained orange, a blotchy fake orange like I had fallen asleep for three weeks on one side on a self-tanning bed, of course I didn't mind, why, it's only a mere blip on a Friday night, celebrating my Mother's birthday with family and friends, with photos and laughter. So let's move on. I shan't dwell on that night anymore. I shan't bore you with the consequences of those lilies that weekend, or the Face-bottom-book photos that circulated the entire globe before I could even get out a wet wipe. No, I save you that bore.

I pressed the laser pad for the lift. And waited. And waited. And waited some more. Since returning, full-time, to work as a PA after an entire yummy mummy year on maternity leave, the lift (or elevator as our Boston counterparts liked to refer, although the level of elevation simply had not been applied in this case, it was rubbish) system had been modified. Now, my understanding of modification is thus *"a change for the somewhat better."* This has, apparently, not been applied to our 'elevators'. Our elevators come when they rather fancy it, rather like trains. The Great British Elevator System arrives just like the Great British Train; late, impromptu, rather haphazardly and, quite definitely, packed when the doors finally open that you may as well try another. This new elevator system was linked to the highly recommended 'appointed real time' computer, supposedly equally distributing usage (does that save on their haulage ropes? I never actually enquired.) So, anyway, instead of any lift stopping at any floor (of which, come off it, the building was hardly a skyscraper; eight floors at best) each lift had a 'mind' and each lift spread the load only dedicating itself to stopping at perhaps two floors per trip (all real time, a passenger could not tell in advance which lift would be affiliated to which floor at any given time as only the human lift (elevator) would determine that information when 'called.' Now, this can appear confusing, so safe to say, it was better (and quicker) to enter any lift (preferably the one that opened first), ride as close to your dedicated floor as possible, and then take the stairs. Done.

Anyway, that given Friday afternoon, when my Pussy Willow was finally given a robust name as Pussy Willow, and not my half-hearted disguise as a Catkin, I called the elevator, followed all the above instructions, and took my daily recommended exercise via three flights of stairs.

I recounted this en-route. Word for word. And giggled.

37 Pomegranate Road

Draycod

Herts

DR3 9SF

England

16th January 1995

Dear Amber,

Another *Overseas Jobs Express* came this morning, so I enclose two copies, and also a large envelope for you (which wasn't stamped!) and a Bank Statement. Rather hefty. You're not over-spending on diet shakes again, are you dear?

Thank you again for the Raclette. Honey was going to translate the instructions and recipes for me but due to going to the Isle of Man followed by Bangor, she didn't seem to have time. I will ask *Tefal* if they can send me one. I like to read all about things carefully before I start! (Unlike Dad who reads the instructions only when something goes wrong and then tries to chase the bin men down the road!)

The Champagne Truffles were also very delicious. There is one left which neither of us is eating!

Please thank Kevin again for the *Anais Anais* perfume and body cream and Dad's Grand Marnier and also the Champagne and cheese, and thanks for thanking his Mother for the chocolates. Sharon had one and enjoyed it. (There was so much to take in all at once with three people I had never met before and heaps of presents that it isn't until everyone has gone that I can think quietly about who brought what!)

As I was saying last night on the phone, poor Great Uncle Kirkpatrick had just popped down the road to buy a pint of milk at the corner shop and had a heart attack. He fell on his face. Small shops don't always have a first aider, but a girl who knew about resuscitation happened to be there. They closed the shop but they couldn't revive him. The emergency department at St Oranges hospital has now closed and all emergencies have to go to Lavender Lane which is where Virginia had to go to identify his body. His face was all cut where he had fallen on it and his mouth was hanging open and his hands were sticking out apparently (so

Virginia's Mother told us during the meal afterwards!) He had to have a post mortem as it was sudden.

He had his diary and wallet on him so the police knew who he was which is why they turned up at Virginia's Mother's. They got past the dogs and came upstairs. She thought they were burglars as they were in plain clothes.

The King William is a carvery. I chose turkey and helped myself to four tablespoons of what I thought was bread sauce (which I love). It turned out to be horse radish sauce which I discovered after putting a whole forkful of it by itself in my mouth! I thought my head was going to explode!

About half an hour after getting home it was time to go to Heathrow. Honey wrote her name on a serviette while we were having a drink before the flight as she was being met by a friend's Father whose house she was staying in for one night. She had two items of hand luggage (your black bag and her rucksack). I had to stand in front of the rucksack as she said you are only allowed one, and if she had put it on the scales she would have been overweight. When she boarded the plane she had them both on one shoulder trying not to look as if she was about to collapse under the weight!

Dad has finished staining the new porch roof now, and we have bought a new door to go between the lobby/lounge which is glass, to let in more light. We hope to go to Telfridges one day this week to choose matching duvet cover/curtains for our bedroom (we went round every shop on the Retail Park and also John Lewisham but couldn't find any we liked!)

I saw a picture of André Agassi last week. He has shaved off all his designer stubble and also the hair on the top of his head. The rest of his hair is short and he has got a beard. I wouldn't have recognised him if Dad hadn't said who it was. I was going to send it to you but can't find it now.

I went with Dad to his hospital check-up about his shoulder blades last week. Mr Kelly was very pleased with his progress and says he has now got 80% mobility back 'which is amazing considering you went such a wallop!'

Your glass dining table and coffee table sound lovely, dear. And also your wrought iron bedside lamp table. And your blue leather chair! About your television, I was thinking after I put the phone down that I'm sure you told me you were watching a video when I rang one evening towards the end of last year. What were you watching it on?!

Honey asked me to make some mince pies for her teachers as they don't have them in France. One of them had asked her to take back a savoury recipe book so I found one in in the cupboard under the stairs from 1953.

She said it was snowing and wondered if I could post her a pair of gloves. I thought this rather an ask seeing as I am already paying for her overweight luggage – again.

Well, it is now 4.45pm so I will parcel this lot up and try and catch the Post Office if there aren't any more interruptions. I am making turkey casserole with sage and onion cobblers and rhubarb crumble - the first lot of forced rhubarb to arrive in the shops.

Nutmeg was very daring and let the hairdresser stroke her, and Coriander was walking in and out of her legs. Muesli is asleep on Honey's bed, Truff is sitting by the word-processor and Twiglet shot out of the backdoor as soon as he heard the hairdryer. Oh to be a cat.

Well I'm afraid I did get an interruption – Penelope Popple rang with some dictation so I will have to post this tomorrow now as it has to be weighed.

Incidentally, Honey said Mrs Williams has won the court case about not giving anyone their house deposits back. I can't believe it. She changed the venue to a different court so we think maybe she has a friend who is a dishonest judge. So now they owe her more money. Apparently she used carpet samples in the shower room when she said it cost £500 to replace the leak caused by drunken students. I didn't realise Honey got drunk?

Anyway, I'll print this out now. Dad sends his love. Glad you had a good New Year celebration. Oh and thanks for the phone card - I have still got some units left on the one I sent off for free with Radio Times tokens so Dad has got it.

Did you know that all branches of Athena are closing down? They haven't been doing at all well and no one even wants to buy them. I shall miss Athena.

Well, the turkey cobblers can't wait any longer so I'll have to go.

The Un-Named-Lady

Of whom I have spoken to so much over the months, it now seems preposterous to actually say *"Hi, my name's Honey. You?"* I mean, the un-named-lady has given me a lift home on numerous occasions, so to suddenly introduce myself would be a little, in the least, ridiculous.

Having said that, she's now on maternity leave, so perhaps her head is so fuzzy with nappies and dollies and her two enormous dogs in her new life that she will have entirely forgotten we haven't had the conversation over introducing ourselves, and she will now, comfortably, be as potty as the next full-time-working-commuter-Mummy-with-S-A-H-D (Stay-At-Home-Dad) and we can start again. If not, well, she looks like a Patsy, or a Diana, or even an Emma at a push, but definitely not an Ange or a Chloe and definitely, not in the slightest bit does she look like a Barbara, Barb. None of these names are particular to anyone I know, and I love everyone I know who is entitled by these names, but it is simply the fact that the un-named-lady does not look like anything the names prescribed.

So, I will call her Alycia.

Nice, I like that name. Alycia.

And then she completely disappeared off the radar once I had given her a title.

The Headmaster

"Morning, Mr Barclip!" I spoke out every morning to Jack's headmaster. Mr Barclip was a character. He was *such* a character. He was mid-seventies to be sure, but he was as bright as a button and not only did he run the primary school of Greater Bungchip, he taught two classes and he ran *Duke of Edinburgh* every spring and summer from as far back as I can remember. Mr Barclip endorsed summer camp and school grounds for the infants was riot-some from age 5. Get that; a headmaster, nine other volunteer teachers, taking pupils, for free, away for an entire weekend? Were they mad? It was just camping in school, but still, an entire weekend, in the summer, so we parents could quaff Pinot Grigio Blush. Once there had been a storm and we parents had been beside ourselves with worry that our babies would come home and find us inebriated, texting to see if it should be advisable to go and pick them up? But, in retrospect, the children heard not a thing and despite roof tiles of most of the older village cottages swinging through the air, and most sheep ending up 17 miles further into Kent, our babies were whacked with weekend activities and Coco Pops that most of the little angels heard not a thing. Not a *thing.* According to my son, two little urchins cried so much there was indeed a flood, but, for most children, the whipping wind perhaps sent them to sleep whilst the aged-old oak trees crashed down around their tents. And, we all waited for the next year for it all to happen again. Infant Camp, it happened every July. We all looked forward to that.

The Fast-Lady

She was fast. She drove fast. She spoke fast. She even blinked her eyelids, fast.

I found out later that she is called Kasey-Louise. Oooooh. *Kasey-Louise.* And she is the fastest raver I have ever met. Her 40th birthday was immense. My hangover the following morning was too. It plays testament to the wildest rave ever. Never in my life would I try to prise myself out of my pit of a bed with such a fat wine-head than that following morning unless I had to. I had to. Drive to Edenbridge, curving a multitude of country lanes, to watch my seven year old play rugby. Fuck. But, in all honesty, thank the bloody Lord for *Storm Imogen.* It blew away the cobwebs like no normal little smackering of a wind could even try, and my hangover was cured (until we got back in the car, shut the doors, the wind ceased and then it was back, back with a vengeance.) A temporary cure. Bugger.

Kasey-Louise was ever so funny. We only saw each other on the odd morning that our trains coincided to London from Greater Bungchip. She'd either shoot past me in her larger than large car, texting and waving (all my way) as she break-necked it over the speed-bumped mile-long *Station Approach.* She was actually aiming for the train before the one I was generally attempting to catch so a glance and a wave and *Darling, Darling* texts later, we were through.

Kasey-Louise was also a Mum. Her children went to the same school as Jack and Henrietta-Divine. So that was nice.

The Eloquent Porsche Boy

The man who drives further down his own drive in his Bentley than the actual drive to the station next door must use an awful lot of petrol; that's what I used to think when I strolled past him the first time, scraping his suspension of his, oh, *Ferrari* along the tops of the speed bumps of *Station Approach*. On a Tuesday, he usually takes his Audi, and a Wednesday his Range Rover, Thursday, he is dropped off, just so as his wife can take the car for its 0.4 mile spin at 07:23am. He is different to the Porsche boy.

The Porsche Boy. He is always timely, it must be the car? It MUST be. How on earth else can someone always drive over the speed bumps towards Greater Bungchip train station, with such etiquette I might add, so incredibly timely each day? From wherever I may be placed on my dashing, hair-raising, crazed, flighty walk, Porsche boy always ascends speed bump number two (of which there are four, I believe) at exactly 07:29. I only see him certain days as I generally aim for the train prior to the 07:32 departure, but on the days when push comes to shove and

I'm running behind, Porsche boy is punctual for sure. Could be mere coincidence but I don't think so.

He's polite, ever so polite, Porsche boy, and we always exchange a nod and a smile and even manage our 'Good Mornings' for good measure (three more things than never seem to dawn upon that Chardonnay woman.) I'm sure I embarrass Porsche boy as he tries ever so hard to hide inside his Daily Telegraph, but perhaps I could help him with the Cryptic Crossword if he ever gave me the chance?

Running Targets

Over the years, I have often tried to beat my targets. All sorts of random given targets. How fast I can run to the train station? How fast I can run back again considering it is then uphill on the return pleasant trip home? How long it takes me to complete an expense report at work? And how long my husband spends on the toilet, and can he really beat his personal best of over half an hour when we only have one bathroom and there are three of us wanting to come in? I can hold my desire for the toilet, for want of a better phrase, but a four year old and a six year old, although can hold on for a short period of time, get rather annoyed when they cannot relieve themselves fairly soon after an enormous cup of pineapple juice.

So, I started to time myself. I started to see if I could better my walk, my jog, my fast adopted run in my wellingtons, from London Victoria to my Mayfair office in Berkeley Square, and, although I do class myself as a fairly intelligent human being, I can be, not out of choice, quite illogical at times. I failed to realise that when I stopped at the traffic lights at a pedestrian crossing, the seconds and the minutes still ticked on regardless. When I began to understand that walking and reality wasn't like a rugby match when the clock stops as the play stops and the South African referee has a conversation about the films he will watch later that night for all the world to hear, and life was more like a football match where the clock keeps ticking and extra time is added on at the end. When I realised this, I managed to calculate that I could shave off seven minutes, seven *whole* minutes, if I timely caught the Green Man at each pedestrian crossing. (Occasionally crossing on a Red Man if deemed safe outside Buckingham Palace, but not in front of other people's children. I'll save you that one.)

Seven minutes (if I missed every Green Man) plus those four minutes we shared earlier over the usage of the Nespresso machine, well, that makes eleven minutes. Eleven minutes late for work (if I do not timely catch that Green Man.) Eleven whole minutes. Well, I suppose, that is hugely better than being a week late if I lived in India and the trains just ran as and when, but I have deduced and I am sure that one day all of us commuters will, most definitely, be hanging out of train windows, waving rags, forcing as many more insane commuters into the aisles as physically possible. Just like in India. Just like that. Families only not falling out of train windows as they are too wedged in to begin with. And seats, seats, they won't even be in existence. Just standing room only. And tickets? Well, never mind, we can't afford them anyway.

No Shame

"It's coming!!!" I ran, tripping over the uneven train platform surfaces, back into the overcrowded car park. *"It's coming, it's here, the train!"* I waved my arms frantically to catch everyone's attention. For some strange, inexplicit, reason I always thought no one else would be looking. I always thought, just because the collection of train passengers sitting in the warmth of their cars listening to Radio 4 were not fretting on the cold platform, I always got the impression that they might not be looking. I always thought that, "gosh, imagine if I had been selfish, imagine if I refrained from leaping up and down and drawing everyone's attention to the train's imminent arrival, imagine if I had gotten a different train that morning, imagine what on earth happens when I'm on holiday for three weeks in the summer? Imagine. All these potential train passengers, imagine. Surely they'd miss the train?"

For some odd reason I cannot seem to help myself. I was never an extrovert. When I was younger, I was never an extrovert. Even at my wedding, even at my wedding to House-Husbandry, my Father Arbuthnot Jostick waded in to long discussions during his speech that I was never an extrovert. **"It wasn't until Honey climbed Snowdon in a t-shirt she became an extrovert..."** and then, **AND THEN** he produced a manufactured copy off said t-shirt imprinted with **"I climbed Snowdon in this!"** for all to admire that I thought about my life. My Father continued. "It wasn't until Honey climbed Snowdon in a t-shirt that she became an extrovert..." I thought about that part of his speech for a long time (amongst other bits like where I drunkenly admitted to everyone in *my* speech that I only married said House-Husbandry because I couldn't reverse the car, *any* car...), yes I thought about that clever, random part of my Father's speech for a long long *long* while and I must admit (although I absolutely didn't realise at the time) that he was right.

You see, I was quite quiet as a child. I had the *bestest* of friends. I really did. Absolutely. My bestest friend was an extrovert. Oh, she was. Karen. She was Suying, her Father Malaysian and her Mother an English Rose, but she was an absolute extrovert. She was a dancer, she was an actress, she was an artist, she was a mathematician, and she was everything to me. She was one of life's treasured, cherished friends and I was her best friend. We stuck to each other like glue. From the age of two, we had been the *bestest* of friends because we just were. She became a surgeon and then an aid worker and she was the most selfless girl I had ever met. We went our separate ways when we were 16. My sister went to Maston University and I used to jet off on the train, introvertly, to surprise her in Birmingham for her birthday. Birmingham. Really? Yes, really. And Karen, she'd be dancing in Portugal, touring with her global company whilst studying how to perform open heart surgery. And, Karen, she succeeded in both. We always knew she would. Me? After visiting Birmingham, I applied to live in Bangor. And, well, let's face it, if I hadn't I may never have got that t-shirt. And, more importantly, all those warm passengers awaiting the train may never have caught it. If it hadn't been for me, me and my learned extrovertness from Bangor, me and my selfless angst pointing to every train when it chugged, horn blasting, into Greater Bungchip, if it hadn't been for me, a quick glance down for those passengers, well, they would have missed the train. Let's face it; the next one was in six minutes. Ample, appropriate train timetable spacing was not delegated to the correct person.

That Day the 07:21 was cancelled

"Morning," I smiled and nodded to each person, each character but they didn't know that, as I entered the train station one morning; *that* morning. That was a morning I am lest likely to forget; ever forget until I stop my commute; but perhaps not even then either. Until I ripen with age? Or get dementia? It would have to really be a dramatic brain incident to make me forget that morning.

"Morning," each and every character grumbled in reply. Everyone looked annoyed. Not at me, I hasten to add. The characters, I must stop calling them that, the *passengers* looked annoyed that morning, tutting in unison, peering at their watches or their smart phones, BUT NO ONE DARED TO PRESS THE LARGE WHITE BUTTON ON THE WALL. Yes, each person, whether alone or in a gaggle of geese situation, looked more than displeased that morning.

I looked around. It was quite packed, quite packed for Greater Bungchip train station I surmised. I would say, perhaps, that about half a per cent of the village population were waiting on the platform that morning. I continued to saunter along. The platform was immense; long and thin and if you were fit and liked to be the first off the train at its destination then you'd walk to the furthest point of the platform ~ half a mile, at least, from the free car park.

"Morning, how are you? I thought I was the only sucker who worked on a Friday," I just chatted as I walked along. I couldn't help myself. I wasn't the type of person to see the same faces each morning and just pass them by without so much as a "Morning." Other people, all of the other people for all I knew, might have been completely different and have much preferred to have a quiet, uncommunicative, social-less, morning. Who was I to even think about THEM? I needed my book, my Best Seller, my stories, and for some unexplained reason, most, I shan't say all because that would be a blatant lie, but most, more than most, people replied back with at least the same as me. 'Morning, Honey."

I mean, how could anyone not? How could anyone not want to converse with me? How could anyone not want a chirpy, happy, laughing, chatting (repetitiously) person; every morning? Nope, surely, surely everyone adored my approach. No? I mean, I was cool? Yes? Everyone knew me, no one mistook me for anyone else, and even the USA baseball-jacketed dressed Brain Surgeon knew me. He could even spot me from 3 miles away, before I had even left my cottage, he saw me (or my pink and grey tea cosy teetering on my twisted messy-haired bun which appeared before me in my heeled black wellies.) I was cool, I was the quirky perky soul of the commuting village empire, I was renowned for my tales and sharing my Revels, I was tall and jolly and smiley and everyone always enquired as to what I was on, I was.......

SPLAT. On the floor. I was on the floor. I was lying, my messy-haired-hatted bun bouncing my head off the platform concrete, on the floor. I was not, not really, not then, not entirely at that point of the quirky perky morning, cool then. Not even *I* tried to brush it off. It wasn't just a little slip, one of those little skids whereby you manage to save yourself the unenviable task of severe pain but an even more unenviable task of severe embarrassment, it was a sheer, complete, massive crumble to the depths you couldn't possibly fall any further fall. **Crash.** Flask bounced. Coffee in flask splattered, mostly on me. Bag crunched, that would be the shared Revels, head hurt, finger bent back, elbow cracked and funny bone, well, that searing pain not even I could disguise with a further "*Morning.*"

I just lay there. My head went fuzzy. My body was burning up like I had tripped into a volcano. My sweating skin would even make a sauna feel like an igloo. I couldn't hear. My vision was blurry. I was extremely hurt. My funny bone was buzzing with shooting pains, but my pride, my pride was abashed, and I just wanted to be back in labour. And, the 07:21? It was cancelled.

Consolations

In consolation to my train being delayed on Wednesday, and cancelled entirely on Thursday, it decided to leave early on Friday (to make up.) I am not sure this is entirely acceptable behaviour (for a train), especially when the only message of consolation was completely unrelated to the ailment. The robotic tannoy spurted out "I am sorry for the short formation of your train this morning, of only four carriages. I was also unaware until I looked out the window at Quarry East and asked myself where the other eight carriages were."

How can I have possibly let scenario after scenario pass me by, probably through all of my adult years, without noting it all old school style, with a pen and paper. That is what I do, you see, I scrabble around in my overly-sized bag that is full to the brim of 99 items I never need, and never actually appear to take out of my bag, but my train pass seems to be perpetually at the bottom, under a winter coat I use as a pillow in a 30 degree C un-air-conditioned carriage, three pairs of less than appropriate shoes for work, a well past its best rotten banana, stylish pens that each, respectfully, look nice but have no ink, and a purse bursting at the seams with pennies which I have scooped from the floor in Berkeley Square, Mayfair just so as I can conjure up some luck. I chant to myself, despite strange looks from strangers, *"Find a penny pick it up, all day long you'll have good luck,"* but the more I rehearse my song in public, the further delayed my trains seem to be, but I can't help it anyway, and I'm sure that will always be the case. Perhaps the train driver of the 16:52 service from London Victoria to Ashford International really *is* stuck in the queue of Starbucks waiting for his outrageously-priced frothy caramel topped buffoon of a caffeine drink? I used to think that this type of reasoning was an excuse of sorts over the train tannoy to make passengers laugh; or titter, or just plain sigh with disbelief, but I actually witnessed my blue uniformed driver alight my train service on one occasion and return with a smile on his face, an iced Frappuccino in one hand and his whistle in the other. That was fine; passengers on delayed, redirected and cancelled train services can get a refund, of sorts. Just fill in an overly long form and you will receive a voucher by post within ten days that can never, that I have worked out, be exchanged on train trips with excited children. These vouchers are now part of my overly-filled up purse, and I tend to use them to play *Hangman*.

When trains are always late, one starts to prepare oneself for their inevitable tardiness. I say "prepare" as I haven't quite yet fallen foul to accepting the tardiness as absolute reality, but one day I am sure I will aim for the 07:32, which always departs at 07:36, and miss it. That will be the day it decides to leave on time.

Those minutes, those precious minutes in the morning are invaluable. But, if I am to be honest, the trains are not entirely to blame.

Imagine, and I only really want to imagine, if you lived in one of these far out places in, is it Tibet or a random rural (in the loosest term) village in India where trains depart once a week, on a certain day, and perhaps at a certain hour of that certain day if you're lucky? Well, then, I wouldn't place such precise timing on the train's departure. I'm sure it's acceptable (I might even go as far as saying unnoticeable) to be four minutes late for work, but a day or even an entire week late to ones desk because the train departed not to schedule? Not so sure about that.

Anyway, back to the four minute thing. I mean, it takes me that long (in fact far longer if I'm to be entirely honest) to work out the Nespresso machine as I have mentioned. Does the top red flashing button mean 'heating water', or is it 'please top up water dish', or does it mean it is actually 'preparing to pour'? If the third option is the correct answer, then I generally forget to timely place my Espresso cup beneath the nozzle and the thick black gunge pours out all over the office kitchen. If I'm lucky, my boss will walk past, although I am sure he is vision-impaired as why would you then request one of those delicious coffees, add a drop of milk and bring it into a meeting, Honey? How I manage to carry the cup slurping with coffee, a china milk jug, a brown sugar bowl, a 'nice' teaspoon and exactly the same list above replicated again for his colleague at the same time whilst opening the heavy door with my elbow, avoid the door then shutting back onto my elbow and try not trip over the doorstop, of which I always fail to notice? Beats me, but, well, I am a PA. What else must one expect?

Anyway, this is my downfall, going off at tangents, so I must now scroll up to see what point I was trying to make earlier. Where was I? Oh yes, precious morning minutes. Yes, those minutes which you think are plentiful but the microwave clock's gremlin has suddenly changed the time (again; it also happened on Tuesday, on Monday and every day last week too.) Fifteen minutes have passed but all I have achieved is finding my hat where it was thrown after a 'fashion show' at teatime the night before. So, yes, children. Children and timing are to blame for tardiness. Yes, children and timing, and aiming for a particular train for work each morning (despite said train never truly departing on time) do not really, do not ever, and marry up. I used to have plenty of minutes, ample time that it did not even compute in my brain that minutes could ever at all be precious, but that was before children. Don't get me wrong, I love the brats to heaven and back. I love the loud, continual bickering, and the constant sense of always being right, and the overwhelming desire just to leave them to make their own porridge whilst House-Husbandry gets those extra fifteen precious minutes in bed, and I get those extra fifteen precious minutes finding hats and having childish conversations about deciding which spoon Dolly must have for breakfast, and finding Dolly a chair and a bowl and an apron during my precious fifteen minutes each morning. Of course, I adore making sure the milk isn't poured so fast (by

Dolly) that most of it ends up ON Dolly, oh yes, I love exaggerating by forced smiles each morning whilst I find an extra reading book for bloody Dolly. Oh yes, I enjoy every one of those precious fifteen minutes so much that I actually forget what I have achieved and believe all that I have actually achieved is finding my hat. Okay, sorry microwave gremlin, perhaps it was not you who fast-forwarded the clock, it was just, just, just……adult life. Whilst House-Husbandry still dreams of large houses and holidays, Wifey pulls on odd Wellingtons in summer, fumbles with the stable door, slurps first of many Espressos far too quickly creating brown tidal marks up sides of mouth and up cheeks (even as far as touching the ear lobes at times), stumbles past the side cottage window to blow air kisses to son, daughter (and Dolly plus a now rather enlarged increased collection of elephants, dogs, bears and Power Rangers) through said side window, lollops towards the steepest steps in the world to climb from the top of the cottage to the bottom.

Then peace.

Awash with peace.

Nothing but the dawn chorus intercepted, if you listen very carefully, by the soft snores of Daddy Daycare still quietly dreaming of his children dressed, breakfast-fuelled, homework completed, and ready for school. I am sure I can quietly hear him say "what beautiful, non-demanding siblings I have created." Or am I dreaming? Nope, dreaming is not, really it is NOT, part of my daily routine. If I daydream, those precious minutes will tick away, and the 07:32 WILL depart at 07:32.

So, trains are not to blame for my sudden lack of morning minutes. I run (or try to look mildly less stupid by adopting a fast walk like all these legendary people who *do* seem to have an enormous amount of precious morning minutes) to the train station (1.3 miles from my stable door, but sometimes further, sometimes nearer depending if I take the overgrown grassy route through the cow field and feel obliged to address each cow with a *"Good Morning"*.)

Upon arrival, I say my obligatory *"Good Morning, don't you look lovely today, it must be your new beard?"* to everyone save Chardonnay and life is happy once more. Oh my goodness, the random collection of people is so inspiring. And my chirrups write a thousand words. Flattery seems to get me everywhere. Flattery and continual sacred interest in each and every daily commuter's life at Greater Bungchip will get me everywhere; everywhere and further up the shelving on a Best Sellers Book Shop. You don't think so? Well, you're reading this, aren't you? Seriously though, Greater Bungchip commuters, don't track me down, don't track me down for your share of my profits. You can see it a different way. You can see it as free advertising for yourselves and for your beards. Just think, you are mentioned, you are mentioned in a book, an Authoress, a quite normal Authoress deemed your life superior enough, exciting enough, brilliantly funny enough to write about you, count your stories and count your little chats highly enough in her thoughts to actually put pen to paper and write about you. Aren't you lucky?

Precious minutes in the morning in parody compared to 1 hour and 29 minutes on the train. 1 hour and 29 minutes on the train is sitting there, looking out of the window at the cows gnawing the meadows, and the sheep following other sheep following other sheep, the front sheep walking much faster than my train which is generally crawling. That was the play-off. Loads to do in the 15 minutes I gave myself in the morning (granted, that was entirely my fault, I could have gotten up far earlier, but well, no excuse, I didn't), and then nothing to do, of much real great importance, on the train, with all this time to spare, with all this wasted time ticking away (11 and a half hours to be precise on a return trip to and from London, five times a week) as I trundled through fields and headed into tunnels darker than the darkest volcano yet to erupt. That type of thing. Until, one day, one strange day when my son brought an inanimate toy monkey home from school (smelly and sticky, and probably infested with other people nits), until that day when we had 'Toby' the inanimate toy monkey to stay for an entire weekend so we could take photographs and write copious stories of what Toby and family did. Granted, I hoped that the point of this was to get the children to learn to write and to describe and to build up a bank of vocabulary by the age of 4. I hoped it wasn't so the teachers could pry on what we did at a weekend, I mean, we could really go to town, we could really big ourselves up and say that Toby had gone to Florida, that Toby had gone to the moon, that Toby had been rammed up a cow's backside and luckily Mummy had noticed and washed Toby before the next school victim took it home. (God help those parents who had Toby over the Christmas holidays.) It was not until that day, not until that exact day that Toby appeared at our stead-fast stable door that I had a striking thought. The most striking thought. This thought was more striking than the church clock on holiday at Wells-Next-The-Sea, when I was a kid, which used to chime every hour, on the hour, twenty-four-seven without a glitch in the world (unlike the trains); this thought was more striking than when the best footballer, so famous that his name escapes me, scored a hat-trick in the World Cup (one infamous year); this thought was more striking than when I was told I had gotten a Distinction at Bangor University (no, not for mounting Snowdon in my t-shirt, but for achieving the highest score in my year for talking French at Degree Level, I obviously just did not shut up.) Yes, it was *that* striking. Less striking than my ginger hair at aged 2.5, but none the less, quite evidently striking. That was it! Strangely, before children, I used to be so incredibly tired getting up at 6.30am each weekday morning that I used to spend the entire 1 hour 29 minutes (each way), five days a week, which makes ten train journeys if you add them up like that, asleep on the train, asleep on the train in one of those old fashioned carriages where a collection of 'rooms' snuck off from side-passageways, and each little 'room' had six enormously comfy armchairs. No wonder I used to sleep all the way, and it was a great wonder anyone actually ever woke up at all at the end destination, as each armchair was so incredibly soft and each little 'room' was so incredibly hot that I am, genuinely, surprised all the commuters did not end up back at the depot at Ashford International. Genuinely surprised that did not happen to me, ever. I mean, the Nurse. Monica, the Nurse, for instance. Monica the Nurse on the train, on my return journey, who is kind, kind enough to give me a lift home. She'd wake me up, wouldn't she? Followed by a lift home whilst House-Husbandry chats with the dolly.

Coal Miner?

I am a top class PA, honestly. Underneath the cladding of pink and grey tea cosy, and clay-coated wellie boots, I work as a Top-Class-Bilingual-Multi-National-Financial-PA. Seriously now, I am not pulling your leg. I mean, I must be *okay* at my job. I have been doing it for 18 years or more, and I'm still here. I'm still calculating Korean expenses on my fingers. I'm still on first name terms with the cleaner. I'm still gaining members to join my team. I call it my team, my team of Investment Professionals, and I am their right-hand-woman. I mean, how would they make it to the Nespresso machine without a map, if it wasn't for me? How would they decide what to eat for lunch, if it wasn't for me? How would they, get this one, how would they find their staples for their over-sized, over-priced stapler, if it wasn't for me? Answer: they wouldn't.

And, I am super-organised. Get that. Me, super-*uber* organised. In the work place, that is. I am sensationally-smashingly-unparalleled-unsurpassably-peerlessly organised. At home; well let's glaze over that one. We have House-Husbandry, and that's all we need to know.

So, back to the work place. Me. Always punctual, repeatedly multi-tasking itineraries for global travel whilst whipping the chaps into shape, pushing them here, and pulling them there with maps and timings and Visas and Estas and Passports and Expenses and Proformas and Chauffeurs and masking telephone calls and sending out world-wide dial-in instructions and printing calendars and shaking yellow post-it notes under noses when *Instant Messenger* does not appear to be working as the recipient is staring out of the window. Yes, under that tea cosy hat and beneath those enormous winter wellies worn in summer, there is me. Just me. Little old me.

But if I was not me, then the taxi for the plane for that meeting for that importantly scheduled Investment Deal, for that continuous ebb of reunions for years and years to tide over simply would not turn up. Yes, the taxi at the correct time of the morning for the business man to make his super-*uber* planned trip just would not happen. So, yes, I must be getting by at my job. I guess. But, if that 07:21 was cancelled, and the 07:32 was delayed, well…..

We smiled at each other most evenings. Me and the Coal Miner. We smiled. Then, a smile was added to by a nod; I from my position alighting the train carriage exactly lined up with the bridge steps (only because I followed the **Banker** one day, and he *always* seemed to be able to know which carriage would line him up with the steps.) Then a *hello* was added to the smile and the nod. Then a combustion of conversation overflowed which we tried to fit in as we walked up the concrete steps, over the bridge, down the other set of opposing concrete steps if they had been well-salted and we were not all to tumble down (my wellies were not built to withstand that amount of tumultuous falling.) And that was how that relationship began. A nod, and a smile and a personable *hello* (because Perdita started it all off.)

He had a hat, you see. The Coal Miner had a hat. A mid-blue hat that slotted onto his hair with a big hard peak at the front which cast a shadow completely across his chiselled face and stubble, and I wondered what on earth he did for a job. You see, we (Perdita and I) we were obsessed. We were obsessed with trying to figure out what people, all these commuter people, did during the day, during their days in London, dressed as they were. All these commuters must have been wondering for *years* where on earth the local cattle farm was in Mayfair. I mean, I dressed every morning like I was just off to milk cows, or herd pigs, or brush horses' manes and shovel shit. I wore over-stretched leggings, black wellies, generally my tea cosy hat, and no make-up.

But *I* was a Business-Woman; a Business-Woman in disguise. I did not do it on purpose; dress like I was about to start my rural farming shift. It was just what I did. My alarm sounded out, and I whizzed downstairs to shove my head of crow-dyed black hair into the sink, scrub my face and arms with a brightly coloured exfoliating glove, grab whatever tea towel which was unlucky enough to be lying to hand, towel dry hair, find hat, shove it on over wet hair (or coiffured hair if I was lucky enough to have leapt out of bed all bright-eyed and bushy-tailed that morning to allow a hair dryer to be part of the ablutions routine), whizz up the children's porridge to look like a rancid sweet milky

Demerara filled breakfast but as long as Mummy had 'cooked' it, it really didn't matter about the presentation or the taste, slurp my ever-so-black-beautifully-tasting coffee-gruel so it generally flew up my face...

...and go.

I would fast-pace to the train station in fewer minutes than it should reasonably take, to catch that train. Any train. Any train that took me in the correct direction. Any train that went to London Victoria.

And so we looked, we looked at those commuters, Perdita and I, and we tried to place them. It was probably more fun to try and place commuters in what we thought they did as a career, than what they actually did. But, anyone who was unlucky enough to alight at Greater Bungchip was probably not lucky enough to miss my casual *Hello*, or my inexplicit *Good Morning*, or my supposed unpremeditated *Good Evening*. So, that commuter, most likely, only had a small window of opportunity to be anything other than what they were.

The Coal Miner was only a Coal Miner in my eyes for a few days before he became, when probed, a Fine Art Auctioneer Restorer. Now, I couldn't have made that more of a fairy-ending tale if I had tried. His actual job was entirely awesome. Unless, that was, *he* was playing the same game as me. A man, a man though? A man, playing a premeditated game like me, the Business-Woman? Surely, unless the Coal Miner was also writing a book on the side, gathering fictitious, embellished information whilst he travelled, unless he was also doing that, then no, I think he was telling the truth. He was indeed a Fine Art Auctioneer Restorer. And, even if he wasn't, that was good enough, *more* than good enough for my Best Seller.

"What do *you* do, Honey?" Miles asked.

"Me?" I replied, flicking my hair flirtatiously and wondering how he knew my name. "Me? Oh, I'm a Pilot."

"You speak French then when you're piloting?" Miles replied, inquisitively, as we approached the bridge steps.

"Yes," was all I could say as, obviously, I spoke French if I was a Pilot; some people, but I smiled sweetly and asked him what he did.

"A Fine Art Auctioneer Restorer," Miles replied. He didn't flick his hair, it was stuck down by his coal-mining hat. "I'm a Fine Art Auctioneer Restorer. Not half as enthralling as a Pilot, though, Honey, eh?"

"Gosh," was still all I could say, wondering how he knew I spoke French, and knowing entirely that he knew I wasn't a Pilot. I *was* trying to talk and ascend the steps simultaneously, so *Pilot* just slipped out. When I said earlier that I could multi-task, I didn't mean anything beyond mental things. Anything physical, like driving a car (holding the steering wheel and changing gear) was not really for me. And talking was taboo when overtaking a lorry.

"Indeed, Honey," Miles sniggered, shaking his head and glancing at his watch.

Did he know my game? I thought I was clandestine? And, looking at his watch? Wasn't I interesting? "That sounds interesting, a Fine Art Auctioneer Restorer, tell me more…," I flourished up a grin. And he did, but not before asking me about aerial spatial awareness, flight plans, fuel level balance safety, pre-flight checks, take-off and landing noise regulations, aircraft technical performance, positioning and log books.

"Yes, we have all of that and more," I smiled.

Each day, Miles and I talked, but not about planes, thank God. We talked so much, in the three minutes and 17 seconds it took to ascend one side and to descend the other side of the train station that I learned all this:

"Hi," Miles waved, approaching the steps with me that first or second or was it third nice, crisp mid-December evening. "My baby. It's due soon, very soon."

"Oh, how lovely," I replied, and immediately thought Miles must really like me and already believe that I was probably a kindred spirit of sorts to let me into such a personal discussion about his private life. Or, he was just raving scared. "Your first?"

"We already have a daughter, she's so…exuberant," Miles frowned, sounding like he actually needed me as a stranger to cry on. I imagined he was looking to use the word "hyper" but didn't feel it quite proper. I now absolutely knew his views on my kindred spiritedness were true. I was a kindred spirit and so was he. So, I absolutely poured over him and I tried to be kind and a good listener, and a believer in Karma, and yes, I was preying on his ideas for my money-making Best Seller, but I listened to Miles and I tried to look positive, tipping my head to one side and opening my eyes wide. "And, she, my first, my daughter, Petunia, she never used to sleep as a baby," Miles sounded progressively worse and we had only surpassed 18 seconds of the three minutes and 17 seconds it took to climb up and then climb down. "And we thought we wouldn't have any more, so we sent this one, Petunia, to an Ivy League school."

"Oh, that's…exuberant."

"And we went on some of the best holidays, cruises, diving, even booked a trip on one of those up and coming flights into orbit…"

"…very exuberant," and I glanced at my watch this time.

"And we came to the conclusion that we were really to have an only child. We love travelling. Then, Penny-May, my wife, she fell pregnant just like that. A shock it was, such a shock."

"A *nice* shock though?" I tried to sound pecker and make Miles feel normal at his lack of knowledge of the Birds and the Bees.

"Suppose. Hope it sleeps," Miles looked to the floor and scuffed his shoes. We were still only on step four. Did he not want to get home? "And, apparently I'm to triple paint the new nursery in my 'spare' time." He sounded quite desperate now. "We've test pots everywhere, from the kitchen to the parlour to the stairs and even in the en-suite, *my* en-suite, and I haven't even begun to think about colours and co-ordination," Miles sighed, slowing down even more. I had heard that snails can sleep for three years and I thought we were heading down that route.

"But, you're a Fine Art Auctioneer Restorer," I replied, thinking that would of course cheer him up, but I soon realised it didn't. It sounded more like a nagging wifely-thing to say. "The second, the second baby is always easier, and the third, well, that's simply a breeze," I consoled even further, I thought, the Coal-Miner. How could I actually even know the third baby was a breeze, I only had two children myself. But he then, actually then, came to a complete stop at step seven. "Oh." I stood with him. Holding my breath. I jiggled. I really did need the toilet. I thought I was doomed.

A wave came from the end of the platform. It was Perdita. She had been on my train after all, and had been stuck just off the platform, just in the second to last carriage which did not fit entirely into Greater Bungchip, hence, for safety reasons, Perdita could not alight immediately. I hadn't actually realised the train on which we had been was still sitting there. It had budged, slightly, further up the cranky train station edge, and then stopped again. It must have done this so surreptitiously that I had not even noticed.

"Hi," Perdita announced.

"I'm pleased to see you," I replied, smiling back at Miles, still thinking about being doomed, and we all changed the subject to the non-gritted steps. It was a frosty night and health and safety had not really played its proper part. We were all to slip on the safety-edges and plummet under the next fast-speed to Paris. Well, that was not ever-so likely to happen, but it would have been mildly more exciting than trying to console a depressed male in advance of a pending second child.

The following evening was bright.

And so was Miles.

Perdita had texted to say that she was on Jury Service for the impending future, and was therefore unable to offer me a lift home. I believed her, of course. We did both have outlandish vivid imaginations, and we really did love to be exuberantly embellishing in our stories, but she was not a fibber. Perdita was the least person to ever, *ever* tell a white lie let alone a big black one. Oh how exciting, how provocative, how enticing and indulgent that train story was to be. *Jury Service.* I wondered what she would get? Would Perdita have to send down an Axe Murderer? Would she have to stand up and show her face and say *"guilty, tough titties"* to a Petty Thief? Would Perdita have to give an Armed Robber a life sentence with no appeals? Wow, how I *am* glad I was her friend.

"Evening Miles!" I shouted. Miles and I never managed to sit in the same carriage. I did look through the windows to see if I could see his coal-mining hat, but perhaps he hid from me. I didn't blame him; really, I'd hide from me if I saw me coming.

"Evening," Miles replied. He was fairly chipper, for a Fine Art Auctioneer Restorer pending a second child who would, apparently, never sleep. "Nice day?"

"Yes, I went…,"

"…mine wasn't…," Miles replied before I could move my lips faster to reply to him.

"Oh," I replied. I had been wrong. Perhaps he wasn't chipper after all.

"I found out it's twins!"

St Mary Pray

"Two kids, one dog, half term, on the train in rush hour. If my mum phones again, that's it, we'll never speak until we meet in heaven."

That is what I heard.

Ring ring.

"Sit dog, Honey SIT, but not on that man's foot. She has no clue whatsoever. Mum. No clue…"

I still couldn't believe this man's dog was called Honey. How **could** *they?*

"I'll tell her to her face, that's if we speak ever again, that's if she comes to her senses and realises how difficult answering a phone is when we're packed in like lemmings, packed and squashed on this train so much I can't even eat my crisps. Can you, Gemma, can you move your arm to eat your packet of crisps?"

"Nah."

Ring ring.

"That's it, *never* gonna speak again. To my mum. She's so inconsiderate. How can she think I can answer my phone? And the kids, they haven't eaten. Bet *she* has. Bet she's eaten. She's eaten that pasty she found in her bag. Bet she's eaten that for tea. Bet she has. We need to get off."

"Digger, digger…"

"Yeah, Sonny, it's a digger, we need to get off."

Ring ring.

"Digger, digger," and all I can see is a sticky child in an all-in-one winter suit pointing out the window. He's unable to move anything but his index finger as he is so padded up; compressed like an astronaut.

Ring ring.

I sit opposite the family from St Mary Pray and try to close my eyes.

RING RING!

"Seriously though, she doesn't think. I say to her, I say *'You don't think.'* Two kids, no, three kids, one Staffordshire terrier and seven bags from Primark, I say to her *'You don't think.'* How can I answer my phone with four kids, three dogs, a wife, twelve bags from Primark and only one leg? She doesn't think, I say *'It's half term, commuter train, six children, five dogs, fifteen bags from Primark and a peg-leg at that.'* How can I *possibly* answer my phone?"

"Dunno, she doesn't think, your mum, does she?" Gemma replies.

"Nah, that's what I say, I say *'Mum, seriously, you don't think.'* Oh no, we've got to get off, it's our stop. Sonny, stand up, what are you doing sitting on that man's foot? Sorry, mate," Trevor said.

"No problem, old chap," Crispin answers, searching desperately for a seat which was sufficiently far enough away to avoid any more chit-chat. Crispin smiles again, awkwardly. "Getting off now, are we?" Crispin hopes. "Aren't trains fun?" He was sure he had heard that man, the turquoise shell-suited man, bellow to his astronaut son to get up as it was their stop. "Nearly there, then you can have your tea. That'll be yummy," Crispin tries another smile.

"Chips, chips, I want chips, I want chips NOW," Sonny screams at the top of his lungs. The entire carriage, whether seated or standing, either stared into their newspapers, those articles on Insurance Claims in the Workplace were increasingly interesting, or if someone did not have a newspaper, they stared at someone else's. "I want chips, I want fat brown chips, *NOW!*" Sonny was relentless.

"Terribly. Sorry," Crispin realises he doesn't have a newspaper in which to disguise his guilt.

He had mentioned food.

He had mentioned food to a toddler.

He had mentioned food at dinner time to a toddler, a tired toddler, a tired toddler, who was squashed on the floor, over-dressed in a roasting carriage, a tired, hot, seat-less toddler with tired, hot, seat-less, agitated parents during half term on a packed commuter train whose grandmother kept phoning, and now, now, to top it, the packed commuter train, packed with seat-less, tired, hot people of all ages, creed and colour, had broken down, and all, **all** the tannoy announced was;

"Apologies for the slow running over-crowded train this evening, we seem to have problems with one of the electric toilet doors. We will be waiting just outside (yes, a few millimetres outside) of St Mary Pray station until this dangerous situation has been fully rectified. First Class will, of course, be declassified," (although First Class, it was already heaving with passengers due to the other issue of *"Sorry for the short formation of the train this evening of just four instead of eight coaches, the other four have been accidentally forgotten back at the depot. That old chestnut, oh, sorry did I say that out loud?"*)

Crispin sighed again. *"Fat, brown, crispy, oven chips, now, they'll be yummy?"* He'd never learn, and I could not help but stare at the floor, I wasn't really a stare-at-the-floor type of person. I was more of a hands-on-helping type. But, this was simply too painful for even me to get involved.

Crispin, he was on his own.

Crispin, he could see St Mary Pray.

He could actually see the dazzling orange floodlit lights of St Mary Pray just an arms-stretch away, but he had to remind the grizzling starved child of his chips.

Pins and Needles

Oh my goodness, if there is one thing that makes me cringe in pain? It's Pins and Needles; not just Pins and Needles, but Pins and Needles *in public.* And not just Pins and Needles in public, Pins and Needles in public, on a train. A crowded train. I missed my station, I missed my station at Greater Bungchip because I had the affliction; I had Pins and Needles in public, on a train. And if there wasn't anything worse than that, everyone saw. Every passenger who lived so far into the deepest darkest depths of Paddington's Peru, aka Greater Bungchip and further, saw me, with the affliction, saw me with the affliction miss my stop.

You see, I didn't just calmly accept I was about to miss my stop. I had to try and avoid it, I mean, I had been sitting on the train, for 1 hour 29 minutes (if I was lucky, as it was most likely that it had been longer as there had definitely been a kafuffle at Bromley South, and a youth had got his arm stuck in the closing train door delaying the departure of said train; and there had also definitely been some random woman stuck in the toilet needing to get off pulling the emergency cord, and only then realising that the toilet door was in fact electronic so she did only need to press the 'open' button, and the door would have opened widely for all to see, which she then did decide to do, and we all saw her in-between leg bits whilst she still sat on the toilet seat; and there was also, absolutely, a group of school girls so tarted-up to the nines at Quarry East that they, indeed, with their short skirts and their pink lips (and eyes and cheeks and foreheads) distracted the platform conductor who was more interested in looking at those girls than making the train depart on time.)

So, yes, we had more than likely, which is quite a typical occurrence, been on that train for at least 1 hour 45 minutes. A long time to go only 38 miles.

So, it was highly embarrassing, but I did not really try to hide the fact as I am, now, an extrovert. And, I really wanted to get home. So I tried to get off. *Tried* being the main word. If I got up and tried to aim for the door at Greater Bungchip, I would have indeed fallen flat on my face, losing my pink and grey tea cosy hat and smashing the bananas in my bag to smithereens, but I had to try. I knew that if I got up, I would inevitably twist my ankle and hit my head and end up in A&E, but I had to try. I absolutely knew that if I tried to get up, I would just fall back down, but I had to try, and I did. I got up and fell straight back down. And, I missed my stop.

I suppose that was mildly more amusing (for others) than when I actually didn't have Pins and Needles, all I did was bend down, do up my shoe laces, and indeed, by pure accident miss my stop.

Scattered Belongings

"Did *YOU* hear about the nutty girl today, in a lilac tea cosy hat not too dissimilar to your pink and grey one, Honey? She only went and leant all her stuff up against the train door, inside the carriage once she was seated, and didn't even *think* someone else might get on. She lost her entire bag, open it was I might add, just like you, have you got a twin?"

I blushed. "No," I said, trying to look blazé.

"This entire girl's stuff, it fell out, fell out all over the place, onto the platform, under the train, between the rails. Well, I suppose all the passengers could then claim for train tardiness, but my friend said it was such a funny sight. This girl had two minutes, TWO minutes before the train was due to depart, and there she was scrabbling about with the platform cleaner's picky-up rubbish stick thing, under the train, trying to recover her lipstick, her purse, her Annual Gold Card, and a load of other crap. You know a woman's bag!" Milly laughed.

I blushed, and I shot a glance at House-Husbandry. I thought he may be in need of a new pair of trousers. So, I checked House-Husbandry's trousers. They were okay; suitably dry, although the new brown tweed collection which he seemed to adorn of late was rather sceptical, and I did have to shoot him another glance just to make sure the pattern was indeed a tan patchy brown pattern of twisted tweedy material. I convinced myself it was. I blushed anyway. I thought everyone knew; I thought everyone was suddenly against me; I thought they were all, *all*, laughing. At me. I thought Milly's story about the nutty girl who scattily lost all her open-bagged belongings to those demons called railway tracks was aimed at me. *Me?* Why would, how could, anyone possibly think I, *I* would lean my unzipped bag up against the slam-door? (It was one of those old fashioned trains.) I mean, it was an honest mistake. I'd alighted the carriage, found my seat, and relaxed. Relaxed. Is that a crime? Is it? To relax? How was I to know that someone else would also like to get on in rush hour? Some people! I mean, for all the silly things. Other people, *other* people, wanting to travel home? Whatever next? Train drivers leaving on time, that's what. Anyway, how did they know? How could my friends possibly think it was me losing my best lipstick, my open purse, my front door key to the railway?

It turned out they didn't. Nobody in the room, none of my friends that day, in that room knew. It was just a giggle, it was an amusing tale that had happened, happened to someone else. A funny drama which had affected some poor, dithery, careless lady and the tale, it had come full circle back to me, and little did any of my friends, hearing it for the first time, little did any of them know, it had been me. "Oh, what a lax thing to have done," I laughed, and brushed my messy locks away from my watery eyes. "What a careless girl, ha ha ho ho," I laughed along with the others.

"Honey, can I please borrow your lipstick?" Milly tittered.

"Sorry, hun, I lost it under the train tonight." Crap, I'd told them. I'd told them. They stared back. Smiles creeping onto their faces.

"Oh Honey. I'm sure we all knew, really," Poppy owned up. "It's been on the local news."

I blushed, this time profusely. And House-Husbandry, he needed a new pair of trousers.

Would you like to carry my rucksack like a mule?

These were the questions I tended to hear second hand from a somewhat perturbed person in the office. And I really had hoped that the recipient on the receiving end of this question had the laughable sense to reply *"No,"?* I really *did* hope. I never heard the reply first hand, but when I saw the questioner carrying his own rucksack day-in day-out, I had assumed that the recipient had gotten common sense and declined. I mean, hello? Why would you do that type of thing? Why would someone even ask?

The Brain Surgeon

I texted: "Hilarious, Perdita! *Blaise Pascal* he's on this train, and he's asking me to wander about to find him. I have an enormous Christmas cake, again, and I'm not lugging it about. It's got lights. For my Dad's 71st this Sunday. My sis comes tomorrow. To stay, again. Better start using that Fossil bag she bought me to match the Fossil purse from last year," I texted Perdita, again. "My sister, Aunty Amber, she's bound to ask me, no, she really *will* ask me how is my new birthday bag, the one she bought me for my 40th, and I am so not like my husband, he would tell the truth and say he is waiting for a special occasion, but me, me, I just have to lie, blatantly lie. I feel awful. I cannot possibly tell

Aunty Amber that I still have not even removed it from its cloth bag in whence it came. I simply cannot tell her that."

"Liar."

Perdita, she's on a different train to me today. In fact, we seldom catch the 16:52 together in the evenings now. In February the train time table was modified. Better for me. Worse for Perdita. I really needed to run, and I mean *really* leg-it, to catch that 16:52 of an evening, and it was not making for great moods as my black-heeled wellie boots were not always up to the challenge. Plus, I needed to make sure I left the office on time at least, or indeed a little earlier, if I was to catch the early train at 16:52. Now, with the train timetable shake up, the 16:52 was no longer fast, although it did miss out all the irrelevant train stations (to us that was, Perdita and I, not to all the villagers who resided at these particular irrelevant train stations.) The 16:52 was now a slow one, taking in all the sights of the irrelevant train stations. And, and it was packed, *jam*-packed with everyone who resided at all the irrelevant train stations and jam-*packed* with all those weirdos who just spent all their days shopping.

I didn't take that train any longer, the 16:52. I waited for the lesser-spotted 17:12. The 17:12 was now the fast train, and, although it got in a few minutes after the 16:52 to Greater Bungchip, psychologically, it felt like I was getting in earlier. Don't ask. It just felt that way. To me. It felt that way to me.

Other People's Children

So I raced for the train before the shake-up, the 16:52, with my bosses posh box of partially intact free-range eggs, wrapped in a last minute pinched red and white tartan picnic rug, which he no longer wanted, or in fact he no longer knew about, or was in the least bit bothered about, from a paper bag he had been given at a 'Gallery Do' fifteen days previously (the eggs not the rug.) There was also a mini jar of homemade gooseberry jam tucked away in that paper bag, and a nice piece of bespoke pottery of which I could neither make head nor tail, and those eggs. Those eggs, those free-range eggs which were at (nearly at) their BBD (Best Before Date.)

Yuk. Not the free-range eggs, oh no, not them. Yuk, it was packed......packed. The train was steaming, teaming, bustling, if there was indeed any room to bustle, with other people's children! The 16:52 from London Victoria to Greater Bungchip was absolutely ram-packed with someone, everyone else's kids and that was to *die* for, in the *worst* sense of the word. I felt sick; I felt greenishly, vomitingly, chokingly sick at the thought of other people's children being told off by their own over-bearing Mothers who felt it absolutely necessary, obliged even, to shout even when shouting was least required. Why is it that I can only withstand my *own* children on a train journey?

"Are you okay? Not too squashed, Lauren, Lucia, Walter?" one overly-bearing Mother cried at the utmost top of her lungs to her three smudged in dust and stuck with grime from a day trip to London during yet another half term (they came round so quickly) children who were sitting, quite nicely in fact, right next to their Mother. Did we all need to know her question? Touching, in fact, they were. Lauren, Lucia, Walter, and another child although I do not think was of the same breed as Lauren, Lucia and Walter, sat touching their Mother who still had to bellow. *"WE'VE ONLY GOT ONE STOP AND WE'RE THERE, THEN WE CAN GET THE BUS TO GRANNIE'S HOUSE FOR SUPPER, YES?"* she bellowed, even more piercingly this time. Was it really, was it *really* critically necessary to shout so much, so incredibly ostentatiously and ridiculously garishly at her children when they were all so close in proximity? And, and, to top it all, tell *them*, tell the *children* to *"SSSSSSSSSH, WE'RE ON A TRAIN,"* when Lauren, Lucia, Walter, or the child who did not appear to have anyone caring for it, replied back.

So, the eggs. The free range eggs had left the warm, cosy idyllic atmosphere of the office, and they were now, they were now on the hottest, stickiest, most perspiring profusely and that was just the Border Collie next to me, train. I am quite sure that the box in which the free range eggs were happily residing, was now quite happily ready to hatch out its contents in such extreme tropic conditions. The carriage was, without reasonable doubt, *THE* hottest I had ever experienced. Even hotter, although perhaps out of context it did not seem so bad now, surely hotter than the train journey from hell to Waga-ha-Joo (the Satellite City of Palmerston, Darwin, Australia) that time. But, the box of eggs was moving, moving of its own accord, and six (if not eight, as two of the eggs looked far too large to be single chick-residence; twins or even triplets were surely on the agenda) fluffy yellow chicks were about to call me *Mummy*. That was before the Border Collie sat it's hefty, fluffy white arse on the entire lot.

1996

It wasn't until 1996 that I had the pleasure of recreating that *Summer of 1991* again. University was out for the foreseeable duration of forever for me and it was quite a scary thought. *Oh, I had to actually survive alone now. Get a meaningful job which emulated all the essential, marvellous, philosophical prose I had crammed into my brain for the last four years and put it to good use?* So, I had the unenviable task of clinching that career which encompassed minimal amounts of fragmented French Business Law, encompassed with Emile Zola's social demise and the questionable all-powerful realisation of *La Débâcle* and *Germinal*'s insufferable tolerance of either demise or the rise of oneself and his educating the readers with the most important example of the literary school of naturalism, juxta-positioned with a smackering of Anglo-Saxon history and the most very, *very* basic collection of Russian phrases of which not even Gorbachev himself would be proud. So, I became a Receptionist.

But, pah, I wasn't going to rush into things, you know, just sign my contract straight away and start on Monday. Goodness, no. I had to relax a little. Take a break. Go on holiday even? I had to really recover from the nine hours of lectures per week I had been forced to endure. Mme. Ludmilla's bright pink lipstick and three metre long hair wasn't going to just fade away out of my memory overnight. Her tactics of allowing her students to enter the deluge of her tutorial office with *Kum een, Kum een* whereby six eighteen year olds per day trooped in and trooped out an hour later having learnt how to introduce their Father as a coal miner and their Mother as a teacher on the *Black Market* was not going to just fade away as a distant fond memory all by itself. No, no, no job market. You would have to wait. You would have to wait your turn. Be patient. Only Receptionists with years of practical European experimental travel up their sleeves having necessitated a three-month transitional period from slave labour education (it takes time to fully recover from a four year hang over) are worthy. Yes?

So in June of 1996 I signed my contract. And the following September I began. And I didn't have to use any of this that I had learnt: *Adult Russians who are on formal terms usually call each other by their first name and patronymic (middle name). This is a mark of respect, and young people address older people in this way as well. For example, a schoolchild will address his/her teacher as Тамара Павловна (Tamara Pavlovna).*

Then, on my first train to work, I re-read a bit of my diary from my early twenties just so as I wouldn't lose sight and faith that my student life had actually existed. It went like this: *In 1996, my friend and I travelled the length and breadth of France busking, and we drank an entire bottle of Dry Martini on the 09:17 from Avignon to Marseilles.*

I digress. So, that was three months (a quarter of a year) to get drunk all over again. Dry Martini for breakfast on the 09:17?

Pah! I laugh in the face of those who just pour themselves a bowl of Cheerios (whilst I throw up in the on-board loo.)

But compared to the realisation of what I could be hearing and experiencing for the next few years on the London transport system, this sickening feeling of self-induced alcoholic nausea abroad, it seemed mild in comparison. On my first day as a squeaky clean Receptionist in duly ironed pin-stripe suit so as no other person within at least a twenty three mile radius would be singled out, robots that we were (naïve and mouldable ready for the intellectual world not even I could even begin to imagine or compute or entertain at all) pulling into London. On that first day into the office, in a capital city which I had only ever seen through rose-tinted goggles, on that first day, I felt vomitingly imprisoned.

July (and there are certain ruminations that July fused into August which almost certainly fused into the early throws of September) 1996 was awesome.

This time, to gain access to France, we took the Eurostar. That July, July of 1996, *Beaujolais Nouveau* was in full flow and our exuberant trip had begun. Just twenty minutes of sheer black wherever you looked, and then England was no more, the waters above our heads had long since dissipated and the challenges of *Gare du Nord* just by day were about to cruelly reveal themselves. I looked at Lorelei. She looked at me. And we both burst into tears without a dribble of the finest red wine left in any of our three bottles to drown our sorry sorrows.

Gare du Nord. What a shithole.

So we left (not without first filling our rucksacks to the brim with any wine we could afford.)

On waiting for the train to take us to some place anywhere other than where we presently sat I read some ad-hoc reviews on the restaurants located within the *Gare du Nord* region (as if I needed any other encouragement not to stay) and I can only surmise that the critics had either been drugged, held to ransom, were beggars, or in fact all three.

Really good and delicious food! Fresh and biological. Also when I let them know that I had some allergies, they replaced the food parts for me! Friendly, and the place is awesome.

And this one they snuck in in the hope that the discerning reader would be so hungry they would not realise the restaurant was actually in Rotterdam. *Fantastic place in the ZOHO Kwartier, a vibrant neighbourhood in Rotterdam. Located in an old East Germany train restaurant wagon, this cosy and very well serviced organic-vegan restaurant is charming, unique and a very pleasant place to enjoy good company and tasty food healthy for you and for the planet.*

And the last: *As a family of four, we visited the Restaurant Gare du Nord, in Rotterdam on a late November Sunday afternoon recently. I was cautiously enthusiastic at my daughter's strong recommendation of this Bio-Vegan restaurant. As we drove into park the car next to the restaurant, wonderful surprises started to add up. The restaurant itself is in a refurbished East German railway coach. As someone who has always been fascinated by trains, for me this was an intriguing introduction. The next surprise was a true gastronomic one. The Menu is inventive and eclectic and the range of dishes offered is surprisingly wide despite being based on seasonal vegan availability. The service was very friendly, attentive and professional. Each one of us was able to choose a different dish, so that we could taste a range of preparations. Each one of them had character, nicely and artistically presented and sumptuous. The dessert was also interesting and tasty. The range of teas and coffee were also organic. To top up our experience, a cheerful gentleman walked up to us, recognizing our Indian English accent and introduced himself as Hans, the owner and the originator of this concept restaurant that he plans to open up in several locations in the Benelux. As much as his passion for Vegan food because of its eco-friendly footprint and its obvious health advantages, what we found remarkable was his social consciousness in working to uplift the underprivileged youth of the neighbourhood, while at the same time propagating a sustainable and healthy life style. Rotterdam is emerging as a trendy happening place, and this trend-setting restaurant is very much a part of that excitement. Don't miss this experience.*

We still left; but not without experiencing this conundrum first.

There's nothing like viewing a person with a biological condition of nearly deceased to put your own life into perspective. Three fervently inebriated French tramps, with dogs to match but more flaked out on dope than homebrew (someone else's homebrew I can only assume seeing as these beggars did not appear to own a home), lay in old cardboard boxes. The boxes were topped with blankets of varying degrees of dirtiness and they themselves were ripped and re-ripped and taped up again to resemble exactly as they had first appeared (the boxes.) Six grotty hands, trembling inside baggy-sleeved jackets, stretched out in the hope of acquiring some sort of help, but all I had in my elasticated shorts pocket was a hair band, a carrot end and £3.25p in Great British currency which would be best used by these deathly bludgers as a means of starting a fire by which to warm up. So, I threw the dogs the carrot top and the pink hair band in the hope that by the time they realised what either of the items were, Lorelei and I would be well out of expletive ear shot. Anyway, at least one of the vagrants should be bloody grateful as his (I assume they were all male) hair was longer than a shire horse's tail pre-Putney-competition.

With the Parisian walls of *Gare du Nord* well and truly 200 metres in our past, Lorelei and I walked to, well…we weren't sure exactly as our entire plot was to *hang, man and just go where the wind took us.* But, happily, the vagrants of our past had just passed such tremendously bad wind that their organics had blown us *à gauche* and we boarded the first train in eyeshot.

Vempleuve. We should have planned. I'm sure I heard at least two of the tramps laugh and relinquish in their gifts (whilst one choked on the carrot top) voicing, loudly, how incredibly lucky they were to be homeless, scavenging, destitute old buggers as at least they weren't headed for *Vempleuve* via *rue de Clichy.* Bourgeois didn't even come into it. This area of semi-rural Paris did not even warrant a mention in *Slummers Guide for Cheapskates.* Not even *Edition Two* embellished for tourism during the recession of 2008.

Vempleuve, however, did have one famous notch on its doddery old bed post. Louis Bonnier apparently saved the town by revolutionising its architecture and *loosening the restrictions on the appearance of building facades in Paris.* I had miss-interpreted this scrawl in the town's Office de Tourisme as meaning that this Louis had designed something which made all the houses collapse into a rubbled-garish heap, but luckily the population seemed to praise his endeavours to within an inch of their *je ne sais quoi* life. Presumably nobody lost their belongings into the depths of a sinkhole. Louis, thank *Christ,* was an urban planner resulting in the growth of Art Nouveau. So, off we went in search of Private Villas and feature-full train stations and, beneath the crude cerise graffiti was, just about, an image of a lady with an angular bouffant hairstyle and a square-lined skirt with diamond-shaped bosoms pointing out into peaks. Never mind. We boarded the train only a few mild notches less cultured than at our last stop.

The train.

There we were again.

On the train. This time it was enormous. The Eurostar had been enormous in a different type of way. The Eurostar was long, ever so long and you could walk for miles and miles and *miles* through the corridors with the smell of coffee from the buffet bar not getting any nearer whatsoever. In fact, I am certain, at one point it got further away. Never mind. I had my miniscule Espresso at 12:35 Central European Time when I had hoped it would be well inside of me when I left my seat at 09:01 British Summer Time. It was worth it though, that Espresso, as my French accent had accidentally ordered a *Ristretto* which was a marvellous seven times stronger. I was awake for five weeks.

Avignon. We got off in Avignon. Pissed. It was tea-time, and as Avignon was the type of place I knew to be quintessentially sublime as it should be, I thought let's drink cordial; elderflower cordial which I swear the French on-board waiter spiked with rum. Who does that and stays out of prison? French waiters aboard the TGV, I guess. It's their pastime, a passion of theirs, and I guess it keeps them amused. They themselves are probably far more pissed than us, and in retrospect it saved Lorelei and me a shit load of money.

Avignon was as quintessentially gorgeous, more even, than I thought it would be. It was so twee and so beautiful and the surrounding rolling countryside so lush and inviting. My demeanour? Well? Drunk. We were both as drunk as those delinquents at *Gare du Nord* and I sincerely hoped they weren't our ghosts of victims past who had also tried to busk their way around France with juggling balls and a twenty year old flute with a flat B flat. If that was our destiny, bring back Ludmilla and her fortuitous Russian history lessons. In 1147, the first mention in the Historical Chronicles is made about the City of Moscow, which was founded by Russian Prince Yury Dolgoruky. Perhaps he was that vagrant's ancestor with the long hair now happily wearing my pink hairband? I hoped I had made some sort of impact. Eight centuries ago, this Yury decided to make a *huge* feast to celebrate and took his troops along the Moskva River where there was only a few houses back then. They killed the owner, took his wife and daughters and made a huge party on the shore of the Moskva River where the Kremlin stands today. That is how and why Moscow was the first mentioned in the Chronicles. I am glad Ludmilla taught us that as it made me feel far more virtuous (and far far *far* less a wicked-murderous tyrant) that all I was held to ransom on in Avignon was being a little bit tipsy on a drink fit for a sailor.

Lorelei and I passed the next few days in quite a misty haze. After having recovered from the embarrassment of pinging my ring over the head of a guy sitting at least eight rows in front of us and then grovelling between his legs to retrieve it (when the Dry Martini bottle had been fully emptied – we checked three times, each) we sauntered about in Avignon. And then in *Carpentras,* and even headed to *Bijous;* a town aptly named as a jewel-like princess of a dwelling, really hoping we would not bump into the *ring man* from the train as I did accidentally untie his shoelace and he tripped, falling into the female toilets. As if that wasn't bad enough, the female inside the toilets had inadvertently forgotten to lock the door and the man had fallen inside; *his* head now between *her* legs, staring straight up. Anyway, we shouldn't have worried as it was highly unlikely we were to bump into him. He was now serving five years.

Even the guide books in cities *miles* from this quaint little place called Bijous proffered reams of literature telling us, weaning us, in its direction. We arrived. It was closed. That's right. The entire town was closed. It *had* been open. Oh yes, it had been thriving, at some point, as cigarette butts still smoked and Espresso cups were still sitting on marbled tables. But people? They had been shot, or buried or at best told not to come out again until dusk. That was *at best* for them, not for us.

We set up. Set up our busking hat, and practiced, and we really should have taken heed when the only person suitably attired enough to give us any idea how well we were performing was a lost German trying to find the best way out of Bijous. *"If you thought anyone was going to give you any money, you're mistaken. You're crap."* And he left.

So did we.

We caught the train to Carpentras.

Like neighbouring *Orange,* Carpentras is a large town, surrounded by urbanisation. The centre of Carpentras is concentrated inside a ring of boulevards, and in the center of the center, the cathedral and other ancient sites are located inside a circle of little streets. So, as you can guess, we got lost. Not lost as in we just turned left once, said *oops* and managed to simply about-turn and be back on the main street again. No, absolutely, lost. And the best thing about it? It didn't matter one jot! Having found ourselves lost and realising if we spent the entire afternoon trying to find our way back to a better grade of civilisation, we would entirely miss what in effect we had brilliantly stumbled upon.

France. It was lush. Lorelei had stumbled upon a *coin* of this country which we had been in search of for days. Not the 350 different kinds of cheese of which we had aromas stuffed up our nostrils since the day we arrived, nor the copious bowls of hot chocolate which never owned a bottom despite being mopped to within an inch if its life with bread so crusty it broke not only your teeth but your entire jaw line, not *even* the numberless lists and lists of artists like Monet and Cézanne, and Camille and Débussy who popped up everywhere. No, that was not what had made our ears tingle with delight and our hearts skip six beats. We hadn't even just bumped into the ancestors of Louis Pasteur or Joseph Montgolfier (the inventor of the hot air balloon.) We *had* practically met the brother of Napoléon Bonaparte as in a small square of *Le Puy en Velay* (renowned for having the only pink-painted statue of *someone* built out of melted down metal from the Crimean war) the Spanish and the Portuguese holiday makers had revolted against the French waiter with only Lorelei and I as their British support. Luckily, the outburst did not last for six years, but it certainly had traits of the *Peninsular War* in all its verbal gun-fare. This revolt was all over a not quite steaming mug of Café au Lait. *"But at least you got condiments and a biscuit au croquante,"* I had said.

What we had stumbled across was *Pétanque.* I had read that this was extremely French and under no circumstances were we to leave France without having at least watched a game and hopefully played one. Pétanque is a form of boules where the goal is to throw hollow metal balls as close as possible to a smaller wooden ball called a *cochonnet* (literally *piglet*) or jack, while standing inside a circle with both feet on the ground.

Just off *Place Maurice Charretier*, across the tiny cobbled pavement behind *Patisserie Martichon* and a stone's throw from *Passion Béauté* which I can only assume was a hairdressers but the people inside were completely naked so I just turned a blind eye (unlike the gathering of old men opposite who blatantly did not even try to hide their Peeping-Tommery beneath their woolen berets) this game was being played. In fact, a new game was in the throes of beginning. It was a daily public ritual. Now, I don't know if I was stupid or unbalanced or should have merely stayed a spectator, but after being cajoled into joining the game by every local on the *pitch* (is that what you call it?) I was just as easily persuaded to unjoin the game when the locals realised my utter hindrance to their fun.

Pétanque is played in every square of every town and every village no matter how small. But I did just join it that one time in Carpentras as I was too mortified to even get out of bed the next day to see another game having smashed an entire bottle, if not three, of Pernod and the jug of water at its side on every shot at the piglet I took. France is lovely, but it is full of fucking French aristocrats with no hope for the mere British novice.

We took a very slow train home up the east side of France. I felt the need to just stare out of the window to fully recover from my Pétanque scare. Lorelei, on the other hand, thought it highly amusing as she had only managed to break the basement window of one of the tallest houses in the neighbourhood of Carpentras, but seeing as the maid inside was trying to rid the apartment of rats which had resided for many months, the broken window was its release and it was like the Pied Piper when the entire infestation appeared to vacate of their own accord. Lorelei was given the village medal, three croissants, a free Ricard and the opportunity to sleep with as many of the gawping men on the bench watching the naked women in the hairdressers. Luckily, she hadn't completely lost her senses and turned down two of the croissants.

As I continued to stare out of the window, the flat, then sudden stupendous hilly hills traipsed by, and I couldn't quite believe the audacity of mankind. I'm looking out my train window, watching urban squirrels heading for school - that's how much I think the world has 'come on' - when I glance up at a dreadful sight. At a 60% gradient (I'm not entirely sure if that statistic is correct but it sounds pretty steep so just imagine something pretty much vertical) I see fly-tipped items. How can that be true? But it is. I see the ugly creation of a bright pink mattress and the most-part of an oven practically hanging in mid-air; carefully obscured by a tree growing out of the vertical earthy bank to prevent the fall. *Lyon,* it can be quite pretty at times. Even urbanised-suburbia has its plus points; old oak trees, large Victorian houses French-style, masses upon masses of forests classed as ANOB (Areas of Natural Outstanding Beauty), even thin meandering rivers if you look very closely. But people - and it's only the minutest proportion of the population which create such an eyesore - but it's there, and the other 99.97% of mankind have to put up with it.

In 1999, a garage owner in *Skegness* was convicted of fly-tipping after he blocked a road with rubbish from his business. Motarlia Statarthengie (English born and bred) was caught by his local council, the *Skegness Neighbourhood Environment Action Team.* The waste which was left strewn across the street (a mile from his business) was traced back to his car garage trading estate. Trying to cut corners rarely pays off in the motor trade industry, and this is particularly evident when it comes to motor trade insurance when items of random exhausts and engines (logged) are found scattered not far from home. Instead of paying a mere £175 for a bona fide company to legally dispose of his rubbish, Motarlia Statarthengie had to pay in excess of £1,000 and wear a bright orange Community Service jacket as penance. Luckily for him, many young child-bearing Mothers with at least six children each and more Fathers than they could begin to remember, took pity on Motarlia Statarthengie, and he managed to budge off a fair few as the weeks drifted on before he was *willingly* repatriated home.

In later years, Amber recollected she had once read in her local *Niçoise* newspaper – *The Riviera Times Online* - (and she doesn't know why that particular tale stuck in her mind) that Motarlia Statarthengie and his behaviour reminded her of something on local news where a guy tried on a coat in a shop changing room, left his old one in the changing room and walked out with new one on without paying. Unfortunately for him he left a bill with his name and address on it in his jacket pocket so the police turned up on his door step. Stupid Man. But, not as stupid as myself in the last hotel before Lorelei headed for home. We stayed at the brightly-lit, yet rather extortionately-priced, *Etoile* on the outskirts of *Dunkerque* and I asked the bald man in the communal shower area if he had finished with the hairdryer as I didn't want to appear rude and reach across him to grab it if indeed he was still drying his baldness. What was I thinking? Never mind, I slipped on a discarded baguette, hit my arse on the ferry steps and spent the last few hours of re-enacting that Summer of 1991 sitting on a bag of frozen petits-pois. Green balls shoved inside my elasticated shorts was not what I had planned, but that is neither here nor there, and I would have to wait another five years to see if any lesser traumas could occur. You see, I still had my cultural job as a Receptionist awaiting me. Honey was now ready to become another android of the bright lights of London. Who else could *possibly* be so well equipped?

Catwalk

It was a long few months, which rather dramatically turned into an entire year and counting, before I realised I had become one of those zombies I had only visualised whilst scanning the *Next* catalogue – dull grey suits and matt black shoes with the thinnest tights imaginable which laddered before you even took them out the packet. So, as you do, I picked up the telephone and called my friend. She pointed me in the right direction.

I took the Piccadilly Line (that's the navy blue one, I remember now. I don't take the London Underground too often these days if I am to be honest.) Yes, the navy blue line took me to *L'Oréal.*

I remember the offices at *L'Oréal* were immense; shiny, grey, full of windows, tall and rather posh. Yes, they were rather posh. Or *were* they? I had just taken a year out (three months was far too short) travelling to grottos in far flung places like the Outback, Rarotonga, New Zealand, Stanthorpe, fruit picking, like you do when you get to 25 and you feel like you're ancient and have not achieved your life-long goals, your life-long ambitions; whatever they were. Despite being *just* short of a First Class Degree in French Language and Modern France, with a mild splattering of Russian thrown in for good measure to boost your Curriculum Vitae, having climbed Snowdon in my t-shirt, been a Brownie for more years than was actually good for me, having a sister living in Nice so I could visit for free whenever I felt the need (and that flight with easyjet from Gatwick to Nice was quicker than my commute from Greater Bungchip to London nowadays) I had needed to see more. How I dreamed of those sweaty Australian nights once more. To feel the intense gnawing of 1001 mosquitos drilling through your tent, your sleeping bag and indeed through your three layers of clothes beneath because it was mildly better to be boiled alive than bitten to buggery.

At L'Oréal, perhaps I was going to burst free from that zombie-like city-status?

"I can't speak Spanish, just French, I speak fluent French, and a mild splattering of Russian if it's not too hard. I can say My Mum's a Nurse, my Dad works for the KGB, and I have 1.3 siblings who each have spiky umbrellas, if that helps? But I can't speak Spanish," I had said.

"Spanish, Spanish? You won't need Spanish," the jovially gay man had replied as he led me through thinning passageways. *"This way, to the catwalk,"* he had called back over his shoulder, his nose pointed to the ceiling.

"CATWALK?" I had said, but he said nothing in return. *"Really?"* I replied. *"Are you sure? The agency said I would need Spanish, but if I could speak French then that would surely get me by. I'm not so sure, they're both descendants of the Romance languages, I learnt that in Linguistics, but I shan't be able to converse at all in Spanish on a daily basis. Do you agree?"* The man still stayed silent. I continued to talk to him, noticing more and more as I meandered along the longest corridor I had ever had

the misfortune to be walking. He was a very colourfully clad gentleman who pushed open door after door in a very gentlemanly manner, and he led me through and down some extremely grim twisted corridors until we ended up in one simply enormous room; one simply enormous room with a catwalk centrally located. How odd.

"Ronnie, he'll be with you in a minute," he said.

"Ronnie? Oh, the agency told me the interview would be with a woman. Angela? But never mind, it doesn't matter, I'm sure," I said.

"Angela? She's interviewing for a PA, French and Spanish," he replied.

"Yes, that's why I'm here. That's why I took the Piccadilly Line for the first time in years," I said. *"I'm here for that PA job, but as I said, I don't speak Spanish, just French, with a mild splattering of Russian. I did say that,"* I said whilst I strut in my thin heals, a scarf thrown around my neck, down the catwalk.

"But, but…" the man looked like he was about to cry. *"What about my catwalk? You're just the nymph-style fairy look we need. It's all the rage…"* and from a distant corner of the office, I could hear a girl shouting *"I can't speak Spanish, I told you I can't speak Spanish, I can toss my hair and place one foot ridiculously in front of the other without falling over, and I can pout and I can batter my eyelids, but…I…CAN'T…SPEAK…SPANISH."*

*"Can **you** speak Spanish?"* the colourful, jovial man asked me.

*"Er, **no**,"* I said. *"But I do know where the Piccadilly Line is now."* I had missed my interview, but that really didn't matter as I couldn't speak Spanish, and, despite wanting to perhaps try the catwalk, the jovial man had already disappeared leaving me to find my own way out of this maze. All I could do was find the entrance to the largest broom cupboard from which I did not reappear until *L'Oréal* had locked up for the evening. Thank goodness the Piccadilly Line ran long into the night.

Waga-ha-Joo that time

If you remember, I mentioned I had travelled; again. This time to further climes; just to see.

Before I knew what was what and which Sheila was shacked up with which Bruce we were interchanging at Singapore airport destined for sunnier climes. *Australia.* Oh dear. With the girl who had recommended I take the interview with *L'Oréal.* I should have just gotten on that catwalk. I could have been a C-List celeb by now.

So, we were trundling along, or were we? Bloody hell, no we *weren't,* we weren't trundling along at *all*. We were *bombing* it along, bombing it along the straightest, bumpiest, red-sanded-track in Waga-ha-Joo that stretched for 17 days and 33,000, 000 kilometres, but not as fast as those Road Trains. Bloody hell, those *Road Trains.* Were the drivers of those seven carriage long, 11 feet wide Road Trains completely insane? Oh no, they were just Australian.

Occasionally, actually let's rephrase that, *continuously* our coach driver twisted his neck right around to make conversation. It was insane. Not only was it hair-raising enough to be travelling slanted on just two wheels most of the time, clinching to our seats and falling into the dusty aisles, we had to try and make decent conversation with the driver. Okay, after 17 days it was highly unlikely I was ever going to cross paths with this freak ever again so decent lines were not a necessity, but still, his questions were phrased in such a way that it would have been rude not to have at least answered them. *"Did I tell you about the time Gracie and Jackson skinned that kangaroo alive? It was insane! It was dinner time and just as they were about to go to the market that 'roo just jumped out in front of their yoot. Pucker!"* I had no idea what a *yoot* was and to this day I just spell it phonetically, but apparently that is what happened and I can only imagine the story ended with dinner being quicker than Gracie and Jackson had planned. Pucker.

You see, Nellie and I, we thought we'd go to the twinkling, turquoise sea waters of the Australian coastline to swim with Angel Fish, to dance with Dolphins, and to find our Dream Man during our mid-twenties. In truth, we disabled our fingers cherry-picking; we slept in bizarre; sometimes hot, sometimes freezing, and sometimes weird, sometimes just plain spooky conditions in hostels. But today, or that night, under the huge bright white starry night sky with a navy blue background, we were doomed. Doomed by the Road Train which did not allow us, any of us, on that coach to dare to take a peaky, sneaky shut eye, despite our tiredness beyond belief demeanour.

I had chosen the film.

I was the tallest, skinniest, most naïve person on board our Australian Greyhound coach. I had stood up. I had taken the most stupid decision, the most wreck-less, most erratic action, and I had stood up. I had stood up, on the Greyhound coach, to change the 'video tape' on the screen whilst we were being overtaken by *a Road Train;* a Road Train driven by an Australian. I was indeed, without a shadow of a doubt, the most naïve 26 year old to have lived. Or died; nearly. Everyone cheered. I thought everyone was cheering my fabulous choice of film, *The Full Monty*, and I was the most proud 26 year old to have lived, for precisely four seconds. Then, after those four short seconds of glory, I became the least proud, and the most credulous, simple, innocent sucker to have lived; and nearly died.

Its horn was phenomenal. That Road Train's horn, which was most probably on the longest, rustiest, metallica-est chain possible, was outrageously deafening. Its blast was so rip-roaringly loud, that I fell over. The Road Train, it had not hit us, not yet, but its blaring echoing blast has not left me to this day. I was marooned. I was startled. And I was on the floor.

Bang.

I hit the deck of the Greyhound coach like no other 26 year old travelling in the tropics of a beautiful island like Australia had ever hit the deck. But, that didn't seem to matter, not really, as most people were either now oblivious to my fall, watching *The Full Monty,* on drugs, or all three. That was best. We had not stopped, but we were merely travelling with more bodies on board than when we had set off. From where had these extra passengers appeared? Moreover, did they know what was in store in precisely three minutes? Another Monster Road Train from hell.

Monkey Mia was the destination, but not for those kangaroos. Bloody *hell.* Nellie was not to meet the man of her dreams tonight with her mascara dripping off her nostrils. It was a blood bath. And that Road Train, it was now nowhere in sight having left death in its trail. But the kangaroos, and *You Sexy Thing* and me, *ME* they were all still larger than life.

"Excuse me, *excuse me!*" I cried from the depths of the Greyhound coach floor. "Sorry, *what* was the reason we took this method of transport and not the plane?" but my voice was second to none as the third, fourth and then fifth Road Train suddenly crushed and rattled and gruesomely rumbled past our tiny coach in comparison, and *You Sexy Thing* still rang out plain as light. And, those poor six-footers, those poor taller than life itself kangaroos tried in vain to avoid our coach, but goodness knows their fate as Nellie's mascara dripped from her nose, and the Australian driver rubbed two large, thick sticks together, as he held, loosely, the Greyhound coach steering wheel with his randomly placed foot, and licked his lips for dinner for which I can only assume he was having free kangaroo steak.

The gallant moon shone.

A star twinkled.

And I dreamt of Linda McCartney and her vegetarian sausages. Now, they *were* to die for. But vegetarians, vegetarians on a road trip in Australia were more absurd, more nonsensical than selling ice to an Eskimo. Not that I had ever tried, but that was what I surmised. Not at the time. But now, now writing this, I surmised that selling ice to an Eskimo would be far, far, *far* easier than feeding the gargantuan of this Australian coach driver a vegetable sausage. Not that I had a vegetable sausage in my ancient ruck sack but that was my analogy.

We pulled in to *Alice Springs.* I had, somehow, managed to regain some sort of composure in my seat. Luckily I was no longer flat on my back on the coach floor, but reasonably positioned next to my travelling partner; her black mascara streaks set-in. I pulled my Australian *Rough Guide* from the depths of my sister's rucksack (the one which had seen us through Paris, Pisa, Florence, Rome, Lucerne, Brussels and Oooooostendeeeee.)

Chapter 15; Alice Springs. There was a rough sketch of the biggest whole rock on the planet on the first page. It was a black sketch. Next to the black sketch was another set of black sketches. Faces. Aboriginals. There, I *KNEW* it. There was Nellie's face. Practically exactly the same endearing pattern created on the face of an authentic, traditional Aboriginal drawing in print in *The Rough Guide* had also been randomly etched on my travelling partner's forehead, cheeks and chin. I shook her. I shook Nellie. I had to tell her the news. It was surely destiny. We had travelled half way around the world in search of love, a soul-mate, our life-long partner, and hers, Nellie's, was so very nearly in sight. I shook her again, a little harder, perhaps a little bit too brutal for a wake-up call, and she opened her eyes. Oh dear. She looked rather annoyed. She *had* been asleep after all, and I must admit, I'd had quite a good night's sleep, for a coach trip, but I had absolutely no clue if Nellie's nap had been the refreshing one I had pleasured or a pure crap one which she had to endure. I guessed the latter looking at her wrinkled, freckled forehead. And, not knowing how to reprieve the situation, I chose to shove page 297 of *The Rough Guide* into her blurry line of vision. "There he is, your life long partner!" I blurted out. "Well, what do you think?"

Now, I was quite chilled. I didn't have a crick in my neck. Come on, I was only 26 years old, not like now, pushing 44. Nope, I had achieved a pleasant, very pleasant in fact, night's kip (somewhat anxious that the Monkey Mia stop had either never happened, or we were all so drugged up on eucalyptus that we had no recollection of the so-called prettiest little bay half way up the West Coast), but anyway, I was chilled, refreshed, raring to explore the oldest site in Australia; aka Uluru.

She wasn't.

"Get that out my face!" Nellie demanded, as she thrashed her arms in front of her body, in the small amount of space that had been allocated for each coach passenger.

"But *look,*" I replaced the book with a little mirror. It did not really help my cause. A book, followed by a mirror brazenly in your face when you'd been awoken, abruptly, by a so-called friend with no explanation. I mulled it over. Mmm, perhaps it was a bit much. Nellie looked at her reflection.

"Bloody hell, what happened to *you?*" Bobby, our newly befriended travelling companion, and worse still he was an Australian, peered his eyes through the gap in our coach seats. He could see Nellie's reflection, her sullen, black mascara-reflection, staring back at him. "Two rounds with that six-footer was it Nellie? That beast of a red kangaroo a few hours back? Who came off worse?" he laughed.

I laughed.

Perhaps we both shouldn't have laughed.

"Get stuffed," was Nellie's over-friendly reply as we all piled off the coach.

It was hot.

Boilingly hot.

Burningly boilingly hot and we all piled back on to scrat about for our overly large sun shades. My hair was so thick, tangle-filled, in dire need of a wash that my cream floppy sun hat did not quite fit properly, but who cared? Who on earth was there out here, in Alice Springs, in the bracken, dry, sandy, wire-fenced little town called Alice Springs to care about my hair?

"G'day girls?"

Oh, he was quite nice.

I looked again.

I blushed.

On second thoughts, perhaps it was just his accent? I was rather a sucker for a manly, brash, deep Aussie accent. But looking, looking for the third time under his extremely hard-brimmed kangaroo-skinned hat, perhaps he was not quite my idea of Crocodile Dundee from the '80's.

"G'day girls!" this mystery tour guide spoke again. Nellie blushed too and soon realised that perhaps *The Rough Guide* in her face was a good idea after all. She grabbed it back from my dirty paws and shoved it where it had been nine minutes previously to cover her mascara-filled face from this fairly nice, good-looking man. Or was it, was it still just the eucalyptus taking its toll, and if we looked at this brash Australian hunk of a man a fourth, fifth or even sixth time, our eyes may well see someone entirely different? But Nellie, Nellie was not about to take that risk.

Now, for me, I had already met my man. A backpacker, an English backpacker who really was not in the game to earn a few dollars fruit picking (from where I had gotten the sack numerous times I had actually lost count.) *"I am sorry my arms are so puny,"* I had muttered.

"Sorry? You're sacked. I'm not a charity," and that was that for my finances.

Anyway, back to *my* man. Angus. He was a tall, dark, muscly, messy-haired, strong boy. Boy was he strong. He liked to surf, he liked to chat, he even liked to carry my rucksack as if it was a small bag of frozen peas compared to my procedure shouldering it off-centre, breaking my back and ending up as a turtle on all fours at the airport that time whilst Angus and Nellie continued walking along chatting to me as if I was still alive. Yes, it was apparent that I spent a fair amount of time there of late. On the floor. And Nellie, she met her man that weekend. An Irish man with vocals to die for.

And me? I flew home.

Arbuthnot picked me up.

I aired the rucksack, brushed the dust from my hair, stuffed my *Dear Diary* into the depths of my drawers, and sipped a glass of New Age Chardonnay.

The phone rang. It was House-Husbandry before he was House-Husbandry, and the rest, as they say, is a brutal history.

A letter fell out of my bag on the way to meet House-Husbandry pre-being *my* House-Husbandry that night. It was quite surreal considering I had been just talking about odd travels. The wind blew a sudden fierce hard blow as I trundled along in my nearly sole-less pumps and I practically lost the lost, but I managed a hearty grab and look at the delights still in-store:

Dear Honey – this is just a letter. The computer is being fixed. I remember Amber telling us that she saw a gun in a foreign man's inside pocket. That suddenly popped into my mind. Funny what you remember when mixing the Christmas pudding in April ready to mature. Was this, the gun escapade, when she with you or was she with Anne? Or was it you and Josephine? You both do gallivant rather too much with a variety of people, but I guess it's best to get it out of your system before having children who take your life away. No offence. It may have been a policeman who you were talking to in order to feel safer when some local youths were harassing you? Anyway, thought I'd ask so as to get my stories straight if anyone was to ask how you both were.

And you had to spend the night in an old hotel with a man with an axe when there was a problem with a connecting train after spending the weekend with your friend and her husband? I'm at the sherry stage now. The pudding will be very much matured come December.

And being sacked for not being able to carry a full sack of apples? That must have been a bit embarrassing for you, Honey? I did always say to build up those muscles if you were to be able to, well, do anything even mildly sporty. (By the way, your travel writing diary is still in your wardrobe if you want to take it. What's a spliff? It just fell open at that page.)

Oh, and not finding Josephine in France - you said to someone *'Do you know a hotel beginning with A'.* And she found you when you were crying. That's probably another one you'd like to forget, darling Honey?

And someone saying Fritz was coming up the road. Your German fancy-man whom I am sure would have made a marvellous husband if you like that type of thing and dress in leather on a daily basis (you could do a university get-together if these are the people with whom you'd like to re-connect, dear?) Remember when Dad ran over that bottle in the gutter and the glass went over an Alsatian whilst dropping you off in digs that time? We couldn't get away fast enough, but I'm sure you were dying to settle in. And when you said you were stuck at Watford Gap and your friends brought their pit bull terrier to sleep on our settee after the tyre blew? That was an eventful one. The cats had a scream.

What fun you young ones seem to have?

Whatever happened to that Policeman's bag and the Tuxedo that you found on the train? And did House-Husbandry recover from those four injections simultaneously? Why *did* you have to go to Sri Lanka? *Indeed,* I muttered back into the crumpled paper with a…*was it a banana squashed to it?* Oh, and did you get that job with a safety pin holding up your skirt? Do tell. And, please, don't get knocked out by another selfie-stick, Honey. I can't *bear* A&E as you know.

Love Mum x

P.s.   And Love Dad, of course, I guess. I think he's gone to "Pay the Papers." It's all *very* embarrassing when we are on the *black list* for late payment. The milkman always sniggers, and I'm sure he's told the neighbours that your Father pays in old coppers. He does love to save them up in plastic bags, but when we are in a long, hot, queue in Tesco, I wish he didn't use those times to pay for a bottle of wine in 1ps. It is mildly better when he used the 2ps, but he lost count when the cashier sneezed.

 Oh, and then an email fell out too.

From: Arbuthnot Jostick

To: Jostick Amber ; Hollings Honey;

Subject: Hello

Hi both,

Well I'm glad that's nearly over (the builders here). They've only been here two days so far but it feels like two years! They come at 07.45am. Your room's full of things from the kitchen, Honey (the dust gets in the cupboards and I couldn't bear dusty bowls). The litter trays and cat food + food we need for ourselves are in the lounge. Can't really get in the kitchen, but from tomorrow they should be nearly finished and we can begin to clean. It is so much better without that awkward wall. Did I say? The kitchen is now quite huge. I didn't ask Dad as he was having a tête-à-tête with the new Rottweiler from the mansion, so the builders took my word for it and just smashed it down. It was totally thrilling watching the space where Dad reads his paper for quiet-time just rise to the challenge of joining the rest of the kitchen. Dad can always slink off to the shed (although that also goes next Tuesday.)

The builders had to take off the kitchen radiator (from the wall that has gone) and in doing so caused a blockage somewhere in the system and we had no heating. Today they found the blockage and got it out but said it needs a power flush as the water inside the system is black and sludgy. The plumber said 'Is the airing cupboard in Amber's room?' I thought he was one of your old boyfriends, Amber, there've been so many, but then

realised he'd read *'Amber's room'* on your door! He had a tattoo
of a woman and, I must admit, it did look rather like you, Amber,
but only when he bent over.

I got this enormous box delivered by courier today and
was all excited as it said *'Attention - perishable contents'* and
thought I'd won a hamper of food from a competition, but when I
opened it it was just a small tub of margarine - the rest was
packing and ice! I'd come fifth.

Poor Dad got a speeding fine in the post today for our
journey down to Kaitlin's.

Can't wait to start choosing kitchen! I can't put my
calendar back as the wall's gone! Never mind. I shall have to rely
on my memory, your Father's memory, or find another wall for
the calendar. I really can't decide.

By the way, I got a letter today to say my three yearly
breast screening I had the other day in Sainsburys' car park was
okay. We might open that old bottle of Liebfraumilch to
celebrate.

Love Mum x

From: Arbuthnot Jostick

To: Hollings Honey

Sent: Tuesday, November 03, 2009 1:42 AM

Subject: Re: Anna

We gave my best friend a lift to the school reunion - we
got there really early and sat on a seat till 12.15pm then waited

outside *Diazomino* for the others. It's a new Italian. Rather posh. Anna said they were late the last times as Lucia's train was late from Lower Lowest Broomfield Field (I didn't go as I was having my operation and the time before that was the day the cat was put to sleep so I didn't go then either) so we assumed it was Lucia's train again and Anna said they wouldn't go in without us - they'd wait outside. When it got to 12.50pm Lucia came out and called us (it's set back from the road). They'd been inside all the time and were on their second bottle of wine! How happy and flushed they all looked. It was a lovely sight. They couldn't see us from their gorgeous bay window perspiring in the sunshine on the wall. That started Anna off on how terrible it was to go in before we were all there. Clara said they'd nearly given up on us and were about to order the olives.

That aside, *really* enjoyed the meal - I had spinach and ricotta something (like ravioli but not ravioli) in tomato sauce and a large hazelnut bombe followed by filter coffee. I was as high as a kite especially as I'd put up my hand to stretch just at the time the waiter asked if we would all like a complimentary liquor in our coffee. Apparently I was counted twice as I stretched again, the left hand this time. Never mind. It was complimentary after all, and if I had realised, I would probably have said no.

Jane's husband (the millionaires from The Common) was down in Dorset bailing out his brother whose business had gone under and who had just lost everything - even his pension - and had all sorts of people knocking at the door to whom he owed money.   She had taken her daughter shopping in Paris for the weekend for her 21st birthday.   They have got a holiday house in Spain and she and a friend had recently had oysters and Champagne in London (but only two bottles to ensure they weren't being lavish.)

Lucia had lent a book to a friend who was in hospital and had said he'd read it later.   Unfortunately he died on the operating table before reading it and she didn't like to ask his wife for it back.   She hadn't read it herself yet, so she's thinking she'd better buy another. Rather annoying as she'd bought it on offer. It's now twice the price, at least. She and her sister have never got on and she doesn't want her to come to her son's wedding next year.   Glad you and Amber get on so well - it's sad when siblings don't.   (Like Truff and Nutmeg, the cats! Heart breaking, in fact).

I think we're meeting in London next time to make it less of a journey for Lucia.   Clara Osborn couldn't make it today as she is a Town Councillor and had an *Important Meeting.*   She has just been elected beating six men for the post as *Speed Bump Monitor* and sent us all an email to explain. I had another complimentary liquor to celebrate.

Whilst I was with the girls Dad had a lovely walk for three hours and a cheese bap from the bakers. At least he didn't sit outside in the pub garden unwrapping his homemade sandwiches in tin foil like he has been known to do – the neighbours told me, and their neighbours too. And the milkman. And the newspaper boy. And the hairdresser. He seems to be getting lots of fame in his older age.

Love Mum x

From: Hollings Honey
To: Arbuthnot Jostick
Sent: Monday, November 02, 2009 4:09 PM
Subject: RE: Anna

Hope you had fun! *(Not sure what this refers to, but Mum and Father must have been doing more exciting things...again?)*

Sorry I wasn't long on the phone yesterday; I couldn't hear Father Arbuthnot very well as Jack was shouting in my ear and climbing up my legs! He's decided that he loves falling backwards and we catch him under the arm pits, but hope he doesn't just do it one day when we're not standing there! He was laughing so much. Then he decided to ride me like a horse...that'll be an expensive hobby if he gets too used to it, so I put him in the paddling pool, screwed up my face and explained that he must learn to swim so as he can be an Olympian and look after House-Husbandry and I in our old age. He pooed his nappy.

From: Arbuthnot Jostick
To: Hollings Honey
Sent: Friday, November 13, 2009 11:52 AM
Subject: Terence Smith!

Hi Honey,

Hope the poo managed to be cleaned-up or do you have those incredibly new-style nappies which you throw away? I spent ages scrubbing towelling and liners and had *days* of washing piled up to the ceiling when you and Amber were babies. Not that I'm bitter about the youth of today, Honey. You can't help being born into the generation that does everything for you, can you? Dad had arranged to see Terence Smith this morning for his annual review of his accounts. Dad left at 10.40am to be at Terence's by 11.00am. He likes to be precise and would hate turning up early. If we're early, we park around the corner and wait. But, the last time, a huge tractor parked in front of your Father's Rover and he could *not* get around, so that theory is not the best.

But never mind, as at 10.55am there was a ring on the doorbell and it was Terence Smith. *Well I never,* I said to him. He had come to have the meeting with your Father here! I was just about to have a shower and was in my dressing gown! He came in to wait and I gave him three weeks' worth of newspapers to read while I had my shower. He said his Mother had died 10 years ago today and he had to be at his Father's at 12.30pm prompt to go to the cemetery like they do every year.

Well, you never guess? We established that Dad hadn't taken his mobile phone! I made Terence another cup of coffee and began to show him some photos. He has now seen all the ones you sent me of you all and some of Amber plus he has inspected the work we had done in the kitchen. We then talked about holidays and cats and sheep and I was struggling to think what else to talk about when thankfully Dad arrived back home to find Terence Smith with all the accounts sitting waiting at the table. He was rather irritated, your Father, what with the waste of petrol and his favourite wall being destroyed. Never mind, the builders found a Mr Kipling Cherry Bakewell right down in between two of the breeze blocks, so that pleased your Father no end. He'd been looking for it since 1979. They are having their meeting now having established that it had been *'a bit of a cock up'* to Terence's words!

We spent yesterday evening with Ruth and saw Barnaby-Pock's six new puppies - four beige colour and two black and white. Rather sweet.

This afternoon Katie (the new acupuncturist come hair stylist; I don't know how she remembers what she is doing half the time) is coming to show us her holiday photos and have a cup of tea and a chat. I actually have my hair done at Synergie in Applebridge Common now - I much preferred how they did it but was wondering how on earth to tell Katie. I explained it by saying they can fit me in at very short notice (whereas I have to book five or six weeks in advance with Katie, and often have to book the next two or three appointments to fit round her holidays. And I would find that it badly needed doing just when we were going somewhere so Applebridge Common works out much better). She is still going to pop in as she likes my tea. It was hard to find a way to change after 30+ years. Just felt I'd got in a rut. I might dye it pink. What do you think? It will make me feel young again, what with your Father. Love Mum x

From: Arbuthnot Jostick
To: Jostick Amber
Sent: Thursday, May 06, 2010 10:22 AM
Subject: Searching through my bag!
Hi Amber,

Thanks again for the lovely time and all the driving about in France, Amber. Do you have speed limits over there? I guessed not. They called me over to search me at customs. Then they called someone else over as they saw something suspicious in my green hand luggage bag. They pointed to a solid black area and asked me what it was. I hadn't got a clue. A man said did I mind if he opened it and then started getting it all out before I had replied, so I can only assume it was a rhetorical question. It ended up being Patrice's box of four candles in glass containers! The gift I was given by that Evangelist on the way to the airport asking if I could just carry it home to England. He had such a nice face, I couldn't help but oblige. He said it was okay to keep it though, the man at Customs, despite the panting dogs salivating by his side. I tried to explain the *Four Candles / Fork Handles* joke but he was French and just cocked his head in a way that made me feel I was quite insane. There was this man in the queue to get on the plane. When they asked for priority boarding people to come to the front, loads of people surged forward, but a lot of them weren't priority.   A very angry man behind me said to them. "The end of the queue is right back there", and one of the pushing in men said "You always get one don't you?" This man said "Did you say *you always get one?* " and he said "Yes".   He said "And what's your name?" He said "John" and he said "John what?" I thought they were going to have a fight.   Then the angry man said "Consider yourself spoken to", and the other man said "Oh dear" (like he wasn't at all afraid).   The angry man latched onto us and said he had had a wonderful time till he met all these appalling British people.   He said he was moving to France to learn the language.   He asked us if it was always like this at the airport and Dad said *"This is a **good** day!"* He said he wasn't used to standing waiting but they had told him he was too late to get priority boarding.   He said he must have a window seat as he wanted to film the take off.   Dad said "Yes sure", and the man said "You said *Yes sure"* as though you had influence - as though you were the pilot'.   Then he started talking about cars - he'd been to the veteran thing as well.   I was dreading him being next to us all the way home so I asked if he wanted to go in front of us and he said "So I can get my window seat?" and he was really pleased.   We then sat as far away as possible!!!!

Taxi driver had had the right arrival time all along.   Dad must have given him the amended driving time but then we were still going by the original one.   I don't know why they changed

it. It hadn't sunk in when Honey sent us the second
email. Thought it was just reconfirming it. She did it all.

I walked straight into the window of the bookshop - I
hadn't realised it wasn't all open to walk in. Then I fell over
with my hand luggage trying to keep up with Dad on the way out
when we arrived. He didn't notice either thing! I will have to
get a piece of elastic for him as Kevin suggested! It's like
travelling with a deranged baby at times when he just walks off.
Love Mum x

From: Arbuthnot Jostick
To: Hollings Honey ; Jostick Amber
Sent: Sunday, October 18, 2009 11:53 PM
Subject: Kaitlin & Daffyd

Hi both,

Thanks for both your phone messages Amber. We were
at Kaitlin & Daffyd's over the weekend - stayed at a B&B
nearby. Glad you're back safely from your trip.

Went to Boules restaurant for lunch. We were meeting
them there at 1.00pm on Saturday and took a wrong turning
somewhere - intended to get there with about half an hour at least
to spare, before they arrived, but got there at 1.03pm and they
were already sitting at the table! What a rush and panic! I
'wasted' a bit of time in Stow-on-the-Wold trying to go to the
loo! Dad came back from the loo (unisex) and said it cost

20p. My 20p went straight through and I wasn't sure which cubicle it was relating to as the machines for the money weren't on the doors. Then a man came out of the one I thought it was. If you go in when someone has just come out you don't have to pay as the door is already open, but there was a notice that said if you didn't pay you might not be able to get out so I didn't go in! It was really automated and technical. I was just about to go and get another 20p when a woman came out of the other one and I went in without thinking, but I wasn't locked in luckily. You had to press a button to lock the door and another to open the door (rather than a manual bolt). And there was this hand washing thing where the water came on automatically when you put your hands in, ditto soap and hot air, except my soap didn't work. Anyway, another woman went in when I came out (without paying) so it probably carried on like that all day!!

Anyway, Dad had veal and cranberry pie and I had roast veg. and cream cheese tart. Both of us had lovely hazelnut bombes, but unfortunately there was a huge coughing fit behind us and I can only assume there was a nut allergic person nearby so I wrapped up my bombe and left.

Daffyd has to use a zimmer frame now since his stroke and has to wear a padded hat all the time in case he falls over and bumps his head. Went back to theirs and tried helping her get sheep into another field but no luck!

They have got a greenhouse now where Daffyd goes to read.

B&B was very nice. The owners gave us hot scones and tea when we arrived. He went to Cambridge University and knew John Cleese, and she is a famous authoress - their son reports from Afghanistan on the news. They were very friendly and talked a lot. Room was very comfortable. I will ensure to remark about all of it on Trip Advisor when we get home. Even the china monkeys on the bed knobs were rather fetching. They gave us a torch for our night walk to Queen's village - just as well as there was a huge ditch at the side of the drive and it was pitch black! I shan't write that on Trip Advisor.

Saw Ralph on Friday – we took all the latest photos of you to show him (that one of you and Kevin, Amber, at the summer party when you'd just permed your hair. You shut yourself in the bedroom for hours, days it seemed, before you showed us. And, I must admit, it did look rather straight. Did you iron it out after paying £80?) Ralph remembers you Honey as 'a delightful young lady'. He didn't ever meet you Amber but loved the photo and is always interested in hearing about your house and work. He wondered whether you had time for any housework.

Twig & Nut been at *Greyshingles* since Friday - collecting them tomorrow. That's the Cattery, not the new nightclub up the road. We can hear that 'til all hours you know.

I've got that breast screening thing in Sainsbury's car park in the morning straight after the Cattery so better go to bed.
Will be in touch.
Love Mum x

To: Hollings Honey

Sent: Wednesday, September 23, 2009 11:47 PM

Subject: Re: return

Welcome home Honey from France!

You must have had the same tropical rainstorm as happened when I went by myself! Same time of year. It was when the pot pourri from the little shops in Old Nice were floating down the narrow streets and everyone hung their carpets out to dry. I went out by myself to buy something for lunch and the rain soaked right up my trouser legs from the bottom, ran down my top from the top and the wet met in the middle. I was saturated! People from restaurants were rushing to put their pot plants out to be watered and an old man was trying to cycle through it with water half way up his bicycle! It was quite spectacular and water was gushing out of overflows and gutters.

We will look forward to your postcard, and you will get one from us posted in Southwold today. We had a day trip to the sea! We had lunch in a walled courtyard behind Tilly's restaurant, had a long walk and sat on the beach (I wrote a poem for a competition). The night before we went to the Gordon Craig Theatre to see a murder mystery. Your Father hates parking and had just had a reverse parking sensor fitted to the car, but unfortunately just as he was taking it to be done he backed into a wall and did £200 worth of damage on top of the £300 to fit the sensor. (Pity it wasn't on the way home - it would have beeped!)

Goodness you did a lot while you were in France. Poor Jack's head in the railings. Did you have to call the fire brigade? Had Kevin done the bannisters and the bedroom balcony railings? Did Jack go in the pool?

As Katie the hairdresser has just had an operation for carpel tunnel syndrome and couldn't work, I went to a hairdressers in Applebridge Common. They did my roots and a cut and blow-dry and I was quite pleased. Katie was going to ring me after her hospital check up to tell me when she could work again (she has only had one wrist done, the other still to do). Well she rang this evening just after we got home from Southwold and I was giving the cats their pills. Dad asked if she could ring back tomorrow as we'd only just got in. Not sure what to say now. I've known her almost as long as we've lived here. It is possible she may retire in the not too distant future, but she doesn't really want to. Got in a bit of a rut really as we don't talk about my hair much anymore and Applebridge Common have lots of ideas. I went to Applebridge Common on Senior Citizens day. I showed my Medical Card with my date of birth on as when I said my age she looked at me and said *'People don't look their ages these days'* and I worried she didn't believe me.

It was Zara's birthday today. Got her some dark chocolate that she likes. Her daughter Liz has been staying with her to look after her while her husband is away.   She still has one more tattoo to go before the entire group of Bon Jovi are on her bottom cheeks forever.

Love Mum x

From: Hollings Honey
To: Arbuthnot Jostick
Sent: Wednesday, September 23, 2009 9:51 AM
Subject: RE: return

You will get your postcard soon from Amber's but there was a strike so will probably come in the next few days or so!

We had tropical rain for three days and it hadn't rained since May! But then we had nice sunshine for the next five days!

Went to the zoo at St Jean-Cap-Ferrat as it was closing down after 50 years as a rich man has bought it and wants to build a spa hotel. Went into the lemur enclosures and they jump all over you with their padded feet! Jack wasn't too sure but I wanted a photo for his 21st birthday.

Went to Monaco Aquarium, Antibes, Juan-les-Pins, St Laurent-du-Var, Cagnes-sur-Mer, and the der Stepani apartment where I remember you saying Jack cleaned the floor with a broom, dug up the cactus inside, got his head stuck in the patio balcony railings, and wanted all the china ornaments!

Jack loved Kevin and Amber, although I'm not too sure Amber was as keen when Jack sicked-up his pureed avocado, but he's her nephew so that surely is mildly better, and the grimace was probably the Botox wearing gradually away.

From: Arbuthnot Jostick
Sent: 23 September 2009 09:08
To: Hollings Honey
Subject: return
Dear Honey,

I'm glad you had a good holiday and Jack enjoyed himself? Did he nearly drown again this year? Hope not. Motherhood is stressful enough without having that at the back of your mind. He's got more air miles than me now. Will await your postcard, although many years seem to have passed without the plop on the doormat of a glossy photo of a crowded beach? Maybe they all get lost in the post nowadays. That is far more likely. Nice autumn weather here. Keep in touch.

Love   Dad

From: Arbuthnot Jostick
To: Hollings Honey
Sent: Monday, June 28, 2010 12:11 PM
Subject: Good Sunday?
Hi Honey,

Hope you had a good time on Sunday (wasn't it hot? - still is). Dad wasn't sure where Cottage Tenant's Park was so wanted to follow you I think. Hope Dad's okay on his own on holiday.

He better be wearing sun scream although I'd bet his corpse that he's not.

I slept right in the middle of the bed last night. Was really comfortable as slept on puffy squashy part which no one has ever slept on. Didn't need the sun lounger cushions under the sheet either! And could sleep diagonally which I find much more comfortable.

My word-processor screen 'went' last week. Just blue slipping horizontal lines. It was still working - I just couldn't see what I was doing. Managed to print stuff out 'blind' as could remember sequence of keys to press but couldn't really type new stuff. Packed it all up to send to Woking. Wrapped in loads of bubble wrap secured with lots of cello tape, lowered into box with bubble wrap in, put more bubble wrap on top and stuffed round sides, put in loads of scrunched up tissue paper then Dad cut the corners of the box and bent down to make exact fit then I drew round stiff board and cut out to make a lid and used half a roll of parcel tape to secure several times in all directions and stuck address label on. Then Henry rang and said the Codes for the latest survey were the same as the ones I did previously (which was on word-processor!) I had to ring and ask him to fax it to me as couldn't face undoing it all!

Spoke to Canon engineer (it's been there about three times). Once in the past (over a year ago) the screen went like has just happened and at the same time they emptied the little debris tank which only needs doing about once in 3 years. Another time was also screen and tank. Other time just tank. He said he has a screen and also a reconditioned machine and will ring today when examined it to sort out what to do. I will have to get a laptop but must have a working W.P. too as so many things on the discs and must be able to access them. Laptops don't have a printer though.

Felix was waiting for me this morning. He'd climbed over from next door and was stuck in back garden as I'd shut the gate as on my own. Dad usually leaves it open. Felix can no longer jump high so I had to open it for him!

Dad took more for three days than Bruce bought for 4 months! He was saying 'Don't open my marmalade', 'That's my cereal', 'Those are my tea bags', 'That's my salad', 'Don't use that loo roll'. He's been hanging over his list of stuff to take and places to go for days!! I know he's going to want to walk further than Bruce will want to and in this heat as well. He took his walking boots. He hasn't seen an orchid yet. They've either been and gone or not come at all.

I've put the parasol up over the table (Dad never wants it up or even the table out - he'd rather perch on a step or sit in blazing sun up the top) and I've watered the entire garden with the hose and done all the dead heading. Dad said it won't reach round the front - well it does for half of it. I'm thinking of changing our service providers and getting a cocker spaniel (only joking!) (Not joking about the parasol and watering). He is always saying I'm doing everything the wrong way and leave him to do it - well nothing has happened since doing things my way! It is very liberating. I wonder if he'll notice if I buy a new dining table and chairs. What else can I do? I know I'll get all my catalogues out and make a mess sorting them all! And I WILL NOT be buying any pork pies, sausage rolls or double cream. Dad can't go out without getting those and a Mars Bar.

Miss him really! There might be a spider!!

Love Mum x

From: Arbuthnot Jostick

To: Hollings Honey

Sent: Monday, June 28, 2010 12:30 PM

Subject: P.S.

Before he went on holiday with your Uncle Bruce, I said to Dad I'd use the garage tap for the front but he said not to. After a lot of stalling, he said I'd have to lower the tap end of the hose into a bucket under the tap first, then said not to use it at all. I asked if it leaked and he muttered it had a crack in the tap. He then said it wasn't really a crack it was a washer. I said shall I get someone to mend it and he said he'd do it sometime.

Then there is the bucket in the loft. I want to get a roofer to fix it. He didn't check the bucket before he went as *'It is perfectly all right'*. What if it pours with rain? I can't get up there as he won't get a loft ladder. I heard him pouring a full bucket into the cistern once. He thinks a roofer will say it is much worse than it is and charge loads like on those dreadful programmes and would rather keep bucket. Gets cross if mention it. What if ceiling and contents of loft drop on me in bed?

Kevin said if we move to France he'll do all the maintenance! (We're not though).

Love Mum x

From: <u>Arbuthnot Jostick</u>

To: <u>Hollings Honey</u>

Sent: Wednesday, June 30, 2010 11:33 PM

Subject: Re: Tickets!

It's very different on my own. I can leave things anywhere and I know they will still be there later. They won't have been thrown away or used to mop up the spilt milk and the cat's poo.

I watched the whole of that dog and cat operation programme this evening without having to worry about Dad's reaction. (Cat had two new feet after her own were chopped off by a combine harvester, and dog had new foot after own foot disintegrated by arthritis). I also saw *'Growing Old Disgracefully'* yesterday. Dad's face when I ask him to watch it with me as a couple so as we know what is about to happen. I like to be prepared.

- No one is saying *'What were you thinking of having for dinner?'* when I'm not hungry.
- No one says *'Do you want to walk round the block'* just when it is time to start thinking about the meal.

- No one has used the last slice of bread and not got the next one out of the freezer.
- No one has started stacking the dishwasher in an illogical way.
- No cups, saucers or mugs have been chipped since Sunday.
- No one turns all but one light out at 10.30 and goes to bed just when I feel like talking and having some 'quality time' together.
- No one mows the drive.
- No one mows over the flex and cuts it in half having to make a join.
- No one says 'It's the way you turned it on - it never happens when I do it' if something happens when I turn something on.
- I haven't found any pork pies, sausage rolls, pots of double cream etc. in the fridge or Mars Bars anywhere.
- No one has got my used old toothbrush out of the bin to use themselves as it isn't old enough to throw away yet.
- No one has been leaning over next door with long handled secateurs glaring at branches blocking out the sun and chopping them off. And, would you believe it, I persuaded Dad to see about his mole/cyst whatever that thing is on his cheek. (I once swatted it but I realised it wasn't a wasp, and I suppose thank the heavens really otherwise it would most likely have resulted in another trip to A&E.

Mind you, it *is* rather an eye-opener in these god forsaken places, and it does make one realise how lucky one is to have what we have, despite your Father.) I have been asking him for years. He is always in blazing sun and never puts cream on his face even if he puts it other places. He said he asked the Nurse about it ages ago when he went about his ears and she said it was nothing to worry about - not sure I believe he asked because I don't think a Nurse would say that - she'd say see a doctor. He asked again the other day and she said they freeze things in Applebridge Common but he must make a doctor's appointment first. We are hoping he won't be referred to hospital about it and that it won't involve an actual operation. Don't know if doctors at 'the doctors' do biopsies or if one is needed. It is always bleeding - I can't understand how he could not be concerned about it all this time. He says he keeps catching it with the razor but it is on the pillow sometimes as well. It is 6th July with Dr Loeffler 9am. He wanted to 'get Bruce over with first'. Grandpa had a similar thing in a similar place. Kaitlin said Daffyd has got two 'sun damaged areas' on his face and has cream for them.

He's back tomorrow (today when you read this, actually today now, it's after midnight). Glad he got to see Kaitlin. I was telling Kaitlin about the little ivory rat pot that Dad really liked. It was the only thing he really would have liked to have. Kaitlin said Grannie left it to her and left a table to Dad but Kaitlin wanted the table and they swapped, but then Dad gave it to Laurie as it was small to take on the plane back to New Zealand. She said *'The Jostick's aren't sentimental - Arbuthnot wouldn't have been affected by Laurie not leaving him anything in a sentimental way - he just likes the pot'.* Janice Browning rang me this evening. They are having their downstairs cloakroom done. She thought she'd chosen some good wall tiles but Tristin wanted smaller ones. Janice likes the large ones. The assistant had said large ones make the room look bigger. I asked what colour and she said the floor ones are the colour of mud (as that is the colour it usually is after Tristin, Bramble and Asbo have been in there!) and wall ones slightly lighter mud! They were going to get any spiders for me while Dad's away but touch wood there haven't been any.

Oh well better make the most of my last night on the nice squashy bit down the middle of the mattress.

We had decided that we would become hippies before we became too old and I asked Dad if he would consider a camping holiday. He shoved his head forward and muttered something like *"the tent will explode if too much hot air is expended inside."* I took that as a no although I daren't think what he means, and if he is referring to me, then I am glad we will not be cosying up inside the matching frog sleeping bags I have just spent days ruminating over. I must send them back. Love Mum x

From: <u>Hollings Honey</u>

To: <u>Arbuthnot Jostick</u>

Sent: Wednesday, June 30, 2010 4:20 PM

Subject: RE: Tickets!

Is it still funny without Dad? Oh yes, Mick was asking Andrew what the mark was on Dad's face and he should get it checked out! Dad said he has a Dr's appointment in July??!!!! To get it frozen off?

From: Arbuthnot Jostick

Sent: 30 June 2010 16:12

To: Hollings Honey

Subject: Re: Tickets!

Bruce and Dad are both men (in case you didn't know!) I said to the hotel inspector when we checked in. We got a very funny look.

From: <u>Arbuthnot Jostick</u>

To: <u>Hollings Honey</u>

Sent: Wednesday, June 30, 2010 8:36 AM

Subject: Torch

I was creeping upstairs with the torch last night at 03.00am after I'd done all my surveys and I suddenly thought what am I doing, I can put the light on!!

I've just received £30 Tesco vouchers for a drinks and socialising ongoing survey, £5 Sainsbury's voucher, £5 Love to

Shop voucher, £25 Amazon e-voucher, Nectar/Sainsbury's £7.50 and in the post is £5 cheque. I've been going through them all to see if I've got sufficient points to redeem any yet and found I had. Two more I've almost reached enough points to redeem. I'd thoroughly recommend it.

Tesco has changed. You know they're building a huge extra bit on the right of it to make it a gigantic store with clothes etc., well now when you arrive there is a huge tall fence you have to walk past which takes you to a new side entrance. I couldn't get my bearings at first. The magazines are where the old entrance used to be.

I've been watching programmes Dad would hate since he's been on holiday. Saw that *Graham Norton show* and *Tribal Wives, also 'Rev'*. Grandad would have had a fit at that. He took his clergyman's collar off and said 'F... off' !! Did you see it? I was thinking I'd have to record it, but of course I didn't have to record it as Dad not here!!

I'm so comfortable in the squashy bit down the middle of the bed.

As soon as he gets in he will straighten the curtains and rearrange the tablecloth.

Love Mum x

P.s. I won't forget about the tickets. *What tickets?*

The Hoover emitted a terrible smell of burning last week (motor finally gone) and we are in the process of trying to choose a replacement.

Dad has done a spreadsheet of all the makes and models within a certain price range including all the relevant points (like weight, performance, wattage, settings, filters, whether a cyclone type, cost etc. etc.) and I am in the middle of reading hundreds and hundreds of customer reviews of the brands and models on his 'shortlist'. Some of them have got over 1,000 reviews. Someone said 'Got electric shock which threw me across the room'. Loads of people said various of them had a too short a flex and too short attachment hoses. Some were very noisy. Some were very heavy to carry upstairs. Some have tools which drop off while in use. Various people got bruises all over them when it fell on them as it tipped over while using attachments. Handle left a sore, red depression in my palm. Taking it to the dump. Have to lift whole Hoover up to vacuum settee. Got sore shoulder as it is so hard to push. My husband's hankie went up it. I am only 5' 10" and have to stoop to hold it. Have to Hoover over crumbs several times. Picks up dust then deposits it 10cm further up. Generates more heat than a radiator. Dust fell on me when emptying. Furniture and skirting boards damaged as no bump strip. Pulls hair out of your scalp - had to tie it back. Exploded after 7 uses. Had to buy two as first one too heavy to carry upstairs so keep one upstairs and one downstairs. Was sealed up too well and I damaged box getting it open - wanted to keep box pristine to send it back!

I could go on. Doing it all yesterday. We decided not to get a 'ball' type as loads of people said they are awkward to manoeuvre and they got RSI after a few weeks.

There were lots of good comments too. Because it is something you keep for years I want to make right choice. Which one have you got? x

I remember phoning and explaining verbally:

We have got a Dyson, or have we? Oh actually, I'm not sure. I hardly know where the on-switch is, and as far as the attachments go, Henrietta-Divine can work that out better than me.

From: "Arbuthnot Jostick"
Date: 13 Mar 2015 23:49
Subject: Re: Happy Mother's Day!
To: "Honey Hollings"

Don't think I was always right when raising you, but you've both turned out okay, or sorts. For instance, I think I should have suggested to Amber that she might like a nice new grown up bed a few weeks before you were born rather than the day we brought you home from hospital! She wanted to get in the cot that night but you were already asleep in it! Then she fell out of the bed with a thud. Perhaps if we'd had three I'd have got it right by then.

Ruth brought round a pair of reading glasses for Dad a little while ago. They are like a pair her Step Father had with light beams that shine out from both sides at the book or newspaper you are reading. He looks like that alien that comes out of that spaceship with a light shining out of the slit in his head! She's making an enormous fuss about my cold asking if I've got a temperature. I haven't even taken it. She asked me why I was shaking when she came the other day - I just couldn't get warm at all. Is there something going round have you heard? I could have picked it up at the dentist I suppose. There was a really depressing programme on the TV in the waiting room about getting old and what happens to your head when you have an accident! You can't change channels. Dad keeps blowing his nose and sneezing but it hasn't actually developed into anything bad yet.

I'm just psyching myself up before going to bed and spending another night sitting up. Grandad always used to do that if he had a cold. It stops your whole head filling up quite so much. I just read on the internet that they've just carried out the world's first successful penis transplant. It took 9 hours. (I had a cream liqueur a bit earlier).

Going to try the Hoover tomorrow - there's a bit missing but it's for parquet floors so nothing to do with the carpets. We'll ring them.

When Dad went to get the paper, a car was hanging over the edge of the little wall at the footpath edge of the doctor's car park in the wood! Then he walked to *The Range* to get some grit for mixing with planting compost.

We watched a programme earlier about all the huge benefits French people get.

Tommy is putting up a new fence (on the right). Two panels blew down in the strong wind a while back but he wants to redo the whole lot. He told me Jasmine's hamster makes a dreadful noise going round in its wheel (so it's not just Ruth's dogs!).

Well I'd better put some Vaseline on my nose. I look like Rudolph!

Night night. x

P.s. Thank you for the beautiful blue tulips Amber. Very strange. They came Friday and are what I call 'crisp and crunchy' tulips. They are really cool and healthy and upright and not at all droopy. When you cut off the bottom half inch before putting them in the special water they make a satisfying crunchy noise (not floppy.) They look really nice in a round pot vase. In fact they look like a painting (Van Gogh! But blue.)

Had a drama on Saturday! We were just watching a wild weather programme when the bell went and Ruth nearly fell in. She had accidentally locked herself out of the car up by the little branch railway line along Kimbolton (by bridge to Applebridge Common field). She takes Barnaby-Pock for a night time walk up there. Barnaby-Pock was in the car, the keys were in the ignition and her bag, purse, house keys and phone were locked inside. She'd got out her door, shut it and must have knocked the thing which triggers central locking as when she tried to lift the back to let Barnaby-Pock out it wouldn't open.

It was bitterly cold and she walked here (without her stick) and Arbuthnot found the Direct Line number for a rescue man. When she said her dog was in the car they said 'Small, medium or large?'

She took Dad's phone for the man to ring her if he couldn't find the car. She wouldn't let us go and wait with her as it was so cold, but Dad went when she wasn't back in 20 mins.

The rescue man looked like he had just escaped from prison, but he had huge muscles. He forced the door open a crack with a pneumatic thing and put a wire thing in and hooked the keys out of the ignition. So it all turned out okay in the end Honey! (Your favourite saying!)

It is her birthday today and either just me or both of us are going round. Dad is saying his passport has almost run out and he has to go to town for a new form. I think that may be an excuse, but I am not entirely sure.

The postman has just been and the relaxation CD was amongst it - it sounds brilliant. Thank you Honey! I'll try that out later on.

And the flowers also just came - the postman came twice. Thank you - they're lovely. And also a box of chocolates and some more butterflies on stalks which we've put with the others. They're so pretty.

And I adore the pictures of the children on the lovely card. Thanks Honey, dear.

Amber said she is cleaning the windows and has washed the net curtains as people are looking at their house tomorrow. They bought a divan bed for the spare bedroom but can't get it upstairs and Kevin won't let her ask a neighbour. She wanted to put the new duvet cover on for when the people come and look.

Just going to have a spoonful of Manuka honey (from your Father!)

From: Arbuthnot Jostick
Sent: 27 March 2015 10:40
To: Hollings Honey
Subject: Re: Bake Sale
Don't fall asleep in the bath Honey - you might have drowned.
Love   Dad

From: Hollings Honey
To: 'Arbuthnot Jostick'
Sent: Friday, March 27, 2015 9:30 AM
Subject: RE: Bake Sale
Oh! House-Husbandry was watching me in the bath so okay.

I have to let you into a secret that I actually bought the gingerbread men for a bake sale. I was going to bake but I fell asleep in the bath the previous night too.

Hi both,

Further to the nighties news - Dad returned with the exchanged nightie and packed both nighties up to send to the hospital.

In order to know where to address the parcel, he rang the hospital and asked which ward Kaitlin Glen-Parker was in now. No one had heard of her. She wasn't on the list of patients. Very strange.

I suggested he rang Kaitlin's mobile and ask her which ward she was in but he didn't want to as it was a surprise.

He rang again and spoke to someone else. They still had no Kaitlin Glen-Parker anywhere in the hospital. They asked her date of birth - he said 29th September 1941 (it's actually 29th August!). Then I said maybe she checked in as Kaitlin Jostick, and as soon as he said that they said 'Oh, she was discharged yesterday'!! She hadn't told us! But hopefully the nighties will still be useful!

Luckily he didn't send them to the hospital then addressed to Kaitlin Glen-Parker!

Another chapter for your book Honey!

Xx

AND PRAISE!!!! Get in!

I got praise, heartfelt praise, genuine raving successes, they were, those dinners which I booked for our overseas clients - explain the collections of clients. LATAM, Korean, Australian and Spanish. I told my family. Mother replied, *"You're so good at all this Honey. I don't think you get it from my side of the family - when I booked my boss into a hotel when he went to Wilton, he ended up having to sleep on a camp bed as the room had been double-booked!! (Not very pleased!). Suppose not actually my fault as I booked it through our Travel and Visitors Department - guess who was the Manager of the Travel & Visitors Department? - Grandad!!!*

Actually it wasn't done through him - Clara Perryman did it. Grandad did long haul flights etc. So either Clara Perryman or the hotel itself made a mistake. But me and Grandad were at the receiving end of his wrath when he returned with backache!"

Mother then re-enacted her dog walking escapade, a beautiful rendition. *"Well, would you believe, Ruth's lot pulled me over on the zebra crossing in Broadhillock Crescent when Dad and I were taking them to the park! It was so embarrassing. All the cars had stopped both ways and everyone was looking. I still had hold of the leads while flat on my face and they were pulling me along the ground on my stomach. Dad hadn't noticed as he was in front as always. They got spooked by a man in a wheelchair who was crossing the road backwards using his feet."*

- Good luck with your moles Amber. Let us know. I went for a similar thing being held at Van Hages shopping Mall once. Queue right round the garden centre. Being run by medical staff.

- I keep reading about Green Tea. Must try some. It's probably cheaper than Manuka Honey!! That is my favourite health luxury at the moment. Have consumed a whole jar of the 15+ sort I treated myself to! (A teaspoon per day - well sometimes two). But you have to offset the antioxidant benefits of the honey from these super special lovely rare bees against the fact that it contains sugar. Dad found an article which says more 'Manuka honey' is being sold than is being produced so I hope mine was genuine.

- Amber, we posted to you this morning your birthday card and a little present that we know you always like so hopefully something will get there for the actual day - will have a browse round some different places on holiday for something main to send. There are various nice shops roundabout and I discovered a classic car show on when we're there so Dad pleased.

Mr Darcey has been castrated (the dog) then swallowed a bee but luckily Ruth had an epi-pen so stuck that in him as he was suffocating with an anaphylactic shock. She is watering the garden and feeding the birds for us. There is usually a disaster while we're away and I get text messages at midnight!

Yes we'll have a sausage roll for you both (maybe we'll save them up and sneak down for a midnight feast - oh no I'll still be up then won't I!?)

Still doing last minute hand washing and ironing. Cases out and starting to pack. I take my year's worth of till slips and ATM receipts etc. to catch up with my money record on holiday so I take calculator, Tippex, ruler, lined paper, bank statements and print outs from all stuff bought on internet for a year - never seem to have time to do that otherwise!)

Got some books from charity shop by the same authors I liked from last year's cottage (that accidentally fell in my case when we came home!).

37 Pomegranate Road

Draycod

Herts

DR3 9SF

England

30th October 1995

Dear Honey,

Glad you had a good time with Irina.

Enclosed is your collection of things. THE APPLICATION FORM INSIDE THE FT CAREER CHOICE HAS TO BE

RETURNED BY NOVEMBER 10TH IF YOU ARE INTERESTED. TEACHING IS ON PAGE 32 - IT SAYS APPLICATIONS FOR MOST INSTITUTIONS HAVE TO BE IN BY END DECEMBER AND INTERVIEWS ARE USUALLY IN THE SUMMER TERM.

There is also a box of tapes, two bank statements and a Britannia letter.

Glad your sparklers and cosmetic things in box arrived (I sent Amber some sparklers too as she always seems disappointed to miss Bonfire Night), and also your phonecards and stamps and letter from France.

I couldn't believe I'd got three numbers in the Lottery – Sainsbury's only started doing it last week and it was the first time I'd bought my ticket from there - I'll get them there from now on! Ernest rang today and said he also got three numbers last Saturday! Mrs Gray-Compote said she'd got three numbers once and four twice.

We went to Allied Carpets again today with the two samples we'd borrowed yesterday and swapped 'Lava' for 'Peppercorn' but kept 'Nutmeg' as we liked that best. Now it is out of 'Nutmeg' and 'Peppercorn' but I think we still like 'Nutmeg' best.

The exhaust has blown so it sounds as if we are participating in the Grand Prix at the moment. It is being fixed on Wednesday together with the juddering brake pedal. Then it has got to have its MOT.

I hope Amber's leaving party went well and her cakes turned out OK. Kevin said 'What are you doing that for? - I can give you some' but she wanted to make them!

I told you Sandy rang didn't I, for your address, and that Dad has put some money into your account and about the news item which said 'A cloud of toxic gas is drifting towards Draycod from Applebridge Common - residents are warned to stay indoors.' (Poor Twig was out in it.) Ernest said that his sister knew someone whose little boy got covered in it and had to have his clothes pulled off and be plunged straight into a bath. Brian Worthington said it burns your lungs (it was a swimming pool chloride factory which exploded and caught fire - suspected sabotage).

I have now got over £50 value in Saver Points at Sainsbury's (£50 is the most you can save with one card), so I'll ask for it to be taken off my bill next week and I'll have a nice small bill for a change! It's good doing that.

Well, I think I'd better have an early night as Peter Potter has just rung to say he'd like to come at 8.30 in the morning and go through something with me which he needs by 10.30. It has been rather chaotic today as John Pain, Victor Wilderspin, Ann Brice and Johnny Worthington all came with work, I've got a box of it from George Trees, Ernest rang, a fax came for Vic Wilson and we've been trying to choose a new carpet! (Victor Wilderspin keeps his money in a money belt inside his trousers - I wondered what on earth he was doing when he undid his trousers!!!) We also had a *Trick or Treat* little boy this evening. I cooked some Le Puy lentils to have with bacon. (Not for his treat!)

Oh, and the sweetest little baby hedgehog has been coming the last few days. It's only 2 or 3" long and it stands in the cat food bowl while it eats! It loves Whiskas. A medium-sized one has also been coming.

Dad has to keep changing his glasses (if he gets up from his desk or from reading to walk somewhere or starts working after doing something else) as he now has a pair for close work/the computer and reading and a pair for everything else.

You'll never believe it but the Schwahn's next door have got their Christmas decorations up already!! We were just coming back from a walk last night and I said to Dad *'What are all those coloured lights?'* and when we got closer we saw that it was strings of Christmas lights round their conservatory! What do you want for Christmas?!

And there's a new black and white kitten in one of the maisonettes which comes over here a lot, and also a black and white cat just like Muesli where Valerie used to live (we thought it was her until we saw Muesli in our garden!)

Continued Tuesday

Dad took a picture of the baby hedgehog standing in the food bowl this morning. PB was eating out of the same bowl but I moved him to another bowl just in case anything happened to baby hedgehog.   They don't usually come out in the daytime but this one's activity clock must be back to front!

Unfortunately I have missed the last post so this will have to go tomorrow.   Johnny Worthington has been three times today and I've only just finished his work. Love Mum x

37 Pomegranate Road

Draycod

Herts

DR3 9SF

England

27th September 1995

Dear Honey, (this appears to be very out of order but I guess that adds to the humility of it all.)

Thanks for ringing last night.   Glad you're all right and relieved that you have put your name down for Halls of Residence. The dogs barking, the broken glass in the street outside your window, notwithstanding the very strong smell of something which when I inhaled gave way to me dancing in the street for at least twenty minutes, and the neighbour who appeared to be wearing nothing more than a dirty old string vest must all be rather distracting when you are studying to be a ballerina.

"Ballerina?" I replied back to the letter. I think she did inhale too much.

Your clothes parcel is coming separately, and enclosed with this letter is a Phonecard so you can keep in touch, an article on somewhere nice to visit quite near to you (Wrexham is on the map as well - perhaps Sara knows of it). (Say Hello to Sara and tell her thank you from us for helping you move your things. Are they still in the cases or have you temporarily unpacked?) Also a voucher for *Tropicana Orange Juice* and that article I mentioned on the phone about *Toulon.* Also a *Brittania Music Club* letter and a Bank Statement.

The cats were all safely indoors when we arrived home on Thursday, and judging by the size of PB when I saw him the following day and the fact that he wasn't hungry, I think he must have been helping himself to the feast in the kitchen while we were away!

David Davis came on Friday with a full disk of typing (I think he is also trying his best at writing a Best Seller, but I'm not sure the percentage of people who would like to read about Colonoscopies Gone Wrong. I guess I'm rather engrossed as he pays me to type it, but I certainly wouldn't pay the £10.99 he hopes to get for each sold copy. So I was doing that all day until Veronica came at 4.0 to do my hair. I'm really pleased with it - she did it really well with mousse and a diffuser - it looks like a 'messy' perm and is nice and dark again. Next time she comes I'll ask her to let me have a go with the mousse and the diffuser so I can do it like that in between (if I get one) but I should imagine it would be awkward to do it yourself. Muesli was extremely interested (nosey cat!) in it all - she practically had her head in the brown dye when Pam was mixing it up in a bowl!   I thought we were going to have a brown cat!   She said one of hers has changed colour as it has been lying in the sun all summer but with its head in the shade, and its head is still black but its body is ginger!

She said Mr Croxton was really horrible to her when she handed in her notice at the last place and started ringing up other salons to see where she was going.   He told her not to bother to work out her notice.   He used to have eight salons but now he has only got the one as people keep leaving and pinching his clients. Oops! He's having the bailiffs next Tuesday.   Veronica was telling me what happened when that lady's hair fell the last time Mr Croxton let an apprentice do it.   Apparently the girl wasn't very experienced at all and she went to lunch and forgot she had left a client with perming lotion on.   The lady had never had a perm before so thought that was the normal time to be left.   When she came back and rinsed it off all her hair fell out in the basin and it has burnt the follicles so it will never grow back and she sued Mr Croxton for thousands of pounds.

Veronica's husband has just been made redundant from the building merchants where he has worked for 25 years. He is 56 he is worried he won't be able to get another job and is sitting around being depressed.

It was really convenient having Veronica come to the house.   I sat in the kitchen and stood your pine mirror on the surface under the phone and she used the kettle socket for the dryer.   Then while the colour was taking we had a cup of tea and a chat. She had just come from the neighbour with the early Christmas decorations who has hers done every Friday, so it was convenient for Veronica too. And it was only £18 compared to over £30 last time I went in-house. Aren't I being sneaky! Veronica prefers not to take cheques though and I hadn't had time to go to the cash point as I'd been doing Cathy's dissertation on French Poodles all day so I borrowed some from Dad until the next day when I paid for his petrol.

On Monday Annabel came. Her daughter Sandy had taken out six vegetarian cookery books on your library ticket and had asked her to renew them but Annabel was worried they might ask her some questions which she wouldn't be able to answer (about you) so brought them over and asked me to do it. There was a small fine on them. There was also a query which they said to go in about so I'm still waiting to hear what that was. I showed her the Nice and Le Puy photos which she really liked and she asked me to ask you if she could have a copy of the one of you and Sandy together and the one of Annabel, Adam and Mark which you took and she'll pay you for them. She said thank you from Sandy for the one you sent her.

She said she was very cross with Sandy for getting bunnies here rather than waiting till she was settled in the house down there. She wouldn't tell her where she got them from! She let them out for a run twice a day and they chewed the wallpaper which Adam was cross about. She was told they were both female, but one of them starting 'behaving like a male' and she rushed them up to the vet to have them checked and they were both female but apparently this behaviour is quite common. She just didn't want Sandy to have ten instead of two when she collected them! She also rang the RSPCA about their stray cat and they brought a cat trap for her to leave in the garden as although she feeds it won't let her catch it. She was worried about it as the winter is coming and wanted it to go to a shelter. She hopes Sandy doesn't visit when the trap is there. (Don't tell Sandy about the trap and she wants to tell you about the bunnies herself, but as you don't see her much at the moment that might be a long time.)

It is Muesli and Minoushka's 6th birthday on 11th October. Min. is much better now and has put on weight. (These are the cats.)

We had a postcard from Amber which I have photocopied (enclosed). And today we had one from Prudence and Crispin (also photocopied and enclosed, although I must admit I haven't a clue who they are? Can *you* remember? Was it that couple from Bournemouth in 1973? Oh, you weren't born then). I also enclose a copy of the leaflet Bill and Clara sent me to tell me the book I typed for them has now been published. They live in Spain. Shame they can't readily get a copy out there. Never mind.

And a copy of your university loan letter for info. Do you need to pay that back any time soon? Just a brief reminder.

George Georgie George has just faxed through a letter he wants sending to the *Education Attache* of several countries to go with the booklet I typed for him so I'll say *Cheerio* for now. Hope this arrives safely, and please let us know your new address when you move. Hope your lectures are going well and you are not getting too many noisy disturbances. Please don't smoke any of those spider plants which I couldn't help noticing you had growing in silver-foiled wardrobes outside your bedroom. And if you do, I am not being any part of paying the bill for the electricity used when cultivating them.

    Will write again soon.   Love Mum x

37 Pomegranate Road

Draycod

Herts

DR3 9SF

England

14th March 1995

Dear Honey,

    As promised, here is your letter from 'Doctors in Rhythm'. (Are you ill or is it a group?)

    And a picture of snowy Wales!

    Also, I thought you'd like the little cartoon. (I don't know whether you heard about the boy who travelled to Malaysia using his Father's credit cards and passport without anyone noticing after a row about a plate of spaghetti which he had been blamed for leaving on the floor when really his brother did it?! It made front-page news here and The Word (strange programme) took him on a trip to New York which his teachers were cross about as it made him into a celebrity when really he'd been naughty and also he played truant to go! I thought I'd better tell you if not, or you wouldn't have understood the cartoon!)

The man on the corner ended up in hospital with his pneumonia and rang me on Saturday to say he was back home again. He said he was 'very moved' by my concern and offers of help (I had rung his wife nearly every day to see how he was) and that he had a lot of 'acquaintances' but he wanted me to know that he regarded us as 'friends'. He always asks after you.

Paddy is also back home after his stay in Bath hospital with his eye. His next door neighbour has a key for his house so I was frantically looking for things last week.

Peter Potter rang me on Saturday to say the *Proposal* I had typed for him called 'Ammunition '95' in his 'usual last minute panic' was an 'exemplary job' so I was pleased about that. I actually did it mostly during the night while I was waiting up for Nutmeg (who didn't come home). I was so relieved to see her when she returned at 11.00am in the morning. I can't think where she can have been - I walked round the streets for ages rattling her treats and playing the musical cracker!

Corrie and Truff have now got nice clean teeth too. I bought another cat basket from the market for their trip as we normally have to go and borrow one (and pay £20 deposit), come home, put them in it, take them, come home, fetch them, bring them home, then go back and return the basket and get the £20 back. Buying another one seemed simpler! It is beige and isn't actually a wicker basket - it is a sort plastic box (like a large litter tray with a lid on) with ventilation slits all round and a door in the front. The top comes off completely for washing the bottom (just as well as Corrie wet herself!)

Peter Potter came again yesterday. He said he has got a 30-page invoice detailing all the holes he has drilled for someone but he hasn't had time to add it up yet. And Mrs Potter is going to Hong Kong tomorrow.

Love Mum x

37 Pomegranate Road

Draycod

Herts

DR3 9SF

England

18th April 1994

Dear Sandy, *(she's another bestie of mine)*

Hello Sandy-dear! I have got Honey's birthday present to you here. I know she really, really, really wants you to go and stay with her in France but I understand that your fear of flying, trains and the French might preclude that from happening. She has asked me to make sure you know that she really, really, really wants you to go, but she knows it is your Mum's birthday too and you have got 45 essays to write. Rather a lot going against your visit.

Arbuthnot took me to an art exhibition (which was in the form of a video installation) which was showing at the Pake Gallery in Motherwell in March (and will remain there until May 2nd). It is called *'In the Light'* by an artist who seems to have gone right out of my head. I felt it was something which might appeal to you so I am enclosing a write-up about it.

'Thin Mermaids' was the one I went to see - it was really moving. You go into this pitch black room and walk towards tiny pinpoints of light, and as you get nearer to each one in turn, it grows and you realise it is a person. If you stop in front of one of these lights, the person will become life-size and turn towards you, and if you stay there he or she will get up and walk towards you. Their reactions upon seeing you are all different. They will stay with you for as long as you want, until you move away, when they too will walk away, but if you stop as if to walk back, they too will stop and turn towards you again. It is a study into isolation and longing.

Of course, you really need to go when it is not busy, or other people will trigger these figures to walk towards them before you have got to them. Arbuthnot was rushing up and down starting them all off while I was still engrossed in the first one. Then a strange man bumped into me - I think he was more scared than I was as my eyes had become accustomed to the darkness by then. I didn't know anything about his other exhibitions which were in adjoining rooms. One was images of eyes and ears projected onto a pile of open books on the floor accompanied by a scratching noise. Arbuthnot didn't realise that was the masterpiece - he thought someone had left a pile of rubbish on the floor. I looked at it for quite a long time but wasn't sure what to make of it. Then there was a long table with a chair at one end and at the other end was a long screen onto which were projected continuous waves. That was rather strange as well. I sat in the chair but nothing happened. Perhaps I missed it. Then there was a room with three television sets and a row of chairs with headphones attached in front of each. One was a man sitting with his head in his hands. He had cut his thumb and bombs were dropping. Then he started running up the road accompanied by strange noises. It lasted an hour but I only saw two minutes of it due to the expression on Arbuthnot's face! Another was a man making ape-like noises. This again lasted an hour but I only saw about 30 seconds of that one. We didn't put the headphones on for the third as Dad was worried that we would end up in the rush hour traffic and miss the train home. I think he secretly wanted to eat the rest of his cheese sandwiches outside on the sun.

Then there were some more ears and beads of perspiration in a glass case with sighing noises in the background.

Arbuthnot went to wait outside.

It's a shame Honey isn't here for her birthday. I have just ordered a basket of flowers for her so she knows we are thinking of her, so I hope they arrive and there is someone there to answer the door if she has another one of those dreadful hangovers caused by the small mead wine.

If you do overcome flying and the French, Honey would love to see you.

Ciao, darling!

Clementine J xxx

37 Pomegranate Road

Draycod

Herts

DR3 9SF

England

17th October 1994

Dear Amber,

We received your pretty card this morning. Thank you. It's lovely. And thanks for your Get Well wishes to Dad.

I haven't had chance to write and tell you about it properly as I have acquired three new customers recently, and they all came, as well as several of the old ones, the week after Dad's new accident, and I am only just up to date with all their work. I'll tell you about them after I've told you what happened on Sunday 2nd October at 3.0 pm .....

..... I was typing in your room when I heard a bang. I looked out of Honey's bedroom window and saw Dad lying on his back on the ground. I rushed downstairs and found that he couldn't get up and was having difficulty breathing (he had winded himself) and he was in a lot of pain with his back and shoulders. I called an ambulance which arrived very quickly with its siren going. Peter (from Applebridge Common) came to wait with us while he was being attended to. The ambulance-man said 'Is he normally this pale?' They asked me to get a pillow for his head and an umbrella to put over him (it was pouring with rain!), did all the usual tests then carefully slid a stretcher under him in two halves. They then put a collar on (I was really afraid he might have broken his back or his neck and be paralysed) and cello taped his head to the stretcher to keep movement to a minimum. They had to give him oxygen to help with his breathing and to cope with the pain.

Then I went in the ambulance with him and we were put in Cubicle 3 of Casualty. (We had only been watching 'Casualty' the day before - I didn't think we'd be in it so soon!) They had to cut his clothes off because he couldn't move his arms. (He had been stripping the varnish off the porch roof to do it another colour to match the door and the steps must have been on an uneven piece of ground - they must have tipped over and he fell flat on his back from the top with no chance to grab hold of anything).

We were there until 11.30 pm (8+ hours!) and during that time he was wheeled to X-ray on his bed. That was the most worrying wait I have ever had and it was such a relief when they said there was no damage to his spine. But the X-rays did reveal a broken scapula (shoulder blade), and at a subsequent Clinic appointment they decided to send him for another X-ray as his other arm was hurting a lot as well, and this X-ray showed that he had actually broken both shoulder blades.

He was having oxygen the whole time as he felt faint. He fainted every time he tried to sit up for them to put a sling on and they had to keep lowering the head end of the bed and getting doctors to look at him. Once he fainted on me. If I hadn't been there he would have fallen forwards on the floor. He was a dead weight and I was calling out 'Excuse me!' to anyone who might be around and one of the nice young doctors came to help.

They had said he could go home after the X-rays revealed nothing too serious and I was going to call a taxi, but with all this fainting they thought they might have to keep him in overnight for observation. Part of it was the pain - they couldn't give him any pain relief until they had found out the extent of his injuries in case he needed an operation (I shouldn't actually have given him the drink of water he asked for on the ground - you have to have any empty stomach until you know if you need an operation). And part of it was 'The thought of what I've done.' So they then gave him painkillers (pills) but they didn't work and he down right refused to have anything shoved up his bottom. So they then came with an injection which was stronger but he said he would faint again if he had an injection (that's why he hasn't ever been for his MOT at the surgery which he had a letter for about five years ago, as it involves a tetanus booster), so they *had* to give him his pain relief in the form of a suppository. We told him to bend over as he was sitting on the nurse's hand but all of that was a complete lie, and when he was in that position, the nurse just popped it in. He was very annoyed. I could tell as he raised his eyebrows higher than when I didn't bargain more the doughnuts at the fair that time. But he still fainted when he sat up, so at 11.30 pm (I was hoping I had remembered to turn the oven off in the panic or our Yorkshire puddings we had been going to have for lunch would have been rather well done!) they said they would take him home in an ambulance on a stretcher so he could remain horizontal.

He obviously had to stand up when they got to the front door as the stretcher wouldn't go round the corner into the lounge, but he was OK once he got home with the ambulance-man helping him. He just couldn't do anything!

He is having to sleep in your bed at the moment as it is easier to get out of - it still takes him ages though - he has to slide onto the floor then I pull him up trying not to pull his arms.   He couldn't get dressed or undressed at all at first but can do most items of clothing now, except he struggles with socks and shirt sleeves.

And I had to give him a shower and wash his hair at first but he just about manages now (by bending his head down to his hands rather than raising his hands to his head!)

He won't be able to drive for about six weeks and can't do any D.I.Y., or anything involving pulling, pushing, lifting, carrying, moving his arms upwards or backwards.

Needless to say he wouldn't stay in bed, and even the day after he had done it he sat at the computer in his pyjamas all day saying he had to 'get on'. The next day they found this other broken shoulder blade (I thought they had already diagnosed both shoulder blades as being broken, but maybe science has given rise to us now having three?)

At first he was drinking out of a bendy straw so he didn't have to sit up in bed if he was thirsty in the night!

So it's all been happening on the new Estate opposite recently. Not only did Dad's ambulance come hurtling up the road, but a lady from Marely Close was found dead in the wood on the way to the shops a couple of weeks ago. Poor woman.

Sorry it's taken me so long to write to you with the details, only I have been swamped with work the last couple of weeks and what with Dad and his lack of shoulder blades, it takes me an age to even reach the breakfast cereals.

The Italian family up the road have been rather loud recently with an exceptional funeral which I was invited to. Their dog had to be put down and they were terribly sad, but I managed to put a few ham sandwiches in my handbag at the wake so your father didn't miss out. He was really upset when I mentioned that I had eaten egg ones. I calmed him down by mentioning their cat didn't look at all well so I may be going back in the not too distant future.

And Peter Potter's wife (the farmers) came the day Dad fell off the ladder (just before it happened) wanting something by 8.30am the following morning, so I was doing that till 03.00am after we got home! Luckily your Father's suppository had knocked him out so I had peace and quiet.

I am enclosing the last of the present subscription of Overseas Jobs Express. Have you found it helpful? Let us know if you would like us to renew it, perhaps when you know about the job you applied for - Good Luck with that.

Honey's excess baggage came to £74 by the way!

She rang last night and seems to be really enjoying it. The place. Not the excess luggage fee which she appears to have left with us.

By the way, her address is:-

Honey Jostick: Assistante Anglaise

Room 6; Lycee Technique "A & A Pupuy"

La Roche Arnaud - Rue du Docteur Rurand

43003 Le Puy en Velay

France

It barely fits on the envelope.

She said she had received a letter from you with no name and funny spellings!!!

I had to send her duvet on to her as there wasn't one. I put it in two dustbin liners and wrapped it in brown paper secured with yards of parcel tape, and stuck four address labels on it plus there was a Parcelforce label on it, but when she got it all the brown paper was hanging off and it was just in the bin liners with one label left hanging off it.

You should also have received from Dad (he can use his fingers to write and work the computer, but not his arms) some more Overseas Jobs Expresses, a forwarded on letter and a Bilingual Journalist vacancy.

I can't think of anything else at the moment. Did I already say that Kaitlin and Daffyd have moved to a 54 acre farm? If not, they have!

Sorry again for the delay in writing fully about Dad's accident. He is feeling a lot better now though, but it was pretty scary at the time.

Will write again soon. Hello to Kevin. Love Mum x

37 Pomegranate Road

Draycod

Herts

DR3 9SF

England

Re: (April 16th is 'Phone Day'. Area codes starting with '0' will then become '01'. So we will be 01422 768721. And the fax will be 01422 722222. You won't be able to get through unless you add the '1').

24th February 1995

Dear Amber,

I hope your new job is going well. We will look forward to receiving the brochure. And I hope Kevin's gastric flu is now better.

Here is your post - a letter from France, two bank letters, a book club letter (+three of the statements from which I have removed and sent back the slip saying you don't want the Editor's choice), another letter and your Overseas Jobs Express. There are also some cuttings - watch out for poisonous fish masquerading as rocks if you go to any of those places. I thought you might be interested to read about the floods (although you probably already have!) and English vs. French bread. Also one about Henri Leconte and a Sainsbury's recipe card.

Dad was watching the 'Antiques Road Show' from Luton Hoo last Sunday and he suddenly called out 'Come and look at this woman'. It was Annabel (Sandy's Mum)! She had taken along some china to be looked at and they filmed her being interviewed. She rang me after and said she was glad they filmed her bit as it was so noisy she couldn't hear what the auctioneer was saying and she could have gotten a Limousine home if the china had been worth thousands. You don't expect to see people you know, you know.

Dad has put a new door between the lobby and the lounge (it is one of those divided into 15 small panes of glass - including 3 bullions - which lets a lot more light in).

We have just chosen some curtains/matching duvet and pillow cases for our bedroom. It's called 'Mystique' and is a sort of patchwork effect in beiges, black and white of stars, suns, moons and leaves. I know it sounds odd but the overall effect is really nice and the colour goes with the shower room which is still in a state of flux.

Did you know you weren't a Gemini anymore, Amber? They have found a thirteenth sign of the Zodiac called Ophiucus (see enclosed chart) which has caused all the others to move up a bit! I am now a Pisces, Honey is still an Aries (just) and Dad is still just an Aquarius (thank God. He *hates* changes.)

Later this week.

I can't remember if I told you but they have now fitted the shower door so we can now have proper showers (or rather Dad can - I still prefer the bath! I omitted to tell Dad that as he had already started to pay the builder. It was terribly embarrassing as he tried to use up all the old pound coins and five pound notes which I read have now gone out of circulation. But I am getting rather confused nowadays as Dad swears that is not happening for at least ten more years and I should really stop going to visit that Clair Voyant who has set up a tent outside the camping shop). It folds back against the wall when not in use and is smoked glass (the shower door, not the Clair Voyant although Dad wishes she would.)

I hope Honey's scalded fingers were a bit better when she came to see you? She said they had now gone septic and black (where she took the lid off the rice she was boiling and scalded the ends of her fingers under her nails causing bad blisters). Her friend gave her some cream but this didn't work and she had to go to the pharmacy who gave her some special burn cream and remarked on what a bad scald it was. I'm trying to think how she could have done it with the knob being in the middle of the lid.

We took the kittens (!) to have their boosters on the 10th and Mrs Petunia (the new vet lady, very nice) said all of them except Twiglet need to have their teeth cleaned as they have got Gingivitis, so Muesli (who has also got to have it done) and Nutmeg are going on 28th and Corrie and Truff are going the following week (they have to have a general anaesthetic). We had an awful job getting them in their baskets for their boosters (we borrow one from the vets if we need to take all four - two in each) and had to leave Nutmeg behind in the end and come back for her later as she hates being in a confined space with any of the others.

We went to the *The White Tiger* (or was it Lion?) at Lower Grimchurch on Dad's birthday and he wore your nice shirt. It fits exactly. I had rung round all his main colleagues and told them about his birthday and he got a card from them all and a bottle of wine from Bob and Anita. I gave him a Salisbury's voucher as he wants a new briefcase and a book of footpath walks in Hertfordshire. Molly and Harold gave him a blank video and some wellington boot soaps and Mandy sent him some Australian socks called 'Holeproof Heroes' - one pair has got sheep on. And I made him a birthday cake (like the Christmas cake).

By the way, the actor Stephen Oil has walked out of his current play and disappeared. He was last seen on a ferry to France. So keep a look out for him - all his friends and family are really worried.   He has had some bad reviews.   (- added Saturday morning - he has sent a fax to his agent saying he is OK - he had stage fright-).

The tree surgeon is coming on Monday to trim some of the tallest trees. I have just finished the final draft of Wayne Lancaster's Logistics Report on Electrical Retailing (he has

Swiss type which is this, and all the others have **Dotum**

which is this) but I always use Courier font for my own

letters as it seems easier to read) and he has gone away to see if he wants to change or add anything.

Peter Potter is in the middle of having his new house in Cornwall modernised (while he stays at a friend's flat temporarily in Swindon) so all his typing has been about that for the last few weeks (banks, building society, builders, letters to his friends and family explaining the situation - even a letter to the milkman!) He brought his son Markus with him last time he came. (His parents' divorce is affecting his 'A' level study). He sent us a 'change of address' card with a photograph of his new house, thanking us for our friendship during his difficult times.

George Boots (The Robotics Collage Foundation) is busy putting together a brochure describing his new robots (which I have typed a section at a time) and is sending them out to Technical Colleges.

Jerry Jives has now moved back to Mead Lanes as it is nearer to the shops, buses, his old friends and neighbours and us! He has just had a cataract removed but although things look brighter, he has not yet noticed an improvement with regard to reading. Everyone sends him his faxes in really large type. He always asks after you.

Rodney Spotter is very pleased as all his letters and his petition have prevented planning permission being approved for the bungalow his next-door neighbour was planning to build at the bottom of his garden. He isn't very well at the moment. He thought he'd got flu but it turned out to be mycoplasma pneumonia. I diagnosed it before he got the results of the blood test back as I had recently read an article in the *Telegraph* describing it, and how people think they've got flu, and that there was an epidemic of it at the moment which began on the day he first felt ill. I gave him the article which included the appropriate treatment for it. He rang me yesterday to tell me he had just got the results of the blood test and I had been right and that I had missed my vocation (what with that and missing out on being an opera singer, I've started to get those palpitations again!)

Piers Andrews drilled 50 holes yesterday for which he charged £1,400! (He is a diamond driller and looks like something out of Status Quo).

I have just updated Claire Burrage's CV for her as things have changed a bit since I last did it.

I am still doing the Lottery but the most I have got so far is two numbers.

Dad has joined the Herts and Middx Wildlife Trust whose meeting place is in St Urbans. They give talks on photography, flowers, local walks/open days etc. and conservation - this year is the 'Year of the Dormouse' so we better tell the cats to start to respect your Father and not bring them to us as gifts at the back door (at least for this year anyway).

Honey rang at ten minutes to 01:00am the other day (it would have been 10 to 2 in France). She was in the street on her way back from a meal. Just thought she'd check in, she said. I think she must have had a small glass of mead wine as most of the conversation was rather unintelligible. It was the night before she came to see you. Was she suffering? I thought something dreadful had happened when the phone went at that time of night.

Well, I seem to have run out of news for now but I know I'll think of some more when I've posted it. I am typing at your desk and Muesli and Truff are asleep on your bed, Twig is on the warm patch on the landing, Nutmeg is downstairs curled up on a sleeping bag and Corrie is stretched out on the black cupboard by the radiator and Dad is reading the paper although I'm sure his eyes have been closed for three hours. I shan't mention it as he'll be wild with annoyance.

I will have to post this in the morning now as it is 6.30pm - time to go and peel some Jersey potatoes.

I wonder where Stephen Oil is? Or did we sort that one?

I think we are going to get two wooden curtain poles tomorrow for our bedroom window and balcony door. I shall be glad to finally have some curtains up - I'm sure everyone opposite can see us sitting in bed reading, and when it's a full moon it takes me ages to go to sleep it's so bright! Will write again soon. Hello Kevin. Is he asleep?   Love Mum x

37 Pomegranate Road

Draycod

Herts

DR3 9SF

England

17th June 1994

Dear Amber,

Thank you for your pretty card which has just arrived. Have you ever thought of designing ceramic tiles? It is exactly like the tiles we have chosen for the shower room! It's a lovely card - very artistic. I didn't know they had buttercups in France!

I hope your flowers are still blooming in the bidet!

Glad you enjoyed your birthday meal.

I do hope your Star Trek play goes well. I'm sure it will. Looking forward to hearing all about it.

The enclosed job on the FRENCH RIVIERA was in yesterday's *Telegraph* appointments section although I wasn't sure it was quite your thing working in an abattoir? There are two letters for you, and I have enclosed the write-ups of *'Allo 'Allo.* Also a *Young Telegraph,* and a couple of childrens' sections from the *Radio Times* - one shows how to make a leapfrog and the other a Fabergé egg. I see that underneath the frog they recommend a book called *It's a Bitsa* containing lots of things to make. I suppose it's a bit late now you're in your 40's?

Thought you'd like the little cartoon! They had a news programme called *'News '44'* after the normal news in D-Day week, which is what the news would have been if people had had televisions then. It contained dramatic coverage of the landings on the beaches etc. and genuine commentary.

There is also an article on English sandwiches in France I thought you might like, and a thing about Lady Pru who 'helped rescue a man trapped in a cave infested with jellyfish'. (Actually it said the next day that all she did was to ring the emergency services from her mobile phone and hold the man's wallet who had dived in to rescue him!!)

... Pause while I rang you to tell you about the job in case this arrives too late ...

I sent Honey the voucher for a free bottle of wine as it had to be bought from Safeways and we haven't got one. She's got a Safeway so was able to get the wine which I think they have now drunk!

The visit of Gilly's second cousin sounded hilarious! When they were going out she said to Gilly *'I think I'll go and put my pants on'* and Gilly said *'Yes, I think you'd better'*. She actually meant her trousers, but they call them pants in America! She was very extrovert and kept shouting out *'Hi Honey'* to all the children in the park! She has invited Gilly back to America!

Dad has got a roof rack for tomorrow's journey. I hope it all fits. Honey's got loads of stuff including four rugs.

I wish you and Honey had been here to help choose the tiles for the shower room. It took six hours. We went to five different places. Actually we were looking at basins, loos and showers too but the tiles were the most problematic. Dad ended up sitting on the toilet in the showroom while I finished looking. We even had our lunch in there! The problem was that not all the ones called 'Champagne' matched the Champagne basin and loo. They had them stuck to wooden things which you flick through (like the posters in Athena). There were hundreds of them. And they also had some in large containers at waist level.

The balcony door and shower room window have now been fitted and our room has been plastered and the power points and light switch and fittings changed. The lobby has now got a double glazed panel facing the front, a brick supporting pillar and a matching piece of glass at the side of the front door. As I said on the phone, the archway wall has had to be re-built due to it being wobbly, which is what they are doing today. The shower cubicle is having a Champagne colour tray. We haven't chosen a door for it yet.

Several radiators have had to come out for the moment, wall light fittings are dangling in mid-air, there is a thick layer of dust on everything every day despite about 12 dust sheets being put down which I have to shake every evening. I have to hoover and dust after the builders have gone every day. They broke the extension window too so that will have to be replaced. And all the timber for the new roof was stolen one night. It is total chaos. So I think we might have to take up Ernies's kind offer of the flat overlooking the golf course. Everything from the extension and our bedroom is squashed into the rest of the house and it is totally full. There is nowhere for Honey's things to go. So they can go to Ernie's for a week or so until we are straighter. She can use his wardrobes. I know she said she would sleep on the settee, but the builders come at 8.0 in the morning!

When we have recovered from all this, we are going to have a new bathroom. Isn't it exciting?!

Did I tell you I have got a new customer, Carlos Maffei, from Applebridge Common, and a Mrs Dews also from Applebridge Common, and an Italian Teacher from only two miles away? I did 12 pages of dictation for William Loo the other day too. I said *'Can you go slower than usual as the builders are here and it's really hard to concentrate with all the banging'* and he started off slowly and got quicker and quicker. I don't know how I read it back. He didn't even check it. He just put it in the envelope and stuck it up! Oh, and there is another customer called *I can't remember.* He also looks like something out of Status Quo!

Your CV's are enclosed, before I forget, or they will be when I've done them. Good luck with all your possibilities.

Last Friday was really hectic. Five new clients all came at once! I have only got a tiny space to work in at the moment. I tried using the word-processor outside with the extension flex but you can't see the screen properly due to the glare. The sun has got rather large, don't you think?

As I type, I have just heard a loud bang and a cry. The builder has just electrocuted himself on a live wire sticking out of the wall. He didn't realise it was live. There was this dreadful burning smell. I think it was his hair. He had a lucky escape. Dad said *'Perhaps it has charged him up and he'll go twice as fast'!*

Did you know there is an automatic library book return machine now - you don't have to go up to a desk anymore. Dad always remembers when the librarian asked him if he was related to Honey Jostick and when he said he was her Father she said her library book had been overdue for years and he had to pay a huge fine!!!

What a brilliant letter Honey. I just found the letter you gave me ages ago when you were trying to get *"Don't Forget to Pack the Humour, Honey"* published! Can't fail to grab their attention with that. Hope it's a Best Seller! If you need any more ammunition, don't forget Dad is always losing his glasses on holiday (leaving them by that horse in Devon, they fell off going into an art gallery in St Ives and he trod on them, having to get a screw from an optician in Ireland etc.) Holiday: Tomorrow - I know Dad said it was Sunday - he thought we were leaving then - so it was lucky I said! Night.   Love Mum x

P.s.   I have packed the top half of my beaded bikini and am determined to use it even if only for a back massage like those beaded car seat covers from the '70s.

One last parting note that I overheard at London Victoria on the platform next to mine late on a Friday night at the end of my first week back post maternity. Nothing new. Same pair of shoes, just a different day. A destitute lady was now without a sodding care in the world. She was swigging from a half drunk bottle of Sancerre, and she clearly looked like she was a wealthy banker having a bad day. Her mascara was pouring down her cheeks, and her stilettos had certainly seen better days. Her iPad had a rather new looking crack across its screen. She cried into it, *"I love British trains. It is nearly 21:30, but the train from Milton Merton is still expected to arrive at 15:25. Maybe it will come tomorrow? Or another day altogether…"* and I nodded off into a dreamy fog of points failures and three-headed cows on the line to Greater Bungchip leaving the millionaire functioning alcoholic to collapse onto the platform, drowning in Sancerre.

Love Honey xxx

Printed in Great Britain
by Amazon